THE AFTER DEATH AFTERLIFE

AFTERLIFE

OF

RONALD FOSTER

BY

ROBERT D TURVIL

Copyright Notice

Contents

Chapter One

Don't get me wrong. I'm not after sympathy and I'm not making excuses. I made my choices same as everyone else. We all have free will. I guess that's the point.

I could put a gloss on the way I used to be. I'd like to, but you'd soon see through it. You're not daft. But I have changed, finally, though getting you to believe me is a tough call.

As to the end – my end – I don't know, not yet. One thing though: this is my first and final account, my testament. If it gets through, you'll understand. You'll be on guard and they won't suck you in.

As to the beginning, two words: catastrophic panic, a whole gaggle of emotions infinitely worse than being forcibly drowned in a swamp infested with ravenous vermin.

You'd think I'd have remembered what had caused it. You'd think I'd have catalogued it right at the top of the never-to-be-forgotten pile. Fact is, I hadn't a clue. Neither did I know how, why, when or where it had happened, or how long whatever it was had lasted. About all I could recall was my given name: Ronald. I wasn't so sure about my surname. I think it was Foster. It sounded vaguely right. I figured I was in my thirties, maybe, give or take a decade. It didn't seem to matter.

I'd have written off the whole thing as nightmare if it hadn't been for the pains. My brain felt as if hot kebab skewers were poking about on a hunt for tasty morsels – and clamping my eyes shut didn't help. That only sparked off all the other bits that hurt: like my chest and legs and arms. No idea what was up with them, but I'd cheerfully have swapped places with an out-of-condition marathon runner stuck at the crest of his pain barrier.

Bottom line: something devastating had happened, something inordinately brutal and terrifying. Even so, I just had to manage the fallout and wait for by brain to wiggle into first gear, or so I convinced myself. I didn't question how I could be so calm, so accepting.

I realized I was in a whopping great oak-paneled room, and I wasn't alone. The vibes told me this wasn't where it had happened – the panic – though I can't tell you why. There were about thirty people there, men and women, all sorts of ages and all, like me, in armchairs spaced around the biggest conference table I'd ever seen. Well, the biggest I could remember, which isn't saying much. It was highly polished, really amazing. The thing that nagged was the top spot. It was empty.

I reckoned I should have been in it, which was odd considering I could only have sat there like a chump and sucked my thumb. What could I have said to a single person there, let alone the whole lot of them? And *there* was odd as well. The room exuded an uneasy mix of eccentric grandeur, the impact emphasized by an excess of ornate doorways. Though nothing was familiar, I picked up a connection. That was unnerving as well as odd.

When a door cracked open at the head of the room – a concealed door – it startled me, but not for long. Instinct made me stand tall and straight. Impulse made me check my suit. To my relief, it felt right, as did my fine silk tie. Whether by sixth sense or something else, I knew that proper clothes – good quality stuff – made a man, and a woman for that matter. Though I didn't know who was coming in, they weren't about to catch me looking less than my physical and sartorial best. That was certain.

There was a pause as if someone was teasing. In the lull I whispered, 'Not noticed that door,' to the guy beside me. Truth is, I thought I'd forgotten it.

He didn't answer. He was too busy staring at the ageless woman who had swept in while I was talking. He was blatantly ogling. Everyone was, and I did too. Even with my hollowed-out memory, I was certain I'd never seen such black hair, masses of it sculpted into a glorious mane.

I couldn't help it. None too discreetly, I said, 'Wow!' One look had turned me into a soppy pubescent boy.

If she heard she gave no sign. Neither did she flinch at the barrage of other eyes upon her. Made me cringe. Every pair looked scurrilous behind a thin mask of propriety, women and men alike.

Having settled, she gazed back at each of us in turn, saving the best till last. The moment she looked at me my pains faded. Finally I could breath easy. No voice came this time, but I mouthed the word *wow* as if fixated on it, and on her, which I was. As I watched, she filled her lungs, swelling her fiery red dress. My eyes were still engrossed when she spoke.

'My name is Charity, but it's not my original name. I chose it because I'm committed. I feel for those we serve and relish my mission – our mission – to provide unique support.'

Couldn't believe it when some people sniggered. Made me scowl, offended for her. Awful manners, yet the intrusion reminded me we weren't alone. It also nudged a thought my way: I had to know some of the people in the room. I spread a measured glance round in the hope of finding a face I recognized. Others were doing the same. Some looked disturbingly scared. Made me wonder if we all had memory problems.

'A few of you know me,' Charity went on, her voice bewitching, 'but most of you are friends-in-waiting who don't know me ... yet.'

I listened intently. Her voice was exactly as I'd imagined, as undeniably enticing as she was undeniably beautiful. Admittedly I'd nothing but air castles to back it up, but I reckoned I was one of the few who knew her. She seemed tantalizingly familiar, like my fantasy woman come to life, except I couldn't remember having a fantasy woman or any special woman come to that.

Annoyingly, my throat sprang a tickle. Normally I'd have coughed, but multiple instincts cautioned me to bottle it. Then they piled in with all sorts of other conflicting prods. I knew her, they egged. I might have forgotten her unforgettable tresses, but I had more right than most to be there. Why shouldn't I cough and damn the consequences?

I caught myself being stupid, and I couldn't afford stupidity. What mattered was getting a grip. I had to remember *something* else I'd be worse off than a lamb spruced up for the slaughter.

Charity spoke again, her voice like a knife murdering my mental ramble. 'Other charities provide for the blind or deaf in general. We are concerned exclusively with the partially blind *and* partially deaf.' She spread her elegant fingers on the table, her nails perfectly manicured. 'Our aim is to make a difference. We must never forget those who depend on us, and always guard against those who would have us fail.'

To my disgust, the earlier sniggers became open chortling. It came from three people: two in their fifties in impeccable attire, male and female; the other a vamp who looked about twenty. I expected Charity to say something. In her place I'd have wiped the floor with them. It seemed to me I would, yet her perfect poise remained undiminished. She didn't so much as shame them with a glare. She merely waited for them to quieten.

'We are a team and, as in every good team, each of us has a role to play.' She looked directly at me but said, 'Frank.'

Thinking she had crossed wires, I said, 'The name is Ronald. Ronald ... Foster.'

She came back at once. 'Then I'm not talking to you, am I?'

Took me by surprise I can tell you. Made me blink, but I was no shrinking violet. I told her from the hip, 'You were looking at me. I thought—'

She chopped right across me. 'You didn't think. You assumed; you presumed and I find that offensive.'

As she spoke, the pains in my head switched on again, swiftly followed by renewed aches all around my body. I winced, though really I wanted to cry out. I think I said, 'Sorry.'

'Stress. That's your problem,' she announced as if she had a string of sure-fire diagnostic qualifications. 'You poke your nose where it's not invited and get worked up about things that don't concern you.'

That was it. Whoever she was, she was no fantasy woman of mine. Pain stoked my embarrassment up to anger. She was a Class A bitch and needed to be set straight. I pointed. 'Those people were laughing at you a minute ago, but *they* didn't offend you. All I did was—'

'Presume,' she cut in icily. '*Those people*, as you so arrogantly call them, are my friends. You are merely insolent, and insolence is not at all what I expect from a team player of your caliber.'

That spun me off balance. Made me think she might be dishing out some kind of backhanded compliment, but if she was, it was way off target. After humiliating me so publicly, her sop felt more like poisonous nettles rubbed into an open wound.

'You call this a team!' I threw back. 'It's a bunch of idiots, most too spineless to wipe their own noses. The rest are cackling hyenas.'

Couldn't believe it when she smiled, just a faint pursing of the lips, but a definite smile. Then she spoke to this other guy. 'The task I had earmarked for Ronald will now be yours, Frank.'

I remember thinking he looked like a loser: a sheepish, never-say-boo-to-a-goose loser. That was it. A wrenching spasm burst across my entire abdomen. Felt like my intestines had been drawn out and twisted into vicious knots. Couldn't bear it. The pain ditched me off my chair. Had me writhing about, my hands clawing the carpet as I convulsed.

The agony ended as abruptly as it had began, and I was mighty glad. Least I was till I realized I was back in my chair, everyone at ease as if nothing had happened. I was still struggling with this fresh bout of disorientation when Charity's voice stroked my ears.

'Will that suit you, Ronald?'

She was smiling as if we were the dearest of allies. Made me feel like screaming: what's happening to me? I couldn't. I dare not. I already knew. It was fallout from my panic, the bchind the curtain panic that had thrown me into this *somewhere* and ripped my memory to shreds. I guessed I'd been hit by some kind of mini mind lapse, maybe triggered by pain. But for how long? It could have been minutes or hours since Charity had hacked into me.

All I had was one constant: my anger. I'd been demeaned, callously demeaned, and for no good reason. I couldn't let it go. My lips were tight when I said, 'I demand an apology.'

All eyes turned my way as if I'd lost my wits.

'You're joking, aren't you?' Charity asked. 'You're just being—'

I wasn't having it. 'No,' I chucked back. 'You ridiculed me; made me feel— I want an apology.'

She caved in like a soft balloon. 'All right, Ronald. I don't fully understand, but if you want an apology you shall have one, full and sincere.' She stood and smoothed her dress at the hips. 'I apologize unreservedly for any hurt I've caused you. The last thing I want is our friendship to suffer so, please, forgive me.'

I watched her start towards me, her gentle sway compelling. As she drew close, the aroma of her perfume impregnated my whole being. When she embraced me, her warmth stole my consciousness of all other existence – until her kiss pecked my cheek and she pulled away.

Sighing, she asked, 'Am I forgiven?'

I wanted to say, *no*. My anger still throbbed but I'd lost track of the reason. As gracelessly as I could, I mumbled, 'All right.'

She stepped away immediately and returned to her place, then took her own sweet time to settle. When ready she said, 'Good. You all know your tasks so, if there are no more questions, I'll close the meeting.'

Her eyes fixed on me, dark eyes that bore into my hidden core and confirmed she knew I was utterly clueless. I brazened it out and ignored her dare to confess how unglued I really was.

It sounded like a warning when she added, 'I've high hopes for my new Ronald–Susie partnership.'

I frowned at the door long after it had closed behind her. None of my aches were kicking and the freedom scraped years off the way I felt. Around me, people were leaving, none in any hurry. I had to wait. What else could I do? As those minutes dragged by, I'd have jumped at any available fast forward memory lapse just to get out of there. It didn't happen, yet I must have drifted off to my special place since she took me by surprise.

It was the ill-mannered vamp. She had waited till all the others had gone. 'You called me a cackling hyena,' she accused from far along the table. 'I demand an apology.'

I sagged when I saw who it was. Don't get me wrong. She looked pleasant enough, except for her hair. It was dyed red with yellow streaks. Awful! I figured my harvest of bad luck hadn't ended and I'd been teamed with this numbskull vixen. After the way she had behaved with Charity – sniggering the way she had – I reckoned she deserved a slice of payback. 'Sorry ... bitch!' I said.

She stood and ambled over. That's when I realized her dress left very little to the imagination, even less when she perched on the table beside me.

'Apology accepted,' she said, catching me out, but she hadn't finished. 'You're old, aren't you? Even your name sounds old.'

I should have let it go, but I bristled and concocted a put-down. 'For your information, I'm not remotely old. What's more, mine is a family name and, unlike you, I take pride in my appearance.'

'Well you look old to me, sweetie,' she shot back, 'and I need someone who can keep up.'

'Shut it,' I said before things got out of hand. 'We've a job to discuss. You lead off. I'm not having you claim my ideas; and basics first: clarify the task.'

I didn't expect her to roll over, yet she shrugged lightly and said, 'It's about this decrepit hag, isn't it. She's having a rough time ... can't tell half-past four from Friday. We test her limits then point the senile old bat in the proper direction. Right?'

I smiled, relieved to have something to go on, even something so jaundiced. Then it hit me. Why should I help out some doddering old dame who was having a rough time? I was having a rough time myself and nobody was sending out the cavalry for me. I searched round the whole room. Not sure why. Guess I was looking for something – anything – to grab as a mental anchor.

The bimbo didn't like my silence. 'Right?' she repeated crankily.

'Yeah, right,' I huffed at her. 'Have you all we need?'

She pushed out her chest. 'Trust me, sweetie, I've everything you'll ever need.'

Frustrated, I rubbed my forehead. For sure, the last thing I needed was a promiscuous feline with delusions of charisma. 'No, blowhard,' I corrected her. 'You've nothing I need either inside or outside that excuse of a dress.'

She flinched, I assumed from the brilliance of my rebuff. I was so wrong. She recovered quickly, laughing as she jumped off the table and wandered towards the door.

'Well you've had a good eyeful,' she taunted, then she unloaded both barrels. 'I'll tell Charity that when I tell her you're a fraud. You've no idea what you're doing. Helping out some coffin-dodging old battle ax ... huh!'

The bitch had tricked me. I wanted to charge after her and deliver a hefty slap for leading me on, but I couldn't afford the risk. Instead, I stood and called out, 'Sorry. I'm not feeling well.'

At first she kept walking. When she turned, concern creased her face. 'Would you like to rest your poor old head on my lap?' Then she dissolved into laughter. Made me fall back in my chair as if clouted in the groin. She was still laughing when she pranced out.

'Damn you, you spiteful whore,' I booted after her, angry at having again been suckered. No one came back. I was left to stew, and that's exactly what I did. It took a while for me to catch on. Charity had been playing mind games. She had set me up. They both had. But I was no pawn. Right then I decided to fight them, and right then I began to sweat.

My stomach tightened. I'd been gripped by the coldness of rising panic. Made me shake inside and out, but I knew it wasn't like before. I could still think and still trace the time-line since arriving in Charity's oak-paneled conference room, give or take the odd nonsensical lapse. *Before* was something altogether different. I sensed it. Whatever that was still hovered like a pernicious cloud behind bleak shadows, unspecific and impenetrable.

Not sure how long the attack lasted, but the shakes eventually eased and I gulped in a lot of wobbly breaths, then washed them down with a few stark realizations. I was in danger of becoming a victim, someone's victim. Cold analysis took a back seat as bubbling intuition told me to discount Charity and the vixen as hirelings. My someone – my nemesis – knew the whole truth and plainly didn't want to share. It was as obvious to me as inspiration to a genius. This someone had orchestrated a perverse scheme and singled me out to play headless chicken. Why, I didn't know, yet I did know without doubt that whoever it was had thrown down a gauntlet.

I snorted. No way was this *someone* getting away with blowing my life into an abyss of mind-boggling torment. I resolved to find them whatever it took and, when I did, to make their mistake crystal clear in a very hands-on kind of way.

Robert D Turvil

Chapter Two

I was still in grim contemplation mode when someone chirped up beside me. 'Looks like you need a friend.'

The voice yanked me from my deep struggle with the unfathomable. A woman stood close, not invading my personal space. She wasn't like Charity and definitely not like that double-dealing little whore. I pegged her at a year or two either side of thirty, probably the wrong side. Her face was kind, sympathetic. I held her gaze.

'I'm Susie,' she said. 'My guess is you're Ronald. We'll be working together.'

Relief squashed my tact. 'You mean that conniving red-haired nympho isn't—' Her confusion stopped me. 'Doesn't matter,' I said.

Her eyes flashed indignantly. 'It does matter if a nymphomaniac is impersonating me.'

Though she'd never have made the final twenty in a beauty contest, she was several points up on plain. Thing was, she had no dress sense. A drab blue sack completely spoiled the pretty decent figure I reckoned she hid underneath. Worse, she'd scraped her hair into a pig-ugly looped bun.

'Sounds like Dimple,' she concluded once I'd explained. 'The red hair and yellow highlights are a dead give-away.' I must have looked quizzical. 'She's rather proud of her dimpled cheeks, hence *Dimple*.' She frowned. 'Watch her though. She's Charity's protégée. You've not upset her, have you?'

The warning unsettled me. 'I may have dropped in the

11

odd home truth.'

'Then we'd best be on our way,' she decreed. 'Your place will do. We can plan our strategy.'

I went with her to the door feeling like a ninny. I had to say something. 'To be honest I'm a bit out of my depth.'

'Nothing we can't sort out,' she said confidently. 'Where do you live?'

It was a damn fine question. I waited until we were in the corridor before mumbling, 'That's the first problem.'

She held out her hand, palm up. 'Not really. Give me your keys.' I did. 'Magic, see? Your address quick and easy.'

That confirmed I was a ninny, a stupid one who kept an address fob with his keys. Saying nothing, I matched her pace till we exited the building.

The next thing was her asking me what I thought. Fair enough, normally, but she was asking from inside an apartment, possibly my apartment, and she had changed into a dull green two-piece that would have depressed a regiment of fogies.

When I didn't answer, her eyes narrowed. 'Are you all right? You look as if you've seen a ghost.'

Ghosts were the least of my worries. I was more interested in how an apartment had materialized around me, especially one that looked so decidedly worldly. A glance told me that everything was bright and ultra modern, the furnishings high on the luxury scale.

I chuckled, tried to. It sounded bitter, even from the comfort of my recliner. Susie was on the sofa next to me, papers beside her and on her lap. I liked her – what I'd seen so far – but no way was I prepared to slobber out my problems just because I'd suffered another memory rift, maybe a chasm this time. I said, 'I'm fine thanks.'

She wasn't buying and asked again what I thought. I had no answer, not even the question, and she knew it. 'Okay,' I fed in cautiously, 'my memory is playing up, that's all. Can't quite get a handle on what we were talking about.'

She gazed back suspiciously. 'Tell me the last thing you remember.'

Her doling out the third degree was a tub of acid I didn't need. I'd just endured a memory jump longer than its conference room predecessor and was still feeling raw. I closed my eyes. Naively I thought I might catch a moonbeam and snatch another jump, just a mini-one. Anything to sidestep her awkward questions. Nothing happened. Nothing ever does when you need it most.

She saw my disappointment. 'I'm still here, but I'll go if you like.'

That wasn't what I wanted, as much as I understood anything of what I wanted. 'It's not you, it's me,' I told her.

Spontaneously she reached for my hand. 'I'm not your doctor, Ronald, but I am a doctor and—'

'You're a doctor!' My surprise blared out as incongruous as birthday balloons around a coffin.

'You know I am. You've seen my résumé as I've seen yours.' She paused. 'I can help if you'll let me.'

I should have followed up what she'd said about résumés, especially to find out about mine, but her claim to medical credentials had tangled me in irrational disbelief. 'You look too ... young,' I blurted like a dork.

Maybe my fatuous wince saved me. Either way she released my hand and spoke softly. 'I was fast tracked through my graduate medical education, so I'll assume you're paying a compliment.'

I stared. My whole face was parading skepticism like flags around a gaping hole. 'Oh,' was all I could think to say, short of telling her I'd have believed a monkey dolled up in graduation gowns ahead of her claim to medical brilliance. She just didn't seem that clever.

She stood. 'We must be honest with each other, Ronald. If you'd prefer to work with someone like Dimple, that's fine by me. But I want your decision now.'

I shook my head. 'Not Dimple.'

She sat again, but stayed perched on the seat ready for a fast getaway. 'Then tell me what's wrong so we can work through it together.'

I felt like a juicy pumpkin trapped between a runaway train and unyielding buffers. I still thought twice before saying, 'It's not easy.'

What came back scraped the marrow from my bones. 'No kidding,' I heard. 'You made a right mess of it!'

I squeezed my eyes and tried to bury the impossible. The voice was undeniably familiar, but it wasn't Susie's. Instinct told me I was lying down, my only covering a thin bed sheet. When a knee crashed into my back, it energized every dread I was wrestling to expunge. A clutch of sharp fingernails followed, all clawing viciously into my thigh. Hurt and fuddled, I turned. All I could see was a few yellow-streaked tufts of red hair. More than enough. I sat bolt upright and threw back the sheet. Dimple's and my own nakedness lay exposed.

'Impotent git!' she jeered, her eyes vehement with scorn.

As I shuddered in turmoil, she seized the moment to flaunt herself, shamelessly cavorting.

The best I could do was croak, 'How did you get here? Where's Susie?'

'Want a threesome?' she sneered. 'What for? I've seen more grit at geriatric sleepovers.'

'Answer me,' I gasped, desperate for anything to crack the inexplicable.

'Well, sweetie,' she cooed after shifting to kneel, 'let's take each question in turn. First, how did I get here?' She threw open her arms. 'Look about, rattlebrain. This is my room in my house where you came to beg me to work with you ... and beg me to be friendly, in a sexually explicit sort of way.'

That emptied my lungs I can tell you, left me grappling with the inconceivable. She took advantage and whacked me ferociously across the face. As I careered sideways, I became easy prey. At full force she shoved me out of bed, then maneuvered to foot pummel my head.

'As for Susie,' she yelled, 'who the blazes knows and who the blazes cares!'

I'd absorbed a whole bevy of kicks before my wits regrouped. I made a grab for her feet. Took most of my strength to keep her flat on the bed. Even then she squirmed on her back trying to break my hold on her ankles. When she failed, she stilled and spat. Her saliva burst onto my face then slid down to mix with blood from my battering.

I could recall wrenching her off the bed, as I could recall my first punch. What I couldn't remember was what happened next, any more than I could remember how I came to be back in the conference room at the low end of the polished table.

Charity was at the head of the room, her beautiful body

snug in a daring yellow gown. 'Do you think you've done well?' she asked.

To put it mildly, I wasn't exactly feeling like a chat yet my eyes couldn't keep off her.

When I didn't answer, she said, 'Are you planning to ask about Dimple?'

A tremor ran through me, more an earthquake. Since last exiting that room, I'd suffered three serious memory lapses, huge jumps that had hurled me from one reality to another. I should have been shrieking from the roof tops. At the very least I should have been thumping my head against the wooden panels. Yet calmness was already beginning to settle me, the same calmness I'd felt in that room before. Not trusting myself to speak, I simply arched my eyebrows.

Charity went on serenely. 'She's doing well, considering the beating she's suffered. A most violent attack.' I gulped. She sighed then added, 'We've asked, of course, but she won't say who did it ... though we're sure she knows him. Must be someone she likes otherwise she wouldn't be protecting him.'

I'd already been so trounced that my confusion was boiling in high pressure overtime. The added steam of Dimple apparently liking and wanting to protect me almost blew a gasket.

Charity's tone didn't change. 'I see your hands are rather messy, Ronald, and – if you don't mind me pointing it out – you have bruising around the eyes and your nose is ... nasty. In fact your whole face is a disgrace.'

My blood ran extra cold as I steeled myself for the inevitable.

'Tell me,' she asked with no emotion, 'why do you suppose the attacker copped out and failed to kill her?'

I simply gaped and she simply waited.

'Not fair I suppose,' she said when our silence had churned on long enough to make butter. 'How could you know what the attacker was thinking, unless you were the attacker?'

She banged the table. Had I not been zipped in, her shock tactic would have shot me from my skin like a bullet out of an oily barrel.

She just carried on calmly, the bitch. 'Thing is, unless

Dimple changes her mind and testifies, the attacker will get away with it. Circumstantial evidence – such as knowing a person to have been with her near the time – will not be enough to convict, no matter if that same person bears all the hallmarks of having been in a fight.'

Her smile came and went, its root almost certainly grounded in my blatant relief. Then she hit me with the sting.

'It's to be expected that the guilty man will be extra nice to her, better than nice.' She paused for me to look. 'So, Ronald, what do you think he ought to do, from your purely disinterested standpoint?'

I had to answer. Playing the game, I said, 'Tell her he's sorry, I suppose. Tell her he appreciates what she's doing for him.'

'Is that all?'

'And be nice,' I bolted on. 'Better than nice.'

'Yes indeed,' she agreed. 'Dimple holds the key to this man's freedom and, if I know Dimple, she'll expect to be treated well.'

Susie came in behind me, but I was too busy processing Charity's sardonic message to notice. 'I had a call,' she said. 'I came at once.'

I sneaked a peep and felt a stir of comfort, till the situation butted in. As I figured it, Susie was the only one worth a thread of trust, yet she'd soon be hearing all about me and Dimple. That would make her ram two and two together and she'd be off faster than a peregrine falcon spotting prey.

After waving her to sit next to me, Charity said, 'Our friend here is not himself. He rather foolishly slipped and fell down some stairs. Now he's something of a mess.'

Susie glanced my way, her face unsmiling. Can't say why, but that glance made me think it wasn't the first time she'd seen my kicked-about face. To my amazement she took gentle hold of my hand under the table. Almost made me forget about Charity, yet Susie's bleak gray outfit and the hash she'd made of her mousy hair stalled me. Couldn't help wishing she had just a breath of Charity's style.

Though the stair-slip explanation hadn't struck me as a hint, Susie took it. 'You'd like me to look after him?'

'You are his doctor.'

I knew that was wrong. 'No,' I began, but Susie emphatically cut across me.

'Yes. Following Charity's instructions, I've arranged a transfer from your former doctor. I have your full medical and social history.'

Thin ice or not, there were limits. Angered I said, 'Don't I get a say in this?' They fish-eyed me. Neither spoke. When my brain caught up, I mumbled, 'Whatever.' Not much else I could say.

'Take him home,' Charity told Susie. 'Work your magic and make him fit for purpose.'

That was it. 'I'm not a machine!' I rasped. 'I don't need greasing or pampering.'

Charity's dark eyes held me. 'Trust me, Ronald, no one will be pampering you. Fit for purpose is what I said and fit for purpose is what you must become, or you'll be dismissed from this charitable body and suffer the consequences. Do I make myself clear?'

Susie dived in quickly, already on her feet. 'Come on,' she said. 'Best we get you home. You can't afford any more slips.'

Robert D Turvil

Chapter Three

Susie's frostiness grew as she drove me from the multi-story car park into the evening traffic. To be honest, I'd probably have let her freeze if she'd not been the closest I had to an ally. It seemed to me it was her help or nothing, and I needed all the help I could get to track down the *someone* I was after.

Hoping to thaw her chill before it compacted into ice, I said, 'Reckon I've annoyed Charity. Good you came. Better still when you touched my hand. Made me—'

She barged straight in. 'Why did you do it, Ronald?'

It was obvious what she meant but I still asked. 'What?'

'I see,' she threw back. 'You want to play games, want to pretend you don't remember, that you had nothing to do with poor Dimple getting smashed up.'

Her chucking out accusations stirred my hackles. I joined in. 'Where did you go? I was with you then I was with her. You must know what happened in between.'

'Must I?'

'Yes,' I told her. 'At worst you've a better idea than me.'

'So it is your memory at fault,' she rebuffed. 'How very convenient.'

'No! It's very inconvenient. Someone's screwing with me and—'

'And you want to thump them just as you thumped Dimple?'

Frustration fed my anger so I laid it out. 'If all you want is to be bitchy, doctor, why did you come?'

That stumped her, fortunately, and we drove on in

silence till the road signs warned we were heading for a hospital.

Cautiously I said, 'I thought you were taking me home. Is this where you work?'

Again no answer. Her silence escalated my misgivings.

She stayed silent till she'd parked. 'Dimple is on the fifteenth floor, room A17. I suggest you use the stairs. That'll give you more time to compose your apology and think how to make up for what you did.'

If I'd had a pile of never-see-again people, Dimple would have been right at its loathsome pinnacle. I wasn't happy. Despite my obligations, I bucked. 'You didn't see the way she behaved.'

Susie looked grimly unimpressed. 'But I've seen how you behaved towards her and, frankly, it makes me wonder why I did come.' She gripped the steering wheel. 'Now get out. I may be here when you return or I may have come to my senses.' I started to say something, but she shut me down. 'Go, Ronald. Go right now.'

I did, but there was no way I was climbing to the fifteenth floor. Anything I had to say to Dimple was going to be made up on the spot. The elevator opened close to the nurses' station. When a bright young nurse saw me, she lost her brightness.

'What do you want?' she said with all the warmth of deep permafrost.

I read her name label: Bridget. Meant nothing. 'Do I know you?' I asked, puzzled. Not only had she recognized me, she'd clearly judged me guilty of something Dimple was supposedly keeping secret.

'Stay exactly where you are,' she told me, hurriedly summoning Bernie, a male colleague. Then she asked the same abrupt question.

'I want to see Dimple,' I said, matching her coldness. 'Point me the right way then go chew a laxative.'

Her glare could have cracked a mountain, but she edged off without a word into one of the private rooms. Her return was even slower. 'Can't imagine why,' she huffed, 'but Dimple says she'll see you.'

I figured I'd soaked up enough hassle for one day. 'Listen, nursie,' I said. 'Far as I know, I've never met you and you've never met me. If this is how you treat visitors,

I'd sure hate to be one of your patients, you uppity little tart!'

'Cut that out,' Bernie said, taking a step nearer.

My expression spiked his enthusiasm. I left them gawking. Dimple waited till the door was shut and we were alone before swinging her eyes my way.

Her lips hardly moved but I heard her plainly. 'Come to admire your handiwork, sweetie?'

I could have waded in with a million questions about the hows and whys of our frantic little spat. I resisted. I wanted to get on and get out. But that didn't mean I was going to be mealy mouthed. The little nympho had dropped me straight in the meat grinder and everyone seemed set on pulverizing me.

Dragging over a chair, I said, 'You were being a bitch. You pushed too far.'

Her mouth twitched into something like a smile. 'Made you feel like a man, did it?'

She was still being a bitch. I'd expected nothing better. I kept cool. 'I came to say sorry, not pick up where we left off. I also came to thank you for keeping my name out of it, even though everyone I've come across seems to know more about what happened than me.'

Her smile was fuller this time. 'Did Charity tell you you're safe so long as I keep quiet?'

I nodded.

'And she told you to be grateful to me: friendly, nice, and grateful?'

'More or less,' I said, hackles on the rise again.

She pouted. 'So do you promise to be friendly, nice, and grateful?'

I had to say it, though I'd have preferred a lobotomy. 'Yes.'

She propped herself up. 'Then I'll tell you.'

I waited but she wouldn't go on until I'd asked. 'Okay, tell me what?'

'You didn't exactly fulfill my dreams, right?'

I baulked at that. 'Where's this leading?'

She continued as if doling out a treat, 'Well, sweetie, when you left me I had someone finish what you started; both things you started.'

I gaped, my brain helter-skeltering through fog,

groping to find any sense in what she was saying.

'That's right, sweetie,' she taunted. 'The very worst you're thinking.'

When my voice dawdled back, I croaked, 'You're saying you had someone belt you? What kind of crazy numbskull does a thing like that?'

'You did slap me,' she said as if it explained everything. 'Mind you, only in a lame duck sort of way. I've had worse from candy-coated little girls.' She laughed. 'This is about control, sweetie. You're now under my control. Whatever Dimple wants, Ronnie is going to fetch like a good little doggy.'

I stood dumbfounded, legs unsteady, my mind in a turmoil of somersaults. I'd been convinced of my own guilt. My hands were ugly proof. Worse, not a soul I'd met since had believed me innocent, and not a soul would believe me if I were to tell Dimple's latest story. She'd not even accused me, officially.

'Bit stuck aren't you, sweetie?' she purred.

I glanced. She was enjoying herself too much. I reckoned she'd hatched up a quagmire of lies just to get even. It was too ridiculous. I told her, no messing. 'You're a lying bitch!'

She grinned and inclined her head a little. 'For the record, which bit of being friendly, nice, and grateful was that?'

I'd had enough. I'd turned to go when she added, 'Don't call me a bitch, sweetie. Call me *mistress*.'

I about-faced, wanting to wring her neck. 'I'll see you in hell first, bitch!'

'You say the most gorgeous things.'

Belatedly, I remembered Susie's warning about Dimple being Charity's protégée, not someone to risk upsetting, and I recalled Charity's indulgence of her scurrilous laughter in the conference room. I hated doing it, but I tramped back to my chair and slumped down, not looking her way. Having baited me she kept quiet.

'I don't believe you,' I told her after a full minute, 'but if you were deranged enough to have some guy hammer you, I'll track him down and march him off to the cops ... or to Charity.'

'No you won't, sweetie,' she said, lying down. 'You're

stitched up tighter than a frog's posterior. Whatever you do, you're mine.'

'Jail time is better than having you round my neck,' I retorted theatrically. 'I'll confess, get rid of you that way.'

'What a dear little chipmunk you are,' she mocked. 'A few words from me and you'd get the harshest sentence. They'd send you to the darkest dungeon with the nastiest of the nasties; but I wouldn't let anyone kill you, only play with you every day in every way, year in, year out.'

My eyes shot to hers. Whatever else she was lying about, her jeering threat clanged with an awful peal of truth.

'I'll be nice,' she said quietly. 'You only have to call me *mistress* when we're alone.'

My gaze dipped to the floor.

She hadn't finished. 'Right now though, slave, I want you on your knees. You can kiss my feet and say, *thank you, mistress*. Then you can go. I'll be sure to call again when my legs need to rest on a whipped dog.'

I didn't move, not a muscle, but my brain looped in knots. I had to find a way out of the wreck of a mess I'd landed in. Denying her could reap a whirlwind and, right then, I'd had my fill of whirlwinds. I doubted I could survive any more. Against every instinct, I gulped down the swirling sea of bile in my stomach. There was no choice, not at that moment. I had to humor the vicious bitch-queen in the bed.

Her laughter erupted as soon as I started to kneel and kept on until I'd hissed, 'Thank you, mistress.'

She dismissed me with a flick of her fingers. Any other time I'd cheerfully have strangled her, or so I convinced myself. But I was no murderer, not then. I just wanted to get out of there. Humiliated, I ran, face flushed and breathing so heavily my heart threatened to rupture a valve. The last thing I needed was to find Nurse Bridget and Bernie pacing outside like a duo of pregnant fathers.

'Did you hear anything?' I yelled at them. 'Anything at all?'

All that came back was a horrified look from Bridget. Within a split second, she'd rushed off to check on Dimple.

'Get out of here,' she ordered, almost ricocheting from Dimple's doorway having found her still laughing. 'And don't come back.'

No chance, I seethed inwardly, charging off, opting for the stairs on some half-baked impulse to let physical exertion burn off my fury. It didn't help. I arrived in the ground floor vestibule panting and just as furious.

'I take it you've been nice?' It was Charity. She looked as if she'd been waiting for me. She wore black, the low-cut dress shimmering as if it had a life of its own.

'I resign from your damn charity, or whatever the hell it is,' I shouted. 'I'm finished with you and—'

'What are you talking about?'

My head pommeled mercilessly, but I knew the voice wasn't Charity's. Though it took several seconds longer, I also realized I was back in Susie's parked car. Like an idiot I mumbled, 'I saw Charity in the lobby. I resigned. Now I'm here.'

'Indeed you did resign, Ronald,' Charity announced from the back seat. 'However, I've seen Dimple since we met and she's asked if you'll reconsider, for her sake. I suspect she sees you as a father figure. Someone to respect.'

'That's really nice of her, Ronald,' Susie approved, 'considering recent events.'

I felt my brain collapse. I'd been flicked from one reality to another like a dizzy pea from a boomerang catapult. Everything had happened so fast I couldn't take it in. Whatever was stalking me – memory lapses, reality jumps, or plain perversity – had me well on the back foot. I stared through the windshield. I've no idea why, but I noticed the overgrown landscaping and the bustle of cars struggling to maneuver.

Charity punctured my pointless contemplations. 'You should take a few days off, Ronald.'

I turned and saw Susie nod. 'Good idea. I'll take him home.'

'And I'll get back to HQ,' Charity said, beckoning her chauffeur. 'Our cause demands my attention.'

I said nothing on the onward road trip and would have kept things that way in the apartment had Susie not squared up and wagged her finger.

'Stop behaving like a child,' she told me as if I'd been sulking. 'You've done a terrible thing but Dimple seems prepared to put the whole incident behind her, and so must you.'

I snorted. Susie didn't know the half of it and I was too confounded to explain. Hoping she'd go, I sprawled out on the nearest comfortable looking sofa and said, 'Yes, doctor.'

'Don't be sarcastic,' she threw back. 'I only agreed to Charity's request because— forget it.'

'What?' I asked, rolling my head. 'You might as well tell me and make my day.'

'They were going to commit you after what you did. They wanted time to check the state of your mental health.'

My head rolling switched to slow shaking. Whoever *they* were had slipped up and, like it or not, they couldn't have it both ways. I decided to rub their anonymous noses in it. 'But I didn't do anything, did I? Dimple hasn't accused me, so I'm as guiltless as a babe; except everyone thinks—'

'Stop it!' she barged in. 'Your self-delusion is disgusting.' Instead of going, she sat stiffly in an armchair and notched up a gear. 'You seem highly stressed, which is hardly surprising *if* you have genuinely been suffering random memory lapses. Whatever the truth, you're clearly not able to manage your personal situation. In my view you need medicine. You need help to calm down.'

How very impressive, I thought. A fistful of medical qualifications and she comes out with something as trite as me needing pills. 'Will your medicine make manipulative bitches disappear?'

'Get this straight, Ronald,' she countered. 'I can have you hospitalized just as easily as your former doctor, and I will unless you start being open with me.'

I couldn't help it. 'Deja vu,' I needled. 'Remember before: you wanting to know what's wrong *so we can work through it together.*'

That clipped her wings. For a moment she sat quietly, then said, 'I remember quite distinctly. It was just before you ran off to see Dimple.'

That clipped my wings. 'I ran off to her!'

She didn't answer for a while. When she did she was unnervingly subdued. 'You left me cold, if you must know, feeling very let down and under appreciated.'

I didn't respond. I sensed she had a bite to deliver. When she shivered lightly I knew it was coming.

'That's in the past. What concerns me is the here and

now of your mental health. Therefore, we'll use the break days Charity has offered to sort you out.' She looked hard into my eyes. 'So tell me everything, no matter how bizarre it sounds and no matter how painful or embarrassing it is for you. The gloves are off, I'm afraid. You're all out of chances.'

Chapter Four

I gazed at Susie, my mind wrestling with a thousand options. Bottom line: to keep her onside I had to go through her hoop. Besides, I had to concede, she was only trying to help, even if her bedside manner was as delicate as a rampant bulldozer. But I wasn't born yesterday.

'You're officially my doctor, is that right?' I waited for her nod. 'So anything and everything we say is confidential?'

Her comeback was guarded. 'Subject to appropriate disclosure to other professionals and—'

I cut her off and told her flat. 'Nothing I say goes beyond you. You're to write and sign a note to that effect so I can get you *unfrocked* if you breathe a word, or whatever it is they do to doctors who mouth off.'

She didn't like it. She liked my finger wagging even less.

'As you wish,' she said curtly once she'd accepted I was serious.

I watched her pluck a notebook from her purse and begin writing. Having had no chance to change, she still wore the gray abomination I'd first disliked in the conference room when she'd held my hand. Seeing it afresh made it seem even more bleak. Undoing the jacket would have helped. Undoing a couple of buttons on the blouse would have helped much more.

She caught me out. 'What are you staring at? I'm not Charity and I don't appreciate being eyeballed.'

'Charity does,' I flipped back, not exactly my finest riposte.

She looked impassive. 'Here is your note. Read it and be satisfied. As far as I'm concerned, this is a professional relationship and I've no interest in anything more.'

I couldn't resist. 'So why did you hold my hand under the table?'

She came straight back. 'Foolishness. Let's get on.'

My choice was stark: either reveal my head-load of off-with-the-fairies disorientation, or dream up a fistful of halfway plausible lies. What nagged was what I already knew: keeping things to myself had achieved exactly zilch. I decided to stick one toe in and see how she reacted. Trouble was, I paid more attention to her than to what I was saying. When she soaked it up without clogging my flow, I opened up a bit more, and then more again. Ended up telling her everything I could remember, including all about Dimple's duplicitous game.

'And that's it?' she asked as I fell silent. 'You're not holding out on me?'

Not feeling particularly proud of my soul-baring exposé, I answered crankily. 'Wouldn't have told you about Dimple if I was, would I?' Even then I couldn't tell what Susie was thinking. She just sat back.

After a while, she said, 'All right. Let's stick with Dimple for a moment. If what you say is true, she can easily be neutralized. You need only record what she says when next you meet. She might even make it easy and brag about her scheme. If not, you can always playact to make sure she repeats the key points. Either way you'll have something to support your story.'

'Would have lined that up myself given half a chance,' I grunted, annoyed I'd not thought of it.

She stiffened. 'Then I'll keep my non-medical ideas to myself in future.'

Reluctantly, I climbed down. 'You know I didn't mean it like that.' It was a mistake.

'I know you're disturbed,' she blasted at me. 'You, on the other hand, aren't certain who or what you know or don't know.'

'I don't ... didn't know you.' I was stupid to toss one back. Should have known she'd want the last word, the last chapter and verse as it turned out.

'True,' she agreed, gobbling up my impetuous counter-charge. 'I can definitely confirm that we met for the first time after what you believe was your initial meeting with Charity. That was yesterday, agreed?'

I'd set her off. Worse, I wasn't entirely sure the meeting hadn't been earlier that day, but then I didn't know how long I'd spent with Dimple. It seemed safest to nod.

She preened. 'The key has to be your strong feelings of having panicked, the feelings you had right at the beginning.' She glanced. 'I should say, from the time you see as a beginning.'

I kept silent, hoping she'd finished. She hadn't. She was in the zone.

'Interestingly, yesterday's meeting does seem to have marked a change in you. You're more fully aware of specific memory lapses, though not necessarily what happens during them. The unchanging bit is your ambivalent feelings of familiarity and unfamiliarity.' She sat forward. 'Is that a fair summary?'

I didn't like her undertone. 'What do you mean: I don't *necessarily* know what happens when my memory jumps. I *don't* know. There's a gap. I thought I'd made it clear. That's why Dimple's bitchy shenanigans are so frustrating. I absolutely don't know what happened.'

She didn't like my overt tone. After sucking in a meaning laden breath, she rummaged in her purse. 'You're lucky I have these. Take one.'

Scornfully, I cold-shouldered the pill bottle and decided to test the hunch I'd had earlier. Dangling my hands, I asked, 'Had you seen these before you came for me?'

'Take a pill, Ronald.'

It was my turn to be on a roll. 'No. I want to know. Had you seen my kicked about head and skinned knuckles before you came to the conference room?'

'I'm not the enemy,' she said quietly. 'I'm trying to help.'

'So tell me.'

She blistered at that. 'How could I possibly have seen them? You're making no sense.'

The bit was still between my teeth. 'Someone knows what's going on.'

She stood. Despite her drab appearance she looked tantalizingly formidable. 'Take a pill now or take it under restraints in hospital, your choice.'

I'm not sure what got into me. I took eight, gulping them down before she could react. 'There,' I said. 'Satisfied?'

She huffed, underwhelmed. 'They'll make you sleepy, and we have work to do.'

'Charity gave me time off,' I jeered. 'Screw working.'

She scolded like a schoolmistress. 'Time to get better, not laze around. You need to take on an easy case and build up to where you were before.' Giving me no chance to question, she went on, 'There's an elderly lady living nearby. She's partially blind and deaf and, sadly, a little confused. We need to make sure she understands properly and doesn't get the wrong end of the stick.' I stared until she had to ask, 'What's the matter?'

'Deja vu,' I said. 'When I thought Dimple was you, she said about a decrepit old hag who didn't know half-past four from Friday. Said we were to test her limits then point her in the right direction.'

'So?'

She had a point. The similarity had seemed far more significant in my head than out of it. 'There's too much coincidence,' I persisted even though it sounded lame.

'Only if you're paranoid,' she declared weightily. 'Are you paranoid, Ronald?'

To stump her, I moved swiftly across the room. 'Let's go visiting.' Only then did I realize we couldn't. 'Damn, it's too late to go now. We'll have to see her tomorrow.'

'What are you talking about?' she said, baffled. 'It's mid-morning,'

I knew it couldn't be. Confidently I said, 'We were at the hospital earlier this evening. We can't have been talking all night and then some.'

She was peremptory. 'I warned you that those pills would make you sleepy. You dropped off.'

I shook my head. 'No way. We've been talking all through.'

'Ronald, listen. This is the absolute truth. You fell asleep. I went home and spent the whole night there. I came again this morning and suggested you take on an easy case and build up to where you were before. I then told you about the old lady needing our help.'

My head felt numb. All her prattling wafted over me.

The evidence lay in plain sight, and it made me cringe. No longer was she wearing her dire gray clothes. Though I hated to believe it, they had undeniably been replaced by a dull blue suit and taupe blouse.

'You might also have had another episode,' she added somberly. 'Do you want to talk about it?'

Did I hell! 'No, I don't want to talk and I don't want any more of your damn pills!'

She didn't reply, unless you count walking out and gesturing me to follow. I did. I was too confused to do anything else. We traveled in silence, tense silence. Fortunately the road trip was short. Even so the area seemed a million miles from the luxury of my apartment.

Belligerently, I said, 'I'll catch something if I go near anyone here.'

'I shall ignore that remark, Ronald, and I'll stay here while you go in alone.'

'Hey, come on. I was joking.'

She wouldn't have it. 'You weren't joking and neither am I.'

I held on hoping she'd change her mind. She didn't. 'All right. What am I supposed to do for the old bag?'

'She is not an old bag. She is Mrs Bessel and she has an appointment with Richard Smithy, a financial consultant.' She glanced at her watch. 'In about five minutes. You can slip inside with Mr Smithy.'

I couldn't help it. I laughed my sourest laugh. 'Don't be stupid. Nobody here knows who I am. They'll never let me *slip* in, especially with my mangled face.'

'Your face isn't mangled, merely lightly marked; and I am not stupid, so I'll thank you to be more polite.'

'Sorry, doctor.'

'And less sarcastic.'

'All right, but—'

She cut straight across me. 'If you're as clever as I believe, Mrs Bessel will think you're with Mr Smithy and he'll think you're with her. She's partially blind remember.'

I thought my ears must have been chomping on magic mushrooms. I'd never heard such a crazy idea and couldn't understand how she could have dreamed it up. Playing safe, I dragged in my first principle: clarify task. 'Aren't we a charity supporting the half blind and deaf? There must be an easier way.'

'There is,' she shot back at once, 'but you'll do it my way regardless. Understand?'

'No.'

She sighed. 'I want you thinking on your feet, Ronald. You're to engage with reality. That means doing things that aren't all about you. We need this dear lady on our side.'

She was talking piffle and I knew it. I tried a dose of posturing but eventually had to say, 'Okay. Tell me what you want and I'll do my best.'

'No half-hearted promises,' she warned before crisply laying out her stall.

My unease grew as I listened. Not only was her scheme lunacy masquerading as half-baked therapy, it offered nothing whatever to help my cause. For two pins, I'd have cut and run. I should have. Instead I shoved the hunt for my nemesis aside and, like a flickering fool, did as I was told. I even remember feeling smug about the way I nonchalantly slipped into Mrs Bessel's house. A surprise was inside: Bill, the lady's son.

He looked about my age, maybe younger. Not wanting to be challenged, I kept my gaze off him and said nothing. Besides, I'd been pumped so full of Susie's absurdities I was still reeling. From any standpoint the charity's perverse interest in financial products was off-base. All I could do was let consultant Smithy launch into his pitch.

After the first forty-five minutes I could cheerfully have clamped myself into a medieval head crusher. I truly wished I'd not behaved like a wimp and let Susie divert me from my own critical quest. By the time Smithy shifted up a gear, I was aching to bury him in his own twaddle.

I groaned when he announced grandly, 'This is a fantastic opportunity, Mrs Bessel. It'll double your money in no time and buy you all the things you deserve.'

'I don't get it,' Bill said. 'You've shown us masses of figures but none explain the—'

He came straight back. 'I'm here to help your mother, Bill. It's her money after all.'

Bill didn't like that. He 'yes butted.'

Unable to stomach any possibility of Smithy going through it all again, I tried telepathy, in desperation more than anything: for pity's sake, Bill, shut up and let muscle-mouth finish. Let's end this torture.

'For pity's sake, Bill,' Mrs Bessel said at once. 'Let the man speak. He's the expert, not you.'

That made me laugh, though I had to smother it. She'd regurgitated my improvised psychic thoughts as if she'd really heard them. Too right, girl, I applauded. Your boy's more interested in his inheritance than in you having a last hurrah.

'I'll do what I want with my money, Bill,' she echoed indignantly. 'It's mine. I shouldn't have to be miserable just so you can live it up when I'm gone.'

Bill gasped. So did I. Not sure which of us was the more surprised.

'That hurt, Mum,' he said softly. 'I want your well-being, not your money. This so-called fantastic opportunity sounds very dicey to me.'

'Well that hurt me, Bill,' Smithy said, appropriately offended. 'If that's what you think, I won't put your mother in for the free bonus; and I'll not be responsible for the thousands of dollars she'll lose year on year.'

'Hear that, Bill,' Mrs Bessel said. 'Thousands of dollars you're costing me.'

Sounds from the front door breathed anticipation into the room and made her pause. When a woman appeared moments later, Bill looked more relieved than a pigeon escaping a pie dish. He said, 'Glad you're here, Gabby.'

'Hello, Bill ... Mum,' Gabby said, her pleasant features creased with concern. 'Bill sent me a text.' She looked round. 'He told me the salesman was here.'

Another offspring, I sagged, yet I was distracted. A light had flashed so brightly it had completely stolen my sight. It was frighteningly dark afterwards. Though too spooked to move, I could still hear, and it sounded as if I'd missed a sizable chunk of conversation.

Gabby was speaking. 'I'm a Christian woman and—'

I heard no more. My entire body felt as if it had been pitched headlong into an intense firestorm. Then all my consciousness was wrenched away.

Chapter Five

It's hard to describe nothing. I'd hit a complete blank. The only reason I knew anything about it was its end. Gradually, I became aware of floating as if encased in a black cocoon of soothing waters. Noises infiltrated, softly at first, then louder until they filled and threatened to explode my head. I think I yelled. More truthfully, I screamed like a sissy. Don't know if my bawling affected it but, either way, the cocoon ruptured.

I was left flat on a hard surface – cold – the blackness replaced with the special darkness of night. My eyes were wide open. Despite heavy disorientation my instincts must have been savvy. They forced me to soak up my surroundings, keen to sling a hook into anything familiar. Nothing. I was outdoors, somewhere. It felt and smelled decidedly urban with me in the gutter, sprawled out, dumped and abandoned.

Most of my aches had returned which made it a struggle to sit up. A solitary street lamp flickered. It revealed barbed palisade fencing, high and forbidding. It could have been keeping me in or out, and I needed to know. Forcing my legs, I staggered a few paces. I was in a yard, a big one. I guessed a depot. Trucks were parked separate from their trailers. Huge buildings loomed in the background, their purpose unclear. All I cared about was getting back to a place I knew, at least somewhere I recognized.

Not sure how I passed through the fence, but I walked unimpeded into a wide alley. There were more lamps, none very bright. I'd been right about it being urban, the guts of a town, maybe a city. Ranges of mixed industrial buildings towered both sides, all black inside, all silently menacing like formidable specters. They spawned an intimidating passageway.

Fifty yards ahead stood a dark clothed man. He was carrying a machete, its cutting edge glinting despite the poor light. For a second I stared, my head cocked like a bewildered rabbit. Then I turned ready to run for my life. I didn't go anywhere. Three other men were the same distance behind me, all ambling closer, all armed. When I swung back, the first man had been joined by four others.

I ran. What else could I do? I lit out of there as if hounds from hell were at my heels. And it nearly killed me. Intense pain ravaged my body as I charged and swerved to avoid their immediate attack. My arms swirled like a demented dancer's. None of it made any difference. Within moments I'd been surrounded. Seconds later, I'd been shoved onto my back and had men holding fast to each wrist and ankle. The others all whooped at me, machetes in hand.

'You brain-dead or something,' the leader said. 'No one comes to The Blades' territory without paying tribute, unless they're invited.' The others rumbled out their own brand of agreement. 'You been invited?'

'No he hasn't, Grub, but then neither have I.' The female voice was so soft I was sure I'd imagined it, except that Grub's eyes had bolted down the alley.

'You are welcome,' he said with a tremor that hinted fear. Made me feel like a bystander.

'Thank you, sweetie,' Dimple said. 'That man you're holding is mine.' At once the men pinning me down jumped clear, each jostling to avoid her direct line of sight. Made me feel like a bonded peasant bystander.

Grub too avoided her gaze. 'Didn't know,' he said. 'Just caught him.'

'Of course you didn't know, sweetie, but you still touched him and you shouldn't have done that.' She laughed. 'Pick one of your men.'

I watched Grub tense. 'No, Dimple, please.'

'Are you volunteering yourself, Grubby, you brute of a leader you?'

Though she seemed to be merely teasing, Grub hurriedly grabbed the nearest of his men, fighting until he had him subdued. 'This one,' he panted.

Dimple stepped close to the captured man. 'What's your name?'

'In The Blades, I am Throot,' he gasped.

'Are you?' she mocked. I saw his eyes drop. 'Guess you think that sounds macho.'

For a second he looked at me. Dread had locked his features into a desperate grimace.

'Got to tell you, Throot,' she went on, 'your name sounds more like a disease. You'd have done better calling yourself Gertrude.' He began shaking. 'Never mind. This is your chance to be brave, so stand free and be brave, my little Throoty.'

As Grub released his grip, Throot moved like a zombie to where Dimple was pointing. After swallowing hard, he shakily offered his machete.

She smiled and took it. Then her gaze fell on me. 'Ronald, get up and stand next to me.' I shivered as if I'd been wrenched from the spectators' gallery and tossed into a lion filled arena. 'Tell them who I am,' she said. 'I mean who I am to you.'

Despite the anarchy in my brain, I knew what she wanted. 'You're my mistress,' I croaked, hoping she might also be my savior.

'I am indeed, Ronald, so down you get on all fours, doggy style.'

Needn't tell you how I felt. Humiliated didn't come into it. I'd never been more scared. For all I knew she was lining up to be my murderer, not my savior. When she turned to Throot, I didn't know whether to spiral into relief or terror.

'Bare his buttocks for me, Throoty,' she purred. 'He shouldn't be here so you may thrash him for his naughtiness. Use your belt.'

I gaped like a dotard, but then so did the others. And Dimple loved it. She positively glowed, feeding on the wild mix of cringing emotions she'd so effortlessly generated.

'I want him nicely purple,' she added. 'Red won't do. Black will be best of all.'

Even if I'd had the presence of mind to run, I couldn't. Grub's boot came from nowhere and crushed my face against the asphalt. Within a heartbeat, it was Throot's turn, his moment of glory. And he was out to impress. I still reckon he squeezed every atom of strength into every lash from his belt. I make no excuses. I lost it. I shrieked like a yellow bellied wimp. Not that anyone cared.

Despite everything, I could almost feel Dimple, what she was doing. She was like a potent organism stuck in my brain, an entity that watched dispassionately, all the while goading Throot with sadistic jabs from his own machete. Finally, not even the jabs could keep Throot from collapsing. He dropped on me like a clutch of crumbling bones in a sack. I must have reacted since he rolled off, slightly away.

Dimple sighed. I remember that sigh: an incongruous mix of disappointment and satisfaction. 'Well that seems to be that,' she said, not in any way shy about scrutinizing Throot's work. 'What do you think, Grubby?'

The gang leader peered guardedly. The second he shifted to look, Dimple slashed open his cheek. Before anyone else could move, she'd virtually severed Throot's neck. Immediately, the all but decapitated body spewed blood, the pool rapidly spreading to within an inch of my face.

The fright almost killed me. Not even at my mental peak would I have tagged Dimple as such a merciless and arbitrary killer. When she tossed down the machete, the clang resonated like my own death knell.

Her composure didn't waver. 'Won't need that any more,' she said, 'assuming you boys are happy to stick to the rules.' Straight away I heard a chorus of reassurance from the survivors. 'Good,' she acknowledged. 'Now dress my slave and pop him in my car. I'm in the mood for dancing.'

After yanking up my pants, they dragged me along the alley and chucked me in the trunk of Dimple's car. The darkness was the final straw. I knew I was already broken, that I'd utterly lost it, yet being caged in that asphyxiating blackness totally wrecked anything I had left. Merely to keep afloat I'd have willingly groveled before Dimple and called her *mistress* as often as she liked, as publicly as she liked. I'd have done anything she asked, anything.

The road trip in the bleak gloom tortured my senses, merging with the agony of my beating. When the trunk reopened, bright lights from Dimple's favored nightclub clawed into my eyes, making me shrink back and howl worse than a teething baby on starvation rations.

Dimple's instructions to two burly attendants rang out with fearsome clarity. 'Get this collar on him and make him presentable. He's not trotting behind me looking like that.'

The men hot-footed to pull me out, their brutal handling instantly re-energizing all my pains. Begging for mercy, I jerked from foot to foot desperate for relief, but they were on their own mission. Ruthlessly, they stripped off my clothes and replaced them with a fancy-dress pirate's outfit. How or why I bothered to notice is beyond me, yet I did. The stupid clothes were merely one more humiliation in my sea of torment; one that would, I desperately hoped, amuse Dimple enough to keep me alive.

I shuddered when she looked at me, assessing. 'Better, but your sniveling has to stop or you'll get something worth sniveling about. Understand?'

I didn't hold back. Like the most submissive and grateful of slaves, I dropped down and whimpered, 'Y-yes, mistress.'

'I think he's coming round,' Susie said, her voice like spontaneous thunder in my head. Her concern was palpable.

'You're right,' someone else agreed, coming nearer for a better look. 'He's one lucky guy.' As I discovered soon enough, that someone was Dr Burns, a hospital physician. I must have peeped because I remember him crossing the spotless and expensively equipped medical room, heading for the door. 'I'll leave you a while,' he said. 'You know where to find me.'

Susie nodded her thanks before looking back at me. We were alone. 'I should be cross,' she scolded. 'You've had us all so worried.'

Though my situation had so obviously changed, I couldn't expunge the memory of the murderous Dimple leading me into a nightclub: beaten, broken, on hands and knees in a pirate costume. I ached to ask what had happened but my nerves were still too shattered.

Jokingly she said, 'Suppose you thought you'd get another couple of days off by injuring yourself.'

I had no space for humor. 'I'm scared,' I said, my voice barely audible.

She melted. There was already moisture in her eyes and

it rapidly became tears. To hide them she lay her head on my chest, her shoulders delivering small quakes as she took and gave comfort. 'No need to be scared any more. You're exactly where you should be.'

I needed all the comfort I could get. I'd been utterly churned up. 'S-sorry if I've been rotten to you,' I stammered like a drunk overflowing with emotion. 'Didn't mean to upset you. Didn't mean to be difficult.'

'It's all right,' she soothed. 'Important thing is getting you well, properly well.'

Suddenly unable to hold back, I erupted like an awakening volcano. 'You've got to tell me what happened, Susie.' It was a moronically overblown outburst. Took me till later to blame it on the drugs they'd plugged into me; but that was moronic too.

Susie merely clasped my hands. Hers were shaking. 'You had a shock.'

With the top already blasted off my mountain of compressed trauma, words gushed like a pyroclastic flow, surging through anything in their path. 'Shock!' I blurted. 'Shock nothing! I've been attacked by a bunch of machete wielding thugs. They would have hacked me to pieces if Dimple hadn't turned up. And there was me thinking she was in hospital! Don't ask me how or why but she scared the steam right out of them. She was a bitch to me as well though. Had me beaten with a belt till I cried like a girl. But that's just part of it. She killed a guy, mutilated another, then – calm as you like – had me dragged off to a nightclub. Stupid bitch dressed me like a pirate then paraded me about on a lead. Real trouble that girl is.'

'Whoa! Whoa!' Susie cut in as I gasped for breath. 'Slow down. Calm down. This is important.' Releasing my hands, she leaned further back and grabbed a notebook from her purse. 'I need to understand, Ronald, so I'll jot down all you remember. We can go over it later.' She smiled encouragingly. 'Start from when you went to Mrs Bessel's about her house adaptations.'

I frowned, confused. I'd forgotten about the old lady and knew nothing of any adaptations. Susie refused to be sidetracked.

'Do you remember being outside her house? Me asking you to go in?' I nodded. 'Go from there.'

I began babbling at once, setting out the lowlights of my ordeal from the excruciation of the salesman to Mrs Bessel plucking out my thoughts. When I mentioned the daughter, Susie interrupted.

'Did she speak to you?'

I was a bit hazy on that. 'There was a light, I think, soon after she arrived. Made me miss bits of what she was saying, though I remember her saying she was a Christian. After that something put my lights out. No idea what. When I resurfaced, I'd become fresh meat-on-the-hoof for the machete boys.'

Susie looked sombre. 'Go on, Ronald. Tell me exactly what happened.'

I hesitated. I'd only just fully registered how remarkably well I was feeling and how tranquil I'd become after my frantic outpouring. That's when I naively thought to blame the drugs.

Smirking like an adolescent trying to submerge a dirty joke, I said, 'Whatever they shot into me has made me high.' When she didn't answer, I conceded. 'All right. You want the whole loaf before you'll tell me anything. Fine. Anything you say ... doctor.'

Half smiling, she settled to listen, only occasionally slipping in a question. By the time I'd finished, I was feeling far from tranquil.

'I'll tell you straight,' I said. 'I don't want any more to do with Dimple. I'll resign, retire, join a monastery, drop to the bottom of the ocean; I don't care. I just never want to see her again.'

She nodded and set down her notebook on the locker near my pillow. 'I quite understand. If I'd been through the things you've described, I wouldn't want to know her either.'

'And I'll not testify against her,' I added emphatically. 'No way!'

'We need to go back a little,' she nudged gently. 'You say that I told you to sneak into Mrs Bessel's house by pretending you were with a consultant–come–salesman and th—'

'You insisted,' I chopped in. 'I said there had to be an easier way but you wouldn't have it.'

I didn't like it when she stiffened. I liked it even less

when she said, 'You must be calm when I tell you this.'

I felt my heart accelerate. 'What?'

'Mrs Bessel is an old lady who has trouble seeing and hearing. She is also a widow of long standing with no children and no family we're aware of. There was no salesman, no son, and no daughter; Christian or otherwise. I asked you to tell her that we've approved her case and that we'll be sending round assessors to chat through her needs.' She ignored my slow and disbelieving head shakes. 'I'm sorry, Ronald, and of course it's no insignificant matter, but all you did was electrocute yourself. Somehow you touched a faulty electrical connection ... which we've now had fixed.'

No way was I swallowing that load of tosh. 'That doesn't explain Dimple killing that bloke and having me beaten. My butt is all the proof you need. You only have to look at the belt marks.'

She stayed unnervingly quiet, then took my hands again. 'All right, Ronald, I'll look ... but you need to know this first: I ran into Mrs Bessel's house when I saw her come outside, clearly in a panic. I found you laid out in the living room. I resuscitated you and then had you brought here to this hospital where you've been for about a day now.

'During that whole time I've not left your side for more than a few minutes, and you've been nowhere.' She squeezed my fingers. 'And Dimple hasn't been anywhere either. She's still three stories up, exactly where you saw her. That means she can't have been moonlighting with any machete men or off clubbing with you dressed as a pirate.'

She released my hands and sat back. 'We'll look at your buttocks now, Ronald. It's important you face up to reality. You must if you're to get better.'

Chapter Six

After hearing Susie's hogwash story, I was red-hot keen to get my pajamas off and prove my case. It didn't strike me that, as a side consequence, I'd be branding her a liar, or worse. And, frankly, I wouldn't have cared.

With my butt exposed and her holding a mirror for me to see, she posed the only question worth asking. 'What do you think?'

For a time, I wriggled about trying to see every bit of skin, hunting for tell-tale signs. Nothing. Not the slightest sign of injury: no scratches, bumps or bruises; not even a pimple.

She asked again. This time I rallied enough to shrug.

'I understand your confusion,' she said softly. 'Sometimes our imaginations can go to the darkest corners and convince us of the most peculiar things.' I grunted. 'That being so, there is something you really should face. I should say someone.' I kept my eyes down, easily guessing where she was heading. 'You must go up and see Dimple right now. See for yourself that she couldn't have done those terrible things.'

Susie was rushing way ahead of anything I could cope with. I'd still not accepted the evidence of my own eyes. 'No,' I said.

'We can put you in a wheelchair if you're not up to walking.'

I stopped that idea with a glare. Not so easy was working out how I'd been so comprehensively duped. Pondering if time alone had done the healing, I asked, 'How long did you say I've been here?'

She sighed. 'Cover yourself and be logical. If you'd been beaten as badly as you believe, it would have taken weeks for your skin to look as good as yours, and that's ignoring the probability of scarring. You've been here a day and Dimple is still here. She would have been discharged ages ago if you really had been here long enough to heal.' Another sigh. 'It's vital you see her for yourself ... and see her bruises. You can then more honestly decide between fact and fiction.' She reached for her purse. 'I've brought something to encourage you.'

It was my turn to sigh. 'Okay. I'll bite. What is it?'

'A micro audio-camera. Easy to conceal so no problem recording Dimple: what she does, what she says.' She held it out of my reach. 'It's yours if you agree to see her now.'

'So you do believe me,' I said, clasping at straws.

She waited for me to sort out my pajamas and sit upright. Pain hit my legs as I moved. I exaggerated for effect.

She looked skeptical, but handed over the miniature device. 'It's what you believe that matters, Ronald. If Dimple really is toying with you, you can catch her out, just as we discussed.'

I held the camera like a minuscule rose in my palm, then studied her intently, wondering if she truly was as golden hearted as she seemed. Until that moment I'd not noticed, but then it became screamingly apparent. Her blouse, as ever, had all the buttons fastened. Her suit was dull. Yet the blouse wasn't taupe and the suit wasn't blue.

'You're a brick, Susie,' I said, lulling her. 'You stayed with me the whole time since my accident.'

She smiled coyly. 'Someone had to stop you getting into more mischief.'

'But you stayed, not leaving the hospital?'

Her smile faltered. 'That's right. What are you suggesting?'

I didn't hesitate. 'Your clothes are always ugly, dull, and boring, Susie. That's why they're so noticeable. But, cupcake, you're not swathed in the same garb you had on yesterday. You were in lifeless blue then and now – unless I've caught color blindness along with everything else – you're in tasteless mauve.' I snorted at her. 'Accordingly, doctor, you're feeding me a load of bull. Everything I've said did happen. Weeks could have passed since my alleged electrocution. You might even have given me an ass transplant! Fact is, I don't care. All that matters is what I know first hand: someone really is screwing with my head, and I reckon it's someone very dear to your treacherous little heart.'

I glowered as she rose, her legs apparently shaky, her mouth tight. I was in no mood to ease her conspicuous shock. I'd caught her bang to rights and it took several minutes of deathly silence before she'd recovered enough to speak.

Even then she surprised me. 'Y-you silly ungrateful man,' she stammered. 'I dirtied my clothes at Mrs Bessel's when saving your life. I phoned from here and a friend brought this.' She fingered the lapel on her mauve jacket. 'And she brought another blouse, and underwear too if you want every last detail. I didn't know how long I might have to stay.' She stiffened resolutely. 'But I won't be staying any longer. Good luck, Ronald, we won't be seeing each other again.'

She dashed for the door before I could blink, leaving me alone to ponder. Though reluctant, I had to admit she'd come up with a plausible explanation, a possibility that had completely passed me by. I could have called after her. I didn't. I knew what I knew and my imagination didn't run to dreaming up machete gangs, murderous bitches, and pirate outfits.

I looked again at the tiny camera. It had to be tested. There would be no value in snaring Dimple if the kit was rubbish. Within a few minutes, I'd checked out the device and made a test recording to verify compatibility with my cell phone. Sound and visuals worked perfectly.

By the time I reached the fifteenth floor, the pain in my legs needed no exaggeration. Bridget, the bright nurse I'd met before, saw me hobbling closer. 'Hi there, Mr Foster,' she said warmly. 'We heard you'd had an accident. Are you feeling better?'

I remembered last time. 'Obviously you're feeling less deviant,' I sneered, not dallying for her reaction. I kept shuffling on to Dimple's room and crashed in without knocking.

'Sweetie,' she said, looking genuinely surprised.

I kept half an eye on her and wobbled round to make sure we were alone. She watched from her bed, her nightie low, heavy bruising vivid on her chest.

'Satisfied?' she queried when I cautiously settled in her bedside chair.

'Throot sends his love,' I said, alert for the least reaction.

'Who or what is Throot?' she bounced back. 'Sounds like a disease.'

'That's what you said before. We need to talk.'

She smiled. 'All right, since I've nothing better to do.'

'Clarification first,' I began, but she charged in.

'Oh yes. I remember from the conference room. You like to clarify your tasks. Am I your task now, sweetie?'

I ignored her question. 'I've been in this room before.'

'Are you asking or telling me?' she countered.

'Asking.'

'But why should I answer, sweetie? What have you ever done for me besides leave me frustrated and treat me like a punch-bag?'

'I hit you once, a slap. You've had worse from candy-coated little girls, remember?'

'Whatever you say, you big brutish boy.'

I should have known she'd be contrary. 'Please could you tell me if I've been in this room before and, if so, when and what happened?'

She grinned. 'Since you ask so nicely, no comment.'

Frustrated at getting nowhere, I stupidly attempted to coax out her worst nature. 'Okay, mistress, do you want me on my knees?'

She sat up, arms folded, eyebrows arced. 'You really aren't well, are you?'

'Well enough,' I told her. 'Just give me an answer ... mistress.'

'Idiot!' she said. 'I'm not your mistress. Neither am I your lover, concubine, paramour, Trixie nor Dixie. As far as I'm concerned, you were a bit of fun. Now you're an embarrassing bore.' She pointed to the door. 'Leave now and we'll forget this loony conversation ever took place. If you don't, Charity will hear about it, word for word.'

There was no point in appealing to her non-existent

finer qualities. All I could do was head out with annoyance between my legs. My plan had nose-dived. I'd not even made first base. The last thing I expected was Nurse Bridget to rush at me. Her slap to my face came as a complete shock.

'You're the deviant!' she shouted. 'How dare you!'

Bernie too was on hand. 'Out, Mr Foster. You've made enough trouble.'

I could have said something. I could have punched Bernie square on the jaw and made myself feel a lot better. But I let it go. Back in my room I sank onto the bed, belatedly realizing my mistake. I should have kept my mouth shut, not faced Susie with her lies. She might then have been slower to charge off and warn the homicidal bitch-queen upstairs, as I was entirely convinced she had.

Angry at having wasted so much energy, I snatched the camera from my bath robe ready to throw it at the wall. It stayed in my hand. I was wondering if Dimple had been too clever. She'd not only said about Throot's name sounding like a disease, she'd also said *brutish boy,* just as she'd said *brute of a leader* to the chief of The Blades. It wasn't much, but enough to hint that she'd been taunting me. Quickly, I linked the camera to my cell phone, hoping for something more.

My screen showed Dimple's surprise at my arrival and my check of the room. Not long afterwards, I heard my own voice, saying, 'Throot sends his love.'

My mouth gaped at her response. 'Doubt it. Last I saw he was dead and gushing blood in your face.'

My soul screamed as if pierced by a pickax. Pure reflex shut off the playback as I told myself I'd misheard, obviously I'd misheard. My glib rationalization blamed the pain killers. They had confused my mind, made me see what I expected, not the truth. It was an aberration, nothing more. Even so, I couldn't resist.

The playback continued with Dimple, no longer in bed, but standing imperiously, no sign of bruising. 'You came to test me, didn't you, slave?'

The images that followed showed me dropped to my knees. 'Sorry, mistress.'

She cuffed my head. 'You want another beating, is that it?'

I heard myself say, 'Please, have mercy.'

'I have no mercy,' she scorned. 'My little demo with the machete should have shown you that.'

I shuddered, powerless to tear my eyes from the screen, utterly nauseated. 'That's not me,' I said aloud, seeing myself cringe and whimper worse than the most pathetic wounded animal. 'I'd never behave like that.'

Even as I spoke, my own direct memories of the machete gang impaled my bravado. When with them, I'd so willingly groveled before Dimple.

Gutted and unable to bear any more, I lay on the bed, the contradictions churning like a circulating stampede. It seemed surreal when a strained calmness overtook me. I imagined Susie close by, helping me to be logical.

I quickly became fixated on Susie and on what she'd said. And – if she hadn't been lying about the time I'd spent in hospital, and if she had stayed the whole time, and if she had phoned for a change of clothes – then she had to be right. Dimple's bruises wouldn't have had time to heal, and neither would mine. Since I'd just visited Dimple and seen her bruises – and since I had no bruises to show – that had to mean the machete gang didn't exist. The playback had flipped out and wired into some rubbish in my mind.

I sniffed and sat up, somberly aware of how far I was from anything approaching the whole truth. Everything was too inconsistent, too plain mad, and there were too many unanswered questions. Frustrated, I resorted once more to my first principle – task – but soon found myself floundering. My only unchanged certainty was the conviction that someone really was maliciously pulling my strings. How or why this nemesis was doing it, I still didn't know; and I was no better off about the *who*.

I'd just blasted out a resentful sigh, when the door burst open. Charity stood like a goddess in the clinically white frame, her rosewood dress beautifully accentuating her graceful curves.

'I've just seen Dimple,' she said, 'whom you've managed to upset deeply. And I've had Susie on the phone in tears because of the cruel things you've said.' She paused. 'Anything to say?'

At another time I'd have had plenty to say, but I bottled it and shook my head. This lady was a whole world of mystery all by herself.

She didn't like my pointed reticence. 'Then I'll say it for you: I'm sorry, you will say to Dimple. I apologize unreservedly, you will say to Susie. You will say both these things in the very near future.' She took a pace towards me. 'I told you at the meeting: I've high hopes for your partnership with Susie. Accordingly, I will not tolerate my plans being disrupted by the disgusting antics of a reprobate who can't keep his nose out of hallucinogenic drugs.' Her perfectly manicured finger pointed unwaveringly. 'If you do anything more to compromise my plans, I will unhesitatingly cut you off ... and I will make sure you sink. Am I entirely clear?' I nodded but it wasn't enough. 'I asked you a question.'

'Entirely clear, yes.'

My heart kept racing long after she'd gone.

Chapter Seven

With my heart still pounding like a manic drummer, my head dropped low. Charity had laid it out, plain and simple. I was a recovering drug addict, apparently not a very committed one given recent events. Although she'd not said it openly, she'd made it pretty clear that I'd been partnered with Dr Susie precisely because she was a doctor. I guessed she'd left it for me to work out that the charity's mission also doubled as therapy for people like me. Made me think how badly I'd misread all those scared faces at the conference table.

My doleful thoughts were interrupted by Dr Burns, the physician I'd glimpsed when coming round.

'Not as bad as that, is it?' he asked. I only managed a blank response. 'Fair enough,' he acknowledged. 'Maybe it's time for another squirt of happy medicine ... if you have the cash.'

His greedy eyes told me I'd not misheard, yet my senses still baulked. I throbbed to ask what he meant, but the question would have been beyond puerile. He couldn't have been more barefaced had he emblazoned his offer in neon lights around the walls.

My hesitation made him frown. 'You've already had freebies, my friend. It's pay up time if you want more.'

My brain ricocheted between doubt and inspiration. Gave me a huge mental double-take. Here he was: showcasing indiscretion; unashamedly offering me drugs; and it appeared, not for the first time. 'Give me a second.'

'I won't be offended if you're generous,' he prompted,

watching as I rummaged around my pillows.

'As long as it's the same good stuff,' I said, finding cash I didn't know was there.

'It's guaranteed good,' he beamed, eyes sparkling. 'I'll take half that now, but don't spend the rest. You'll need it tomorrow.'

As the money became drugs in my hand, I tried duplicity. 'I've only been here three days and already you've made me a pauper.'

'Might seem like three,' he corrected, 'but you've only had a day's worth of my excellent service. Good stuff or what!' Grinning, he left me to it.

At first, I felt I'd been given a bonus: unforced corroboration of Susie's honesty. Then something niggled. When could Burns have dished out his freebies? I'd been mostly spaced out with Susie on guard, or so she'd claimed. It didn't add up, unless certain people wanted me to believe I was an hallucinating druggie.

Still puzzling, I checked the micro-camera. Though my fumbled switching it on hadn't caught the whole drug exchange, it had recorded enough of Burns to have him boiled, if boiling ever became necessary. If it didn't, he could flutter off as far as I was concerned. What mattered to me was turning my insight to best advantage.

Despite being hemmed in by narrow options – maybe because I was – it took me no time to decide. I'd play their game: make Charity think I'd swallowed her verdict and her instructions. I'd behave like a good little junkie and trot off to apologize to Dimple, then do the same with Susie. It was the only way to test the water and, hopefully, get a grip on something useful.

I sighed, still unsure how to read Susie, wondering afresh if she'd been telling the truth. For sure she'd been pretty upset after I'd gone for her. My sigh became an angry curse at my own hare-footed rashness. By not giving her the benefit of the doubt, I could easily have shot my bolt with the one person who might help me hunt down my manipulative nemesis. Like it or not, I had to get her back onside.

Blinded by my own scheming, I focused on my first hurdle: getting passed Nurse Bridget. Hoping she'd taken a break, I set off for the fifteenth floor. She hadn't. She spotted me at once. Her glare vengefully declared that I was in for a rough time.

'I apologize,' I said from a distance. 'If I could wind back time and rub out my rudeness, I would. Sadly I can only say how sorry I am.' She remained poker-faced. 'May I see Dimple, please?'

Her mouth hardly moved. 'It's not visiting hours.'

'When would it be convenient to come back?' I asked politely.

As I spoke, Dimple's door opened. Bridget heard and went across. After a few words she stalked off and Dimple waved me to come in.

With the door closed, she said, 'Suppose Charity came to see you.'

'She did.'

'And said how much you'd upset me.'

'I've come to apologize,' I said. 'It's my day for apologies and you're top of the list.'

'After the nurse.'

I rallied. 'Top of the apology list that matters.'

She moved to the bed and sat facing me, her nightie loose, doing little to veil her body. 'Good recovery,' she mocked. 'Get on with it then.'

I couldn't. My gaze was fixed, my imagination alight with the allure of her inadvertent display.

'I said, get on with it,' she snapped.

I couldn't believe I'd been so blatantly unsubtle. A quick glance was one thing but I'd been openly staring. Worse, I'd been caught. Having been wrong footed, my composure cracked. 'Err,' I mumbled. 'Sorry, Dimple, sorry for things said and done.'

'Do better,' she said.

I managed to get a grip. 'Sorry,' I repeated. 'I realize I've treated you very badly. I'd like to start from scratch and hopefully be your friend.'

'You apologize like a habit, Ronald. You must have had lots of practice.'

I forced a smile. 'It's sincerely meant. I hope you'll accept it as such.'

She straightened. 'I do. I do. But now you must go. I've things to do.'

Bridget was outside the door with Bernie close. I merely

nodded and passed them by, my mind set on getting out and squaring things with Susie.

'It's not a wise thing to do,' Dr Burns said when I collared him in the corridor. 'I'll come to your room and we'll discus it.'

Once there, I sat on the bed while Burns paced and talked. 'After your electric shock, you suffered many hours of unconsciousness, which in itself is not good. You've also experienced numbness, tingling, paralysis, vision, hearing, and speech problems.'

'I have?'

'And memory lapses with hallucinations,' he added.

'I don't recall any of those things.'

'Like I said, memory lapses.'

When he laughed, I decided to chance it. 'I very clearly remember you selling me drugs.'

'Like I said, memory lapses with hallucinations.'

'I have a recording.'

He laughed again. 'And I have the authority to commit you.'

'That won't work,' I retaliated. 'I've already sent it to Susie.'

He didn't flinch. 'Fibber! I checked. You left your cell phone under your pillow when you went off to Dimple. Left the camera and cash there too. There's a form if you want to claim lost property.'

'I don't get it,' I said, feeling like a limbless rat in a collapsing building.

He shrugged and ambled to the door before turning. 'Do what you want. Go right ahead and discharge yourself. It'll save me the bother of giving you a permanent good night injection when your money runs out.'

My whole body tensed. I had to have misunderstood.

'No, buddy, you heard correctly.' After a glance at his watch, he warned, 'But go now. I'll give you ten minutes, then I'll be back with a couple of partners. They'll hold you down while I jab you.'

I'd never moved so quickly. Neither did I stop until I was well outside the hospital's main doors. By the time my heartbeat had settled, I'd binned any thought of boiling Burns. No one would have believed me anyway.

Hurrying on, I shoved my thoughts towards Susie, yet

my unkempt appearance increasingly engrossed me. It overwhelmed me. I sensed people staring, making judgments. And no wonder. I'd thrown on my suit without bothering with a tie. I felt compelled to make amends. Wearing a bath robe to see Dimple had been bad enough. I absolutely couldn't face Susie and do what had to be done in anything less than my very best.

I paused, keenly aware of the need to get back to my apartment. That called for transport, which meant finding a driver willing to take a chance on the fare. By the time I'd pleaded and cajoled and finally made it, I was mentally and physically exhausted, fit for nothing except sprawling out along the sofa. I fell asleep.

When I awoke, late morning sunshine was streaming in and I was feeling remarkably in balance, better than I had any right to expect. Goaded on, I chose to thoroughly indulge myself. After lengthy bathing and pampering, I selected a commanding dark suit and teamed it with a new white shirt and classic silk tie. My span of mirrors beamed back the sartorial perfection I'd achieved. I felt proud, until Charity's inescapable demands ripped into my haven.

They sent my mood crashing into muddled foreboding. The apology I'd already given Dimple had been relatively easy because it had meant nothing. Handling the more delicate Susie was altogether different. Yet she was a doctor and, I reckoned, not the type to walk out on a patient just because of a few crossed wires; not a permanent walkout. Besides she was *my* doctor and I still had issues with some pretty grisly things.

Thoughts of my *issues* soon became double-edged, not least my real – or imaginary – encounter with the machete gang. Made me wonder if my alleged taste for dope was truer than I cared to admit.

'No more mental meanderings,' I told myself sternly. 'I've a grip now and I'm not letting go.'

Certain I'd find what I wanted, I strode into my study and looked up Susie's contact details, private and official. I decided to visit her home, confident she would be there.

When I arrived, the whole street was quiet, the individual properties spaced at unequal distances, all decently presented. As I turned towards Susie's house, I mentally – and big-heartedly – praised the local residents for their conspicuous pride in their neighborhood. Truth is, I was putting off the moment.

Having checked my appearance, I pressed firmly on the bell-push and waited, and kept on waiting. Susie took so long, I gave up and started away. I'd taken ten paces before the door finally opened.

'Ronald,' she said, looking surprised and decidedly unhappy to see me. 'I thought we'd said everything we had to say.'

I too was surprised, amazed. Instead of her usual choice of dull outfit, she was wearing a red satin tunic, the buttoned front only intermittently fastened; and her hair was different. It hung loose, ruffled, not scraped into a mousy bun.

Returning to the doorway, I stammered, 'I-I came to apologize.'

'Fine, mission accomplished. Now go.'

I knew that wouldn't be good enough for Charity. 'Susie, please. I want to apologize properly.'

She huffed. 'Has it remotely occurred to you that your wants are of no interest to me?'

To be honest, it hadn't, but I couldn't tell her that. 'You're making this very difficult.'

'Then go,' she countered.

A voice came from inside, a male voice. 'You all right, Susie?'

She answered at once. 'It's just someone I used to know. He's going now.'

Frank came to the door, his thrown-on top and scruffy pants a stark contrast to my fine attire. 'Ronald,' he said, confused. 'Thought you were banged up in hospital.'

Took me a while to place him as one of the faces around Charity's conference table. Even then, I couldn't immediately dredge up his name. I nodded perfunctorily.

'Fancy a coffee?' he asked. 'Might as well since you're here.'

'He's no time,' Susie said.

My mind swerved, not understanding why Frank was the one offering coffee. It was Susie's house. And why should she look so disheveled, specially after taking so long to answer the door. Made me seriously wonder what they'd been up to. Despite dark suspicions and building anger,

Charity's warning held sway.

Casually as I could, I said, 'Coffee would be good.'

Susie's living room was plainly furnished with not very comfortable armchairs, too stiffly sprung. To be accurate, it was a vapid space oozing less imagination than a half-dug borehole.

Handing over my drink, Frank seemed oblivious to the tension Susie bristled my way. 'Susie's a brick, isn't she?'

I stared. In the hospital I'd coughed up exactly the same metaphor, though with far less sincerity. The coincidence itched my skin. Unwilling to laugh it off, I was about to dive in, but Susie was a breath ahead.

Turning to Frank, she said, 'Ronald came to apologize for his desperately hurtful behavior yesterday.'

Frank nodded diplomatically. 'I'll go then.'

'You'll stay. I don't want to be alone with this person.'

That hurt. Granted I had torn into Susie at the hospital, but I'd never thought she could be so selfishly vindictive. 'Susie, please,' I said. 'I know my remarks were unforgivable but—'

'Right! So don't waste time apologizing.'

Like an idiot, I charged back without first engaging my brain. 'I have to. I—'

She was on her feet in a flash. 'What a simpleton I am! Charity told you to come, didn't she? She's the only reason you're here.'

'Not at all,' I protested.

'Liar, Ronald!' Moving swiftly, she opened the door, her indignation hot enough to cook a thermometer.

I held off moving, but then so did she – and she waited me out. Reluctantly, I stepped passed her into the austere hallway. That's when something inside me snapped. I don't know why. Maybe stress had a lot to do with it, or maybe the color of her tunic had inflamed me; or just maybe it was the thought of her with Frank. Whatever, I was overcome with a combination of jealousy, frustration and anger, and I aimed the lot at her.

'I've apologized,' I seethed, 'but you're right. I wouldn't have bothered if Charity hadn't read me the riot act. As for you ... damn hypocrite! You pretend to be too good to be a virgin, then I catch you playing house with this blithering idiot.'

Neither said a word, though Frank did shift closer to Susie. Made me notice her eyes. They were cold, cast down. I couldn't take it and turned self-consciously for the outer door. Then I swung back, feeling like a jilted suitor.

'You've betrayed me,' I yelled. 'You made me believe in you, then—'

'Enough!' she shouted so powerfully it killed my budding tirade. It seemed surreal when she followed on with a broad smile and almost conciliatory words. 'I accept your apology, Ronald. You can finish your coffee then report what a good boy you've been to Charity. Tell her I've forgiven you and that we'll be working together in accordance with her plan.'

I gawked like a duck in a fox's jaws. Though she was clearly pointing me back into the living room, I hesitated, not sure whether to be glad or suspicious.

'Come on, Ronald,' she insisted, still smiling.

My legs dithered as if to confirm my brain's misgivings. I had to stretch for the walls to arm-lever myself forward. Not until I'd dropped into the nearest uncomfortable chair did I notice that Susie and Frank had stayed in the doorway.

'Take all the time you want with that coffee,' she told me. 'Frank and I have unfinished business in the bedroom.'

Chapter Eight

Susie's bombshell announcement catapulted my emotions into overdrive, not that she hung about to watch. She snatched Frank away and slammed the door. I could hear them racing upstairs and their footsteps scrambling into the front bedroom, and I could hear the sounds that followed. Incensed and on my feet, I was about to storm out when an eruption of carnal laughter held me motionless. I felt sick. Sweat dampened the collar of my new shirt. My soul burned, scorched by her flaunting such shameless debauchery.

Without realizing it, I sat down, dazed. My ears were under obscene attack, the sounds growing in intensity. I shuddered, consumed by hate. To me, it was blindingly obvious. Susie was vengefully repaying my few misjudged words spoken at a time of intolerable stress.

Yet her revenge had awoken me to her true colors; and she wasn't the only one able to dish it out. Superior indifference was my initial ploy. I determined not to leave until she and Frank had come down. Then I'd pretend I'd heard nothing and thought nothing. The pair of them had gone upstairs, that was all. Later, would be different. Once I'd had a chance to put a proper plan together, I'd make her suffer in spades for abusing me with her degenerate theatrics.

When I heard her on the stairs, I hurriedly scooped up a newspaper and settled in a pretense of patient composure. I even jolted in make-believe surprise when she burst in. That's when everything turned on its head. My charade choked and foundered. She was stark naked.

Coming close, she said, 'No point me offering you a pop, Ronald. Dimple told me you're as impotent as a castrated panda.'

I couldn't move. I could scarcely breathe. The pains that had spared me for the past few hours crashed back with a vengeance, turning me gray as death.

'Anyway,' she sighed, 'you've delivered your pathetic apology so now you can shove off. Be in the conference room tomorrow. Charity wants us.'

She left, leaving me gaping at the space she'd occupied. The final insult was her giggling excitement as she hoofed it upstairs. All too soon Frank's salacious laughter fused with hers, the crescendo crushing me, forcing me to smother my ears and run.

But I don't remember actually running. I fell. I've no idea when or how, or if it was just a falling sensation. Either way, my leg hurt, but nothing else. Apart from a moderate throb centered on my knee, I felt agreeably well, until a sinking feeling of deja vu gouged a pit in my guts. I'd suffered another memory lapse – or was it an hallucination? It could have been either one, both, or neither. Regardless, it had left me in sleep shorts on the carpet next to my own bed. I didn't know if Susie and Frank really were brazen libertines or if I'd dreamed up the whole sordid business.

While I still struggled with this extra dose of brain torture, a call came through. I answered cautiously.

Without preliminaries, I heard, 'Charity has brought the time forward. We're to see her now.' The line went dead.

It was Susie. At her house, she'd said about meeting Charity so that nudged me towards believing I'd physically been there, not just mentally. But I'd stopped trusting single factors. I still couldn't remember setting off from her place or how I'd made it home. Neither could I be sure how many hours had passed or what had happened during those hours. Worst of all, I couldn't be sure of Susie. Her being curt over the phone had told me nothing.

If I was to find out anything, I had to accept the summons, bide my time, and keep alert; but that didn't mean my rushing to them cap in hand. They could damn well wait for me. No way was I going to hurry. I did the opposite. I took two hours to ready myself before taking a final check in my mirrors. As expected, they confirmed I looked my best, yet they also delivered a shock.

For a second, I thought I'd glimpsed Susie's reflection; the naked Susie. She'd looked so gorgeous I knew it was my imagination. She wasn't that stunning normally, and she'd not been especially stunning without her clothes – if the fornication episode with Frank had really happened. Only then did it hit me. Not directly about Susie, but a memory of when I'd apologized to Dimple. I recalled being transfixed, gazing deep into her nightie. Thinking back I was certain her vivid bruising had completely disappeared.

Instantly, a shell-burst of grim possibilities exploded in my brain. Dimple could have been playacting from the start. Her sudden lack of bruising certainly put the skids under Susie's glib *my-friend-brought-in-fresh-clothes* story. I really could have been attacked by that gang and kept sedated until I'd recovered. I shivered at the thought; but it was a thought too far. I was making far too much of too little. That's how it seemed then. So I whacked in a mental anchor and forced myself to rationalize. Dimple's bruises had to have been there. I'd simply had better things to look at.

Having brushed aside my doubts, I arrived at the conference room determined to be my own man. Nonetheless, I was wary. That changed when I realized no one was there. On an impulse I sat in Charity's armchair. The view seemed different, more commanding, more what I deserved. Even the oak paneling with its abundance of imposing doorways looked altogether more grand and the table more highly polished; and I could see portraits I'd not noticed before, miserable faces. They made me grimace and turn away.

'Don't suppose they like the look of you either.' It was Susie, dressed to bore boredom, her hair scraped tight. I didn't respond. It was safer not to. 'If you're trying to make some macho point, I can assure you that Charity won't care where she sits.'

I shrugged. 'Plenty of seats.'

'Do you know why we're here?'

What's she playing at, I thought. It should have been me asking that question. I ignored her.

'You're being particularly offhand,' she challenged. 'Have you fantasized about some other betrayal and judged me guilty?'

I almost laughed. Miss Straight-Laced-Whore was definitely playing mind games. Though I still viewed her as little more than window dressing, I felt sure she knew exactly who was screwing with my life.

I couldn't resist speaking out. *'Fantasized betrayal!* Whatever gave you that idea?'

She bridled at that. 'Trust me, I wouldn't be here at all if Charity hadn't insisted. Don't you remember the terrible things you said to me at the hospital?'

I fancied myself saying: trust you! I'd rather stuff a fluttering yellow canary in a lion's jaws. Instead, I said, 'I apologized, didn't I?'

'No you didn't, Ronald,' Charity announced as she swept in, her deep purple dress provocatively displaying bare shoulders. 'Which means you defied both my instructions and my warning of the consequences.'

Taken aback by both her sudden appearance and what she'd said, I just watched her glide to the opposite end of the room.

After picking a chair, she said, 'Nothing to say?'

To me, it was more evidence that they were in it together. I elected to play dumb. 'I'm not well. I forget things.'

Charity spread her fingers on the table. 'I thought you more of a man than to pretend you're ill.'

'I am ill. I had an electric shock.'

She eyed me scornfully. 'Yet you were well enough to discharge yourself.'

Like an idiot, I said, 'The doctor was going to kill me.'

Charity's disdain was conspicuous. 'Naturally. Hospital physicians often fight to save patients only to murder them later.'

'I know it sounds—'

'Ridiculous?' Susie butted in before turning to Charity. 'Do I really have to be here?'

She didn't answer directly. 'I've bad news, I'm afraid. It affects both of you ... all of us.' With us frowning, she went on smoothly, her voice sensuous. 'You'll recall Frank. He was here the other day at our meeting.'

I waded straight in. 'Can't forget our good buddy Frank, can we Susie? Not a guy whose staying power betters that of a prize bull, a guy who makes such great coffee.'

Charity carried on as if I'd not spoken, as if Susie wasn't glaring daggers my way. 'Frank understood the importance of his task; the task I'd originally earmarked for you, Ronald, if you remember the meeting.'

I sniffed. 'Guess so.'

Charity didn't bat an eyelid. 'We've only just found out, but it seems that Frank never made it to the client's home.'

'Whatever happened to him,' Susie asked, immediately concerned.

Grinning I said, 'Reckon he diverted to psych up ahead of his tryst with you.'

Charity's tone didn't waver. 'I can only assume, Ronald, that you've slipped back into your old drug habits. Nothing else explains your disgraceful behavior.' She rolled her shoulders, the exquisite movement captivating me. 'However, I'll deal with that later.'

Despite my fascination, something flipped in my brain and demanded I prick her bubble.

'Wrong guess, cupcake,' I sneered. 'I've come to my senses, that's all.'

Susie gasped. 'You've lost them completely.'

I wasn't having that. 'You've no right to judge me with your sanctimonious twaddle, Susie, not after all that belly rubbing with your boyfriend.'

She gaped, then began to cry.

Charity remained emotionless. 'It'll be all right, Susie. Just a few minutes more.'

I saw Susie nod and sniff. Made me roll my eyes.

'As I was saying,' Charity continued, 'Frank didn't arrive as expected. Sadly, we now know why.' She paused. 'It breaks my heart to tell you, but the poor man was attacked by a gang and murdered. The police have only just identified him.'

My swollen talk suddenly dipped flat, yet I knew there was no way Frank could have been killed so soon after that first meeting.

Thinking I'd misheard, I said, 'When did this happen?'

'I've already told you.'

'That good hearted man,' Susie sobbed in wide open

distress. 'Such a terrible thing!'

Ignoring Susie, I fixed on Charity. It was time for plain speaking. 'I saw Frank yesterday at Susie's house. They were creaking the bed big time.'

Before Susie could gather anything like enough composure to speak, Charity waved her down. 'No, Ronald. The autopsy was clear on the time of death. You couldn't possibly have seen him yesterday, and neither could Susie.'

That spun my head. I sat there feeling twitchy, sure there was more to come. I was right.

'There's more I'm afraid,' Charity added as if on cue. 'Frank was attacked in a most cowardly way by men with machetes. They left him bleeding to death in the gutter.' My jaw dropped. 'The police suspect a gang called The Blades. Apparently, one of their members was killed recently, his head almost cut off.' She hesitated. 'The most heinous thing is a slogan – perhaps a message – carved deep in Frank's chest. It reads: *Throot lives.*'

The more I heard, the more intensely I felt Susie's stare. Her features had shaded to ashen and it looked as if she couldn't speak. To be honest, I was pretty dumbstruck too.

Charity didn't allow herself to be sidetracked by our mute exchange. 'According to the police, *Throot* was the name of the murdered gang member, which is why they suspect The Blades' involvement.' She took a deep breath. 'The police have insisted I ask everyone who attended the meeting to give any information that might assist, anything at all.'

Susie found her voice, a whisper. Still staring at me, she said, 'I think Ronald and I need to talk. Could we have time alone please?'

'Certainly,' Charity agreed, rising gracefully. Moments later she had gone and the room's entire ambiance had changed.

I waited. It was some time before Susie spoke again. 'In your apartment, you started telling me about your memory problems ... alleged problems.' I began to protest, but her hand jumped up like a forbidding stop sign. 'You became agitated when I insisted you be honest with me, then you ran off. As I discovered later you ran off to Dimple, allegedly.'

'Stop saying *allegedly!*'

'Not a word, Ronald. Not till I'm ready.' I grunted. 'In the hospital you told me about a gang of men with machetes. I wrote full notes of everything you said. You accused Dimple of beheading the man who allegedly beat you, and I'm sure you called him *Throot*.'

My head fumed. I'd already had enough shocks and her making two and two equal five was getting right under my skin. Rounding on her, I said, 'Don't you—'

She cut me straight off. 'I'll say exactly what I like and you'll not interrupt again!' She delayed until I'd tersely acquiesced, then she shot-blasted me. 'I think you killed Frank, Ronald, and I think you beat Dimple afterwards to give yourself an alibi.'

Chapter Nine

I couldn't believe her cold-bloodied and hare-brained verdict. I'd kept a lid on my temper till that point, but I wasn't about to soak up that kind of deranged accusation like some masochistic invertebrate. She deserved a verbal pasting and I was going to make damn sure she got it.

I remember how angry I was, how hot and flushed, how I stood and threw aside my chair as if her obscenities had polluted it. I remember trying to speak, trying to release the biting condemnation overflowing from my soul, but no words came. I felt my gullet being crushed. I could feel myself suffocating, dying. I passed out.

My first sensation on waking was a head swimming in uncertainty. Maybe that was the second sensation. The first was: not again! I felt like a sap, a scared sap. Swooning like some emasculated wussy wasn't at all my style. I didn't think it was, but neither could I stop myself flaking out. To be honest, it really rattled me. I hated the memory jumps. I'd endured enough to know that they could land me anywhere, with anyone, and that anything could have happened in the gap. This time, I deliberately kept my eyes closed and tried to convince myself I was comfortable in my own bed.

Susie's voice shattered my cozy make-believe. 'You can't hide from the truth, Ronald.' She sounded really calm and controlled.

I peeped. Apart from being in the recovery position, nothing had changed. I should have felt relief. I didn't. I felt strangely cheated. There had been no memory lapse, good or bad. Susie was still there, still fully deserving to be castigated for her unmitigated foulness.

'There's nothing wrong with you,' she told me. 'So get up and convince me you're not a murderer.'

I stayed motionless. For no good reason, my anger had fizzled. Even she had sounded vaguely conciliatory. I rolled about just to make a meal out of getting up, then plunked into the nearest chair. No one else had joined us.

'I have to tell Charity about this, Ronald; and the police.'

Bitch, I thought. Couldn't believe how mild I sounded when I said, 'But I've your personal note guaranteeing confidentiality.'

She huffed. 'Even if that note hadn't been written before Frank's murder, do you seriously imagine it would keep me silent? From where I'm sitting, you're a dangerous man playing perverted games. You feed off sympathy then sneak away to do terrible things ... and your idiotic cover stories are unbelievably naive. You dish out graphic details and name people as if you're fully bent on getting caught. And you always turn on the people trying to help you ... like Dr Burns.'

'And you,' I whispered, not sure why.

She knew why, or thought she did. 'Don't try that with me, Ronald! I'm not falling for any more of your *poor-little-misunderstood-me* routines. You've made too many wild accusations for that.' Her fingers tightened. 'I've absolutely no idea what mischief prompted you to tell Charity that Frank was my boyfriend, let alone that we'd been together yesterday. That was just sick.'

'I can't make you believe what you don't want to believe,' I answered meekly, bewildered why I wasn't on my feet berating her. 'And I can't explain what's happening to me. Charity says I'm a drug-head, but I've no recollection of ever taking drugs, with or without Dr Burns. And I really don't see my lapses as hallucinations. Sometimes there's just a gap. When I do see things, they're all very real, even if some do turn out to be ... who knows?'

'That's the nature of hallucinations,' she said frigidly.

She wasn't getting away with that. 'You were full on and damn convincing in my last *hallucination* yesterday, and so was Frank. You were going for each other like frisky rabbits in hyper-drive.'

'That's disgusting, and it says more about you than poor Frank and me.'

I snorted. 'Is that your professional opinion, doctor?'

'It's my professional opinion that the police have—'

'Sorry to interrupt,' Charity apologized impassively, her elegance making the room seem shabby. 'There's been an update. The police have now tracked down and arrested all Frank's killers except the gang leader himself, a man called Grub. Apparently, he has a fresh slash wound on his cheek so he's easily identifiable.' She smiled faintly. 'It's good news, but sadly nothing that can bring Frank back to us.' For a moment, she held our gazes, then she was gone.

I deferred for thirty seconds. 'Your turn to apologize.'

She tensed, wanting to make a battle out of it. 'I'd feel more like apologizing if the gang leader hadn't been called Grub, the exact name you gave him in your *hallucination*.'

I'd had enough. There was no point trying to get her back onside. I emptied my lungs, then slowly filled up again. 'Please yourself,' I said. 'I've lost interest in you, in what you think and in what you do. Far as I'm concerned, you can—'

'Not exactly a positive attitude,' Charity declared, returning unexpectedly. 'You're at risk of forgetting our higher purpose: to serve those who depend on us.' She sat half way down the room, her allure like a supercharged magnet. 'This charity does not exist for your convenience, Ronald, or for yours, Susie. We must guard against those who would have us fail, not indulge in silly whims about the people with whom we work.'

Susie kept her eyes down. 'Sorry, Charity, you're right. We have a higher purpose.'

This was just farce. I laughed in their faces. 'Charity, cupcake, I resigned before and I'm resigning again.' I remember standing, knuckles on the table. 'As for Dimple and your sycophantic little Susie, they—'

My next thing was hearing Charity's voice slicing through a fierce clanging in my ears. 'This is the address.'

I felt violated, as if someone had ransacked my brain and left me with disconnected dregs. And I detested that someone. Whoever it was, was playing me like a handcuffed puppet. I had no way to strike back.

Susie charged in with all the sensitivity of an embittered whore. 'It's no use pretending, Ronald. You fainted again, that's all. Not surprising given your temper. Take some free medical advice: get your blood pressure checked, once you've found a new doctor.'

That didn't make sense. 'You're my doctor,' I said, sitting again, my body feeling as if it had been mangled.

'Not any more,' she proclaimed.

I winced, needing to get back to first principles. I tried shaking my head to clear it. Didn't really work. 'I resigned ... didn't I?'

Charity glanced my way. I could feel her contempt. 'I couldn't do much with you flat out, Ronald, but since you're with us again, your resignation is accepted with immediate effect. You have one hour to vacate the apartment ... but I'll be generous. You can keep the suit you're wearing; nothing else.' She saw but ignored my surprise. 'We'll send an account for usage and any damage once a full inventory check has been completed. Good bye, Ronald. It's painful to see you throw away your life's work.' With hardly a pause she turned to Susie. 'As I was saying, this is the address of the client I want you to see.' She frowned. 'Ronald, why are you still here?'

I had a double take. Half of me wondered if she was testing; all her rubbish about me giving up the apartment and being sent a bill. The other half wasn't so sure. I had to find out, so I asked, 'Am I supposed to apologize, again?'

She didn't need any thinking time. 'You know where the doors are. Pick one and go.'

That told me straight, not that I quite believed it even then. Took a few seconds for me to notice that her eyes had darted to the door. Grub had burst in, machete in hand, his cheek flapping open. Yowling fiercely, he hurtled down the room, his blade slicing air in anticipation of slicing flesh.

Susie's piercing scream told me I wasn't seeing things. This was no hallucination. Grub's machete was less than five yards away from me. Terror swallowed my entire being. I could feel my jaw stretch wide and stiff, then see my upper arm spitting blood into my painstakingly selected suit. I must have stood up. My chair toppled. My legs teetered outwards from the table, shooting a foot between Grub's animated legs. I remember him tripping and crashing down. But that's all, until everything suddenly glowed white. To be honest, I thought I was dead, finally at peace.

'He's snapping out of it.'

That voice shattered my illusion of heaven. My heart plummeted. The gutting realization that I'd endured yet another episode was almost more than I could bear. I couldn't even be sure if reality still existed as a constant for me, or if it had degenerated into a bleak series of mind blowing nightmares. More frightening still was not yet knowing where my reality shift had landed me.

Dr Burns spoke again. 'Couldn't keep away from us, eh, Ronald?'

I knew then. I'd merely been transported back to his hospital, his murder lair – not a true reality shift after all, maybe. I rallied all the strength my body could muster, and found only scraps. In the state I was in, I almost wanted him to get on with the inevitable, not torture me by eking it out.

Charity's voice came as a shock, a beautifully melodic shock. Her words took my breath away. 'You did a brave thing, Ronald.'

I had to look. I knew she'd be wearing something wondrous, a dress to rip apart my imagination; and I was right. I stared, all thoughts of death by doctor vanquished. It was a flowing creation in ivory chiffon, its impact delicately compelling. As she stepped closer, her perfume spun my mind.

'You must recover, Ronald,' she cooed, turning to go. 'What you did changes everything.'

We both watched her, neither speaking until the door had clicked shut.

Burns started with a salacious chuckle. 'She's something else, that one. Phew and phew again.'

I glared. Though she wasn't mine to claim, I loathed his drooling, the thought of sharing. My fingers jerked to my head, suddenly aware of something foreign.

'Don't pull that,' he told me hurriedly. 'You'll need that bandage a while longer.'

The way he said it made me pull away. It also reminded me we were alone. There was no need of pretense. 'What do you care?' I scorned.

His eyebrows arched. 'You're my patient. Of course I

care.'

'Yeah well I've no money for your drugs so you might as well kill me now.'

That wiped the hypocrisy off his face. Made him sit beside the bed and pout. Took a minute before he said, 'Probably best if it comes from you so, let me ask: what's been happening to you?'

No way was I prancing to his tune. I just sat up, seething like an over-boiled kettle.

'Okay,' he conceded. 'I'll tell you something first.'

'Don't bother.'

He smiled. 'I'll tell you anyway. We've removed the reason you've been having odd clashes with reality.' I refused to be sucked in. 'You had a tiny – well, reasonably tiny – tumor in your brain right where it could play havoc.' He paused, daring me not to listen. 'That's why your head is bandaged.'

Thing was, we had too much personal history for me to believe a word. As cynically as I could, I said, 'Far as I'm concerned you're an hallucination brought on by second-rate drugs ... your second-rate and over-priced drugs.'

He carried on regardless. 'It might take a while for things to settle but, believe me, they will settle and then you'll have no more memory lapses, hallucinations, or any other far-out experiences.'

'Good try, doc,' I snorted, 'but my head is nothing but a happy family of far-out experiences, so no deal. You're peddling tripe!'

He tried double-talk. 'That's because some of your psychoactive experiences have become embedded in memory, but only some. You've also suffered lapses. Regrettably, it's probable they'll stay that way.'

Despite everything, a smidgen of gullibility sneaked out. 'Proof, doc. I want proof.'

'Fine. I'll get the surgeon to come and see you.'

I didn't expect that. 'All right but, just for the hell of it, humor me first and tell me how long I've been here?'

'A day,' he answered. 'We patched up your arm yesterday when you came in, but the surgeon wasn't happy and insisted on in-depth checks. That's when we discovered the tumor.' He rubbed his chin. 'Truth to tell, you arrived in quite a state, which turned out to be a blessing. We had to sedate you anyway, so took the decision to keep you under and deal with the tumor. And now you're back with us.'

His story was getting more and more stretchy and complicated, yet I couldn't ignore the evidence of my arm and bandaged head. As if awaiting its cue, my arm began to throb. That's when other memories started trickling back; in particular, one of a machete brandishing thug like a character in a slash movie. Grudgingly, I nodded.

'Right you are, Ronald,' he said. 'I'll make a call and get the surgeon in here.'

A few minutes later, the door opened.

Burns stood, both arms extended. 'You already know Dr Fullerton, Ronald, though I dare say you know her better as Susie.'

Chapter Ten

I didn't believe it. I couldn't. Every instinct told me I was in the throws of another hallucination, one I decidedly didn't want. I tried to concentrate, hoping something would happen to drop me back in the conference room with the exquisite Charity.

'Hello, Ronald,' Susie said. 'Glad to see you're—'

'Drowning in confusion?' I interrupted, not wanting to hear or look at her.

'I was going to say, sitting up,' she added quietly.

Burns grinned. 'I'll leave you to it. Don't fancy getting typecast as an hallucination.'

'Funny,' I sneered.

I hoped Susie would go too, but she persisted. 'I realize you've suffered a serious double-blow, but I've been anxious to see you, to thank you.'

'For the chunk you supposedly carved from my brain?'

'No, for saving my life.'

That came as a surprise. Made me look at her properly. Nothing had changed about her dire dress sense except, maybe, the padded shoulders on her khaki blouse had lent a touch of style. Neither was her hair any different. It was her eyes. The way she gazed at me.

My silent thought was supposed to stay that way, but it seeped out. 'You really mean that, don't you?'

'I do. If you hadn't risked yourself to save us, both Charity and I could be dead.'

I huffed at that, too hazy on detail to respond. Yet I'd already had a definite recollection of a madman running at me in the conference room. What I'd forgotten until that moment was the man's face. It hadn't been any old madman. It had been Grub, the machete crazed leader of The Blades, his cheek undeniably bearing the gash Dimple had inflicted before killing Throot.

I felt pain. Without realizing it, I'd been rubbing over the wound Burns had said he'd patched up; the arm wound Grub had given me. I winced, imagining afresh the cut of his murderous blade. 'What happened to the man?'

Susie didn't answer at once. I guessed she was unsure how I'd react. Either way, she took the risk. 'The man was Grub, but you know that. You'd seen him with his gang in some kind of premonition.' She hesitated. 'That's the only explanation. You were as flabbergasted as me when Charity told us about his involvement in Frank's death. Somehow, you knew about the man's awful injury and about Throot being killed.'

I had to say it. 'You've sure changed your tune.' She didn't answer. 'And don't forget it was Dimple who did the killing.'

She sighed heavily. 'That's the part that doesn't make sense, as much as you having premonitions makes any sense at all. All I know is that Dimple was here in this hospital and in no fit state to go off killing people. She simply—'

'All right!' I cut in. 'I know it all backwards, sideways, and inside out, and no amount of pawing over it will make it any different.' I held her eyes. 'Lets drop it, shall we. You play nice and tell me straight what happened to Grub after he slashed me.'

'As you wish,' she said soberly. 'There's no doubt that when he ran into the conference room he intended to kill us all. Charity and I owe our lives to the fact that he attacked you first.' Her gaze dropped. 'Despite being wounded, you had the presence of mind – and the bravery – to trip him and make him stumble. With him off-balance, you wrestled him to the carpet.' She paused. 'You're not to blame yourself in any way, Ronald. It was just one of those freak occurrences. During the struggle, the machete snagged in his clothes and was driven straight through his heart.' She glanced, then carried on. 'By this time, you'd lost a lot of blood and, not surprisingly after what you'd been through, you passed out.'

I stared. 'So Grub's dead?' She nodded. 'And I killed him?'

'No! He's completely responsible for his own death.'

To be honest, that seemed a pretty good outcome from my standpoint. I lay back, not attempting to hide a self-satisfied smile.

'You're a hero, Ronald,' she went on, 'and not just Charity's and my hero. The papers and news programs are giving your bravery massive coverage. Everyone I've spoken to feels lifted by what you did.'

I liked the sound of that. I must have smirked. 'So if I'm Charity's hero, does that mean I'm not out on the streets with no apartment and no clothes?'

She smiled. 'I rather suspect it does, but I'm saying no more about that. It wouldn't do to spoil Charity's surprise.'

'Forgive and forget, is that what she thinks?'

Susie picked up something in the way I said it. She lost her smile. 'I think we've all thought and said things we'd prefer to forgive and forget. For my part, I've tried to make it up. I absolutely insisted they run every possible check when you were brought in yesterday, and I made myself very unpopular in the process. But I couldn't simply ignore the frequency of your recent blackouts.' She nodded slowly. 'And it paid off. We found a tumor and now you're—'

'Hang on!' I bristled. 'You've been meddling about inside my head without so much as a by-your-leave. Aren't I supposed to sign consent forms before you do something like that?'

Her gasp became a smile when she thought I was joking, then she saw I wasn't. 'Yours was a potentially life-threatening situation. In the circumstances—'

'You decided to have a field day by chopping out bits of my brain.'

She gulped at that one. 'That's not how it happened.'

'If it happened at all!' I blasted, sitting rigid. 'I'm not stupid. I know something is going on, even if I can't quite pluck it out. Someone obviously wants me to believe I'm cured. They want me thinking that nothing out of the ordinary ever happened.' I snorted at her. 'Well tough. I'm not buying. I don't believe for one minute that I had a tumor and I believe even less that you took it out.'

'Then it's as well I had the whole operation recorded,'

she retorted, sullenly motionless. 'I had hoped you wouldn't be so—' She took a breath. 'It occurred to me that proof may be necessary, given your recent experiences.'

'Too right!' I bounced back. 'Bring it on. I hope you didn't use B actors.'

After ten minutes of her getting organized and a further ten of me watching intricate micro-surgery, I'd seen enough and stopped it. For sure, my theory had taken a bashing, but I could hardly forget my own recording of Dimple and the barefaced lies that two-faced playback had shown. None too happily, I said, 'Suppose there might have been something in my head but—'

'Stop, Ronald. Stop right there.' Susie instantly moved to stand close. 'Medicine – surgery – can only do so much. You must want to get better. If you insist on looking for what isn't there to prove or disprove episodes that affected you when you were ill, then you're on a very serious downward spiral.' She took my hand. I pulled it away. She continued undaunted. 'I can't make you unimagine what you've imagined any more than I can account for every detail of your hallucinations, or premonitions, or other life memories. But I tell you this: you must move forward and not dwell on—'

'Okay!' I spurted. 'I get the message.'

Her features lost some of their tautness. 'I'm so glad. As soon as—'

'Stop right there,' I said. 'I want my pound of flesh. I was being humiliated in that conference room before Grub charged in, and that's a difficult thing to forgive or forget.'

She looked disappointed more than anything. 'Ronald, you—'

'I'm speaking now,' I cut in coldly. 'I'm prepared to be reasonable, but if Charity wants me back, I want better conditions. For starters, I want a bigger and better apartment.'

'Well done, Ronald,' she scorned acidly. 'You've just blown Charity's surprise gift to you.'

'I'll get over it,' I retaliated, 'just as I expect her – and you – to get over your egotism when you stand in front of everyone involved in the charity and apologize for the degrading way you've treated me.' Not sure why, but I laughed. 'If you've no bottle to do it for the right reasons, tell yourself it's part of my therapy; which I guess it is.' I paused while she dropped into the chair. 'And I want a servant. Charity can bankroll someone for me. A cook would be good as well.'

I was pleased with that. I'd laid out my demands with no dithering about. To show I meant it, I found a spot on the wall ahead and fixed on it, waiting for her comeback. She gave it quicker than I expected.

'If you are serious, Ronald, and not just winding me up for the fun of it, I'll go now and talk to Charity.' She stood, waiting. When my mouth stayed tightly drawn, she edged away. 'It's clear you've no clue what you're asking when you glibly say: *everyone involved in the charity*. Charity herself will be very disappointed in you, as I am. I thought—'

'I was a sap you could wind round your little finger?' I prompted. 'Well I'm not; not your finger and not Charity's.'

Susie left without another word or a backward glance. When the door opened a few moments later, I ignored it, conspicuously. I figured she'd either come back or Burns had been drafted in as reinforcements. The thought it could be Burns made me check. I had too many memories of his penchant for drug dealing and murder threats.

A woman had come in. She seemed ageless, a nonentity person anyone could pass on any street on any day and ignore. Nothing about her deserved attention, not her uninspiring clothes or the bland expression on her face.

Feeling suddenly sweaty, I asked, 'Who the hell are you?'

Truth is, I felt worse than merely sweaty. I hated her on sight. My hackles rose like wary sentries. At first, I wondered if she was one of Burns' drug partners come to warn, or maybe to kill. When she kept silent, my imagination jerked in every direction. I even thought that Charity had sent her, or that she was Grub's mother come to get even.

It seemed an eternity before she spoke. 'Hello, Ronald. There's no need to be scared.'

'Scared of you!' I spurned. 'You're off your head.' Yet I was scared. Full of hate and fear, and I knew she knew it. 'Get out. I don't want you here.'

'I'll go if you like,' she said gently, 'but I'd prefer to talk through some of the things you've been experiencing.'

'Not you as well,' I shot back. 'I want to be left alone. I'm a hero. I deserve—' Something stopped me. It must have been her eyes. I felt naked, almost inside out. As I fell to silence, her expression stayed the same.

'Time is a strange thing,' she said, 'as much as it's anything at all.'

I didn't need riddles, especially from a weirdo who had bounced uninvited into my private room and started prodding at my life; so that's what I told her.

'As you wish,' she said.

For some reason, I felt compelled to justify myself. 'I've been cured. The operation was recorded. I've seen it. I don't need you. I don't need anyone.'

She moved for the first time since entering the room. It was only a half-step towards me, yet it made my heart erupt as if racing for its own destruction.

Quietly, she said, 'It all happened, Ronald, everything, and for good reason. Think on—'

I couldn't take it. 'Get out!' I screamed, hands slammed against my ears, eyes squeezed tight. 'You're a sick hallucination. I'm cured.'

Her smooth tone never wavered. 'I know you're looking for the person responsible. When you're ready, I'll help you; but you're not ready.'

That hit hard. She'd churned me up worse than soft turf under a herd of galloping race horses. Against all my instincts, my eyes opened and I scanned round, needing something. I had no idea what. All I caught was a glimpse of her right shoe as the door closed.

Chapter Eleven

I could have gone after nonentity woman. How I wish I had. But right then, I couldn't. I was too worked up to think straight. Besides, I had Charity and Susie on the run. I'd also just about managed to frog-march all my freakish exploits into tolerably acceptable pigeon-holes. The last thing I needed was a female aberration lobbing grenades and blasting everything straight back in the air.

Feeling more than unsettled, I tossed and turned on the bed, struggling to deny that anything significant had happened. I imagined Susie reassuring me, confirming that the interloper was no more than a post-operation blip, definitely not an hallucination or someone from a time-warp memory lapse. I'd done with those things. Susie's scalpel had cut them out.

I'm not sure when I dropped off. It seemed like a long sleep and I felt better for it. A few subtle changes showed that people had been checking me. I had fresh juice and the lights were fully on. It wasn't difficult to assume it was evening. I remember fretting that I'd slept too long so wouldn't sleep that night. A rustle drew my gaze, and turned it into a stare.

'You're awake,' Charity said from a chair on the far side of the room, a chair that hadn't been there before.

I wanted to say her name, maybe gloat, but my voice wouldn't come. I just looked, my reactions anesthetized as if I were a naive insect transfixed by a deadly flame.

'You spoke to Susie earlier,' she said, her voice beguiling, no hint of acrimony. 'You had some demands.'

As always, her dress seized my attention. This time it was sleeveless, shimmering silver, its mid-length elegantly foreshortened where her legs were crossed.

I gulped. I was sitting up, though I didn't recall making the move. Blood had leaked onto my pajamas where my restlessness had aggravated my arm. I noticed – naturally I did – but I was more concerned that I couldn't speak, and I needed to convince Charity that I wasn't going to cave in.

As mysteriously as my voice had failed, I sensed its return and that it would sound strong and clear. 'Yes, I've demands.'

'It's a pity.'

I listened for more. Nothing. Made me wonder if she was about to cut her losses, yet she was the charity's principal and kicking out the brave soul who had saved her would risk a public backlash. Deciding to be cool, I shrugged.

'One of your demands was for a bigger apartment,' she went on. 'Pity. I'd bought you a very special one as a surprise. Now it's no surprise at all, just payback.'

'Win some, lose some,' I said, unmoved.

'Even so, a pity.' She recrossed her legs. 'However the solution is simple.' She waited for me to ask.

'It is?'

'I'll get you a better one. Then you will have something extra, an expansion of my original gift.'

I felt an inner glow. 'Seems reasonable,' I said, 'considering I put my life on the line.'

'Quite.'

I decided to push. 'Don't I deserve an exclusive and very personal kind of thank you?'

'You do, Ronald. Thank you.'

Typical, I thought. She knew full well what I meant but she'd sidestepped it. Irritated, I said, 'I want a servant as well, a valet; someone who knows about clothes and can do other chores.'

'And a cook,' she added. 'Fear not, Ronald, you'll have staff to satisfy every whim. Apart from your work with the charity, you'll be free to enjoy my gratitude.'

'A car would—'

'Of course, Ronald, but if you keep on, you'll be taking away all my surprises, and that would be—'

'A pity,' I said for her.

'Indeed.' She pouted thoughtfully. 'I must say this: as our relationship has become closer, I've better appreciated your need for recognition and for the finer things in life, the bonuses that lesser people never enjoy. Such people turn up their noses, not because they don't want these things, but because they can't imagine themselves ever having them.'

I guessed she knew what she meant, but it went over my head. It seemed appropriate so I said, 'I don't care about lesser people.'

'My care is for the partially blind and partially deaf. With you at my side, we can do marvelous things. We can serve our higher purpose.'

I sagged. I didn't want her preaching. My head was fully engaged in thinking about all the marvelous things we could do together, and none had the least connection with any *higher purpose*.

The moment didn't last. We needed to get to it, so I said, 'Basically, you want me back at the charity and you agree to all my demands, including the public apology?'

She smiled. 'Ronald, after what you did – after all the things you've done – there are no limits to what I would do for you, professionally, and no limits to what I would do to keep you close.' Before I could speak, she added, 'I'm told you need to stay here a week for initial recuperation. Be assured that, during this time, I shall be arranging a unique reception for you, a thanksgiving event. Everyone from the charity will be there as you asked; and I do mean everyone, including the greatest to the least of our many benefactors. The press too, from every media. Let's just say it'll be a spectacular event with you heralded in as a hero.' Her eyes stayed locked on mine. 'Susie and I will give our testimonies about your bravery and we'll make amends for our mistaken attitudes, words and deeds. They'll be no wavering on this last point, Ronald. Have no doubt, you'll be treated as you fully deserve.'

I can't pretend I wasn't surprised, stunned. She couldn't have been more gracious. I wanted to say something. I knew I should, but I was completely empty of verbal ammunition.

'You're tired, Ronald,' she whispered. 'You've had a hateful time and now you should rest.'

I watched her walk elegantly to the door. With her gone, the room felt entirely different. I blew the wind from my lungs, pleased with myself, yet naggingly dissatisfied. I knew I could, and should, have asked for more.

All right, I figured, she was laying on a big jamboree and had anticipated me wanting a few cherries – like a car – but I'd stopped her being killed. I should have thought bigger. Must get my brain working properly, I told myself. Ask for a yacht next time, a monster with luxury soaked deep into its hull.

I snorted, frustrated that I'd left it too late to call her back, then my arm kicked in painfully, reminding me about the blood on my pajamas. Disgraceful!

To my mind, it showed that someone had done a lousy repair job first time. My laceration wouldn't have reopened otherwise. Angry at being treated so sloppily, I reached for the call alarm, fully intending to let loose the rough end of my tongue.

Bridget, the bright young nurse I'd clashed with outside Dimple's room, arrived within a minute. I was timing it. She spoke before I was certain it really was her. Okay, I admit it. I knew straight off. I just didn't want her thinking she was worth remembering, especially as I'd already told her how much I'd hate to be one of her patients.

'Something I can do for you, Mr Foster?'

I kept pretending she was a stranger. 'My arm ... the one slashed by that murderous—'

She cut me off. 'I can see which arm. We're trained to spot these things.'

'But not to do a proper job in the first place,' I scorned, getting angrier.

After pointedly assessing my bedding, she said, 'Well, Mr Foster, some patients thrash around as if they have bad consciences. They pull their beds about, aggravate wounds, disturb bandages, and generally make a mess. Some patients do these things, but naturally I'm not suggesting anything like that happened here.'

I saw red. 'Sounds to me like your riding for a fall, young lady. Do you know who I am?'

In no hurry, she reached for my medical chart and began reading. 'Just as I thought, Mr Foster, you're Mr Foster, the man with the cut on his arm.'

'I've had a brain operation as well!'

'Good,' she threw back. 'I'm sure if anyone needed it, you did.'

'How dare you?' I seethed, feeling the heat of fury.

'Dear me, Mr Foster,' she said innocently. 'I fear you're showing signs of anger. It's my duty to tell you that this hospital has a zero tolerance policy when it comes to aggressive patients. Unless you calm down, I shall have to call security and have you restrained while I tend to your slipped bandage.' She smiled contemptuously. 'Are you getting angry, Mr Foster?'

'I want someone else to do it,' I told her. 'You don't belong here anyway.'

'What you want and where I belong are two separate things, neither of which you have any option about.'

I sat straight. 'I knew you were a bitch from the second I laid eyes on you.'

'As I knew you were a perfect gentleman, Mr Foster.' Her fresh smile taunted like a burning insult. 'Your choice, naturally, but would you prefer to wallow in your own bloody mess or shall I rebandage your arm while I'm here?'

'I want Dr Burns.' I didn't know who else to ask for.

'The ladies like him as well. Is he your type?'

My jaw dropped. Took a while and even then I couldn't get any words out.

She shrugged. 'Just asking. Obviously you're not the kind of individual to get hung up on old fashioned prejudices. Anyway, we never judge. We leave judgment to those who would have us fail.'

My eyes flew to hers. 'What did you just say ... that last bit?'

'We never judge. We get all sorts in here: women-beaters, liars, cowards, greedy toads, pretentious nitwits. They're all the same to us, all patients it's our duty to care for.'

'No! That bit about *those who would have us fail*. That's wh—'

'Mr Foster,' she interrupted, 'delightful though it is to chat with you, you're not my only patient so, one word answer please: do you – or do you not – want me to minister unto your slightly cut arm?'

'Why are you using such odd phrases?' I asked. 'Who put

you up to this?'

'Not good at counting, are you, Mr Foster?'

Face flushed, I rounded on her. 'Yes, do the damn arm and—' I stopped short when she turned and strolled to the door. 'Where are you going?'

She looked back. 'Patients who seek to belittle staff also figure in the zero tolerance policy. I'm afraid I'm obliged to walk out until you calm down. You must treat me with the respect due to my position as nurse-in-chief to pompous schmucks.' With a final smile, she slammed the door.

I know it sounds crazy, but I lost count of the days I was in hospital and, believe me, I really tried to keep track. The only person I saw was Bridget. Every time, she worked me up into a fury. When she deigned to do anything at all, it was only the barest minimum, yet she always delivered my meals, ensuring they were cold, at random intervals, and indistinguishable; except for startling variations in their levels of seasoning.

Worst of all, was my loss of power. Whenever she was in the room, I could hardly move. It made no sense. When she wasn't with me, I could easily get out of bed, yet the door self-locked and kept me confined. Even the window blinds refused to budge. With the lights constantly on, day and night became miserably blurred, turning my life into a continuous and measureless cycle of surreal monotony.

I almost cried with relief when Dr Burns breezed in with a cheery, 'Morning. You're looking remarkably better than last time I saw you. Hope you feel as good as you look.'

He had to be lying, but I didn't care. 'H-have you any idea what's been happening to me?' I stammered. 'I've been a prisoner here; treated worse than a prisoner by that bitch of a nurse who used to look after Dimple.'

He grimaced before crossing to the window blinds and opening them with ease. 'Not sure I follow.'

I felt cold all over, an ominous tingling. I'd been struggling with those blinds for days. Forcing myself to stay calm, I said, 'Suppose the door doesn't lock either?'

'We don't have locks on patient doors,' he answered with a frown. 'This isn't a mental facility where safety considerations require some patients to be restricted.'

'You sure?' I scoffed.

'Listen, Ronald, I've been away for a week's holiday, but

I'm perfectly happy to check out what you say and see who's been looking after you. We'll go from there. All right?'

I knew it would be a waste of time. Burns would pretend to investigate, then come back with some cock-and-bull story. 'Don't bother,' I said.

'You're sure? It's no trouble if—' He glanced sideways as the door opened and my persecutor appeared. 'Hi, Bridget,' he said, 'thanks for coming in. I wanted to—' He stopped when he saw my face. 'Whatever is the matter, Ronald? You look as if you've swallowed a hornet.'

'Get her out of here!' I yelled, pointing. 'That's the bitch who's been torturing me!'

'My wife has been torturing you?' he repeated aghast. 'Not likely, my friend, she's been away with me on holiday.'

I collapsed inside. Both were smiling, then they were laughing; laughing at me until the contemptible sound degenerated into shrieking guffaws. The pains that had so mercifully left me came back as if desperate to join in and twist the knife. Helpless, I squeezed into a fetal position, rubbing my forehead, crying out. I craved to be rescued by a blackout, a memory lapse, anything that would whip me away from the agony of my hellish torment.

Chapter Twelve

Something happened. I'd wished for it, almost prayed for it, but that didn't stop me feeling petrified. Perversely, at the same time I felt a peculiar peace. My plague of pains had died, yet I could see nothing and, at first, hear nothing. A single sentence – a mental command – kept coming to me: *keep looking for the person responsible.*

I guessed right then it was supposed to be a reminder, some weird intrusion from nonentity woman. Made my stubble rigid, I can tell you. Far as I was concerned, she could get off my back even if she was only in my head. My whole intent was set on finding whoever had ravaged my life, and I didn't need her ring through my nose to keep me on target. Little did I know how far I'd already been sucked in.

Before I could wrench my brain fully into gear, all my agonies flooded back, racking me mercilessly. A terrifying sensation of falling took over, scraping out my soul as I dropped from nowhere into a place that could have been anywhere.

Light suddenly came to my eyes, glaringly over-bright. 'Good morning, sir,' someone said, a man whose voice I didn't know. 'It's a lovely morning and rightly so for your big day.'

I tried to see through the mist of dazzle. The greeting had been friendly, respectful; exactly the way it should have been to someone like me.

'I'll fill your bath tub in about five minutes, if that's agreeable to you, sir.'

I wasn't sure how to react. I heard my own voice. 'Where am I ... exactly?'

The man answered with no hint of mockery. 'At home, sir. You were late last night, very tired. I can ask cook to prepare breakfast if you'd prefer to eat before you bathe.'

Though my body and mind had started to defeat their initial disorientation, I was still a lot closer to turmoil than composure. I said, 'Give me ten minutes alone.'

I felt rather than saw him go and rubbed my eyes. As my vision cleared, my whole being snapped back into shape. Apart from the infuriating itching from my injured arm, I no longer had pains, but that didn't make me any less skeptical of the man's claim that I'd spent the night in the giant bed I still occupied. My pajamas were too uncreased and spotless; my bandage too comfortably in place.

Didn't take long for me to calculate that, somehow, Charity's promise of a luxurious lifestyle had become reality. The grim price had been a memory lapse – a big one – but one that had rescued me from torture. My heart sank regardless. As far as keeping a firm grip was concerned, I was right back to square one. Susie's alleged brain operation had failed, presumably. For all I knew, the torment I'd endured at the hospital could have been horribly real or the perversity of hallucination.

Instead of delving deeper into what might have happened, I grabbed onto the man's words. He'd talked of a fine morning for my big day. To me it was clear. While I'd been held captive, Charity had been preparing the unique reception she'd promised; which meant that things were just as they should be. The man had to be the promised houseman-come-valet.

As the minutes passed, my confidence grew. I deserved it all. I was a life-saving hero. Smiling, I swung off the bed and took a first serious look around. Charity had spoken of appreciating my need for the finer things in life and, beyond doubt, she had delivered by the majestic bucket load. I couldn't have conceived of greater luxury, yet I knew I could have more. Charity had pledged *no limits*.

A gentle tap on the door broke my contemplations and killed any residual misgivings I'd clung to. 'It's James, sir. You asked me to return after ten minutes.'

As I struggled to submerge growing excitement, the

idea of food spontaneously popped into my head. 'I'm hungry,' I said, pausing just long enough to appraise him. 'You can fill my tub and prepare my clothes later. I need to look my absolute best.'

James nodded. He knew exactly how to behave, how to dress, how to pander; and I lapped it up before strolling to the kitchen.

My unexpected appearance in the massive and extravagantly equipped room caught the cook unawares. I shared her surprise. I'd been anticipating a desirable servant. This servant was strikingly desirable in every possible way.

'Good morning, sir,' she said, slightly shaky. 'I didn't hear you come in.'

'Morning, Adelia,' I answered, not thinking how I knew her name. 'What's on offer today?'

As I spoke, she moved within a yard as if presenting herself for inspection, and I was more than happy to inspect.

For some reason I thought of Susie, how unlovely she was compared to my newly acquired cook. Though tied back, Adelia's hair was vibrant auburn, not scraped tight and mousy like Susie's. It had an appealing looseness about it with ringlets of curls laying on her shoulders. Most noticeable was her pure white silky blouse. Barely enough buttons were fastened for decency.

When her hands ran over her hips and smoothed the flow of her tight black skirt, my eyes followed. I have to say it: she wasn't quite in Charity's league, but she was stirringly close.

'Anything in particular you'd like, sir?' she asked. 'Fancy something special for your big day?'

I knew full well what I fancied and, to my mind, she was offering it, practically begging me to take it. Obviously, as her master, it was my duty to oblige.

Grinning, I stepped up and caressed her, at first through her silky top. Within moments, my fingers were eagerly unbuttoning her blouse and wrenching it open. My lips hurriedly found hers.

Lost in pleasure, it was a while before I noticed the rigidity in her body. She wasn't responding at all. Bemused, I paused to look. That's when I saw fear locked into her face.

I recoiled at once, almost stumbling as I retreated. She didn't move. Her mouth was stretched wide as if pegged in a silent scream.

'Is everything all right, sir?' James asked as he walked in, his shock instant, his concern for Adelia just as quick. Within seconds, he'd slid off his jacket and wrapped it over her like a comfort blanket. He glanced at me, his eyes cold as he led her away, her sobs becoming audible, all the worse for their softness.

Completely stunned, I stared after them, yet self justification soon galloped to the rescue. It wasn't my fault. It was hers. She had cold-bloodedly dressed like a provocative tart and could hardly blame me for treating her like one.

The more I thought about it, the more I saw how she'd led me on: the way she'd stood, demanding to be admired; the way she'd flaunted herself, her blouse like an overt invitation; the way she'd spoken, shamelessly offering me a *special* on my big day. She was just another tramp like Dimple; the spawn of pimps and whores.

Once I'd seen the light, I strode after them. James was with her in the sun-filled living room. She was perched on a huge sofa snuggled inside James' jacket. Made her seem all the less consequential and James' loyalty all the more questionable.

First, I decided, James needed to understand who was boss. 'You're improperly dressed,' I told him. 'Correct that right now then leave and fill my tub. This whore is fired.'

He straightened immediately, then bowed in obedience, though he allowed Adelia time to refasten her blouse before taking back his jacket.

It was a gesture beneath contempt as far as I was concerned and I ignored it contemptuously. As he left, I shouted, 'Make sure she's not stolen your wallet.'

His, 'Yes, sir,' was especially crisp.

With him gone, I felt Adelia's wet eyes staring. No way was she getting a second chance. 'Out!' I said. 'Else I'll call the cops and have you jailed for soliciting.'

She ran off, tears in full flow. Made me laugh. I plunked down exactly where she'd been sitting, and soon picked up the aroma of her perfume. The reminder stuck in my craw. I left.

James attended me in the principal bedroom once I'd bathed, his demeanor restored after its failing with Adelia. 'I've asked the chauffeur to be ready with the limousine by 11 o'clock, sir. Is that satisfactory?'

I had to say something. 'It's a lunchtime reception, is it?'

'Yes, sir, a large-scale midday event.'

'Long as I'm there in plenty of time,' I said stiffly, entirely missing the full ramifications of *large-scale*.

'You will be, sir. Arrangements have been made to clear the route so there's no possibility of hold-ups.'

I liked the sound of that. 'The least they can do for a hero.'

'Indeed, sir. For your perusal, I've picked out a number of suits you may like to consider for the occasion.'

With James suitably obsequious, I shamelessly reveled in being pampered. I'd risked my life for it. I'd faced up to a murderer and faced down Charity, forcing her to give in and reward me as I deserved. Soon, everyone would know my name, everyone who mattered to Charity. They would see her humbled and me exalted as her savior. 'And I did it without anyone's help.'

'Pardon, sir?' James said, making me realize I'd been mumbling. I didn't bother to reply. A servant had no place questioning his master.

It took most of the time to the scheduled 11 o'clock departure for me to be ready. At every step, James was on hand to make a difference and, in the end, his small differences made all the difference in the world. My own reflection fired my soul. I looked properly dignified, impressively distinguished, the outer manifestation of the true inner man, self-made and proud of it.

The limousine glided along, its sleek black lines shining as the sun caught its gleaming coachwork. As James had said, the roads had been cleared to ease passage, but that hadn't stopped crowds gathering to glimpse the hero who had saved Charity. To be honest, I was astounded to see so many cheering people and amazed again by the abundance of street display screens – most specially mounted – all emblazoned with Charity's picture, my face beside hers. The headlines all yelled the same key message: *Worker saves Charity*.

It took a few seconds, but only a few, for me to realize I

was being short changed. Anger welled up instead of pleasure. How could they be so obtuse, unless they were being downright insulting? I was no mere *worker*. My name deserved to be on full view. As we cruised passed more displays, the flow of pictures kept coming. As each approached, my image seemed to shrink as Charity's stretched.

'She's swindled me,' I said bitterly, feeling betrayed.

'Pardon, sir,' the chauffeur asked.

I was in no mood to chat. 'Forget it. Are we nearly there?'

'We're doing fine, sir.'

That was a stupid answer. 'I didn't ask how *we're doing*. I asked if we were there.'

'Few more minutes, sir.'

Grudgingly, I sat back. To my mind, nothing stank worse than a woman's vanity and Charity had flaunted personal vanity ahead of gratitude. I remember thinking she'd better have upped her game and organized things properly for my reception. Otherwise there'd be no way I'd respond magnanimously to her apology.

Annoyed that the chauffeur's few minutes hadn't yet elapsed, I said, 'How much longer?'

'Half a mile, sir. Bit less.'

Obviously he'd been lying earlier. Before I could castigate him, a mass of colorful lights illuminated our destination, making it brighter than the sunny day. Forgetting him, I eagerly sat forward. This is more like it, I thought, impressed by the massive picture of my face looming over the entrance, dwarfing the way in. The single word *hero* was written huge beneath my name. I hardly noticed the smaller images of Charity and Susie either side of mine.

I was so engrossed, the limousine door had opened before I'd fully registered our arrival. A red carpet had been laid and, stepping elegantly towards me, was Charity, a teasing smile on her lips, a dazzling golden gown adorning her exquisite body.

'You should have sorted out those street displays,' I told her as soon as she'd pecked my cheek. 'Made me look less important than you. My name wasn't even mentioned.'

Her eyes glistened as she pointed up to my massive

picture. 'Surely this makes up for it,' she whispered. 'You're like a god up there.'

Chapter Thirteen

There was no denying it. I did look like a god up there, at the very least a resplendent king. Charity's words lit a blaze in my head. I felt supreme as I strode beside her along the red carpeted processional route that led into, and then split the gigantic auditorium.

As we appeared, a tumultuous roar deafened me. The sheer size and glory of the welcome was beyond my most towering expectations. It was then that Susie's reproach about my demanding the attendance of everyone involved in the charity came to mind. I'd truly had no idea that Charity controlled such a vast organization.

Graciously, she waved to the crowds. Seeing the reaction, I quickly copied, keeping to her deliberately unhurried pace as we made our way towards the monstrous stage, my face its dominating center piece.

Charity spoke softly yet I heard distinctly, 'No picture up there but yours, Ronald; no name but yours.'

I didn't answer. My attention had shifted to the giant display screens mounted one each side of the stage. Both were broadcasting our slow progress so that all could see. There must have been cameras of every kind everywhere, all ensuring that not a second was lost. The whole while, I could feel the excitement building. The cheers that erupted when we finally reached the stage threatened to blast the roof into space.

At first, I didn't notice Susie standing on the platform patiently waiting. When I did, I forced a thin smile. I couldn't resist appraising her pleated dress, and disliking its peculiar blend of green and blue.

She looked emotional as she came up to me. 'This is our *thank you*, Ronald. We can never repay what you did for us.'

Narrowing my gaze, I said, 'You're just hustling for undeserved credit. You were my messenger. Charity put all this together.'

Moisture came to her eyes. Clearly I'd caught her out. She nodded diffidently and gave a faint bow of concession.

Charity moved serenely to the central bank of microphones then stretched her arms high. Only the three of us were on stage. Her gesture rejuvenated the roar. I could feel its power and, from my vantage point, almost touch the golden gown that tightened so entrancingly against her. Yet this wasn't the time or place. At another time, in another place, it would be different. She had promised *no limits*.

Arms lowered, she began speaking; a deferential introduction. I was all ears, expecting nothing less than gushing praise. I didn't like it when she gave only a brief outline. I liked it even less when she started talking about Susie instead of fulfilling her solemn obligation to apologize.

Though increasingly annoyed, I had to keep listening, but Charity only managed to add, 'Ronald saved Susie's life,' before excited shouts drowned her out and she had to appeal for calm. When the immense audience quietened again, she went on, 'Susie will now share her very personal story and recount how one brave man conquered.' She then paused and beckoned Susie.

In a faltering voice, Susie began. I couldn't be bothered to listen. It was all slush and sentimentality, not enough about the ordeal I'd so willingly taken on; and no sign of an apology. I sighed disparagingly when she finished with a maudlin, 'Thank you, Ronald. Thank you for my life.'

It hit me as pure rudeness when Charity ignored me and unhesitatingly offered Susie comfort. It was sickening to see the two women embrace and steal the limelight. So I showed I wasn't a stooge to be sidelined.

'That's okay, Susie,' I said very loudly. 'Call me any time a machete wielding maniac charges straight at you.'

The crowd responded at once, more so when I raised my arms and waved. The thunderous sound extended beyond three full minutes.

I fancied that Charity became jealous. After giving Susie a final squeeze, she did no more than wait morosely for the auditorium to settle. She then moved to the microphones. Utter silence descended like an asphyxiating shroud. She said nothing at all.

That stumped me. I stared, confused. When I could no longer bear the grave-like hush, I said, 'You were about to tell everyone how I saved your life.'

'No.' The contradiction came from somewhere else, another voice, female. It was controlled and amplified so that all could hear.

Talk about surprise! It felt as if the stage had turned to sea. Hurriedly, I scanned the profusion of faces, seeing so many, yet seeing no one. Trouble was, I had no idea where the voice had come from. Pretty worked up, I glanced at Charity. She was alarmingly still. When I looked towards Susie, she too was fixed dead ahead, her expression curiously neutral.

With them uselessly mute, I searched again for clues among the closed-lip multitude. Something odd was going on. That much was obvious. Even more disturbing, I'd sensed an unnerving familiarity in the dissenting voice, no matter that I'd heard only one short word. Digging deep, I prepared to challenge the challenger. I was about to speak when the crowd's silence ruptured and all spontaneously resumed cheering.

My relief when Charity spoke was immense, yet sour. She carried on as if nothing had happened, skillfully filling in her earlier outline and detailing Grub's violent entry to the conference room.

As if rehearsed, the audience gasped and cheered as the story unfolded, but the shine on my valor had been dulled. My brain refused to be still, constantly diverting to that unnatural interlude. I became obsessed. It hadn't been imaginary, I was sure of it. Someone had definitely intervened and selfishly sabotaged the accolade I'd earned with my own blood. Although churned up, I clung tight to the ace that would crown my triumph. Charity was committed to giving me a groveling apology.

I looked at her afresh. Her narrative was winding to its conclusion. Consciously or otherwise, I steadied myself, expecting to bask in enthusiastic acclaim. I'd just begun to soak up the cheers, when the crowd's fervor haltingly faded. I saw people pointing to the massive screens on stage, a few at first, then hundreds, then thousands. Increasingly perturbed, I turned to check. The shock almost dropped me to my knees.

Both screens were running the same playback: me in my kitchen with Adelia. The cook was standing motionless, conspicuously terrified as I sexually molested her.

Unhesitatingly I howled out, 'No! This is a set-up.'

My protest hit a wall of disbelief. Everyone was fixed on the screens. Not a sound could be heard, except from the voice that had so mysteriously intruded before.

'What about me, Ronald? Was it a set-up when you beat me so badly? Your attack put me in hospital.'

All my grubbing speculation about the voice disappeared; and I dare not let her go on. Instead of thinking, I shouted, 'No! I only slapped you. You had someone else beat you. You wanted control. You wanted to make me your slave.'

That was when Dimple stepped into view from behind the right-hand screen, a tiny microphone pinned to the low neckline of her white camisole dress.

'Listen to yourself, Ronald,' she said, coming to stand near. 'Even a lecherous woman-beater like you must realize how ridiculous that sounds. Be honest. Be a man for once. It was you who beat me, no one else, as you would have beaten Adelia if your manservant hadn't rescued her.' She pointed. 'Look at the disgust on James' face, disgust we all feel.'

I glanced automatically, but my eyes were soon back on Dimple. Despite her red hair, she appeared remarkably sophisticated, the effect due to her full length white dress. Its delicacy bestowed elegance beyond her years; its wispy straps so thin they seemed barely capable of supporting even their slight load. Most noticeable was its cleverly revealing style, absolutely perfect to highlight the bruising over her chest.

Anger doesn't come close. I was furious at the injustice and furious at Charity for sucking me into her elaborate trap. When I turned to trounce her, she was no longer on stage, and neither was Susie.

Blanking out where I was, I spun back to Dimple, my

index finger jabbing the air. 'You bitch!' I bawled. 'Those bruises are fake. I looked down your nightie in hospital and you had no bruises then.' She didn't flinch when I moved closer. 'It's make-up. That's all it is. It'll rub off. I'll prove it.'

As my hand shot out, she lurched forward. Instead of merely brushing her skin, my fingers became caught in the flimsy material. In that moment, she recoiled sharply, ensuring the dress ripped away, leaving her all but naked.

My whole body tensed as I belatedly saw the craftiness of her ambush. I couldn't let her get away with it. Grabbing her, I rubbed at the bruises, fully expecting the make-up to wipe away and expose her as the cheating liar she was. Her screams hardly registered. Neither did the stage-hand who rushed to her rescue, until he knocked me cold.

When consciousness returned everything felt so muddled I was sure I'd suffered another hallucination, a painful one. I took a deep breath, not wanting to open my eyes. When I dared to peep, the staring crowd noticed straight away. Their contempt erupted in venomous catcalls that quashed the throbs from my jaw. A minute must have passed before my mind cleared. I realized I'd been strapped onto a cheap wooden chair at the front edge of the stage, facing outwards. Though I couldn't see anyone behind me, instinct told me I wasn't alone.

I make no pretense: I was well freaked. They could have done anything to me. I craned my neck, expecting to spot one or all three traitors, expecting to find them gloating. I'd risked my life and they'd repaid me with public humiliation. The lies of a degenerate hussy had poisoned Charity's mind, Susie's too. What may have begun as a spoiled brat wanting revenge, had reduced me to helpless victim. Yet I knew another Dimple. I thought I did; and this one was a murdering and unrepentant sadist, probably. All I could think was how much she deserved to die for her toxic double-crossing antics; for her bringing down such unwarranted degradation on someone of my stature.

I shuddered when Charity's voice rang out and silenced everyone. 'For years Ronald has been an ambassador for us, proving himself time and time again. Imagine my profound distress on discovering his terrible secret. I feel for Dimple as if she were my sister. For him to abuse someone so unsullied and inexperienced – and to do it so violently – is as unfathomable as it is depraved. Like a virtuous angel, Dimple trusted him and he—'

I couldn't take any more. Dismissing her reference to ambassadorial service as boastful embellishment, I dug deep and screamed out, 'You're blind, Charity.' Yet I was the blind one. I was the one who didn't understand. Like a lunkhead, I just let fly. 'Dimple is lying!' I persisted. 'She's just—'

Susie chopped me off. 'Dimple is lying! What about your lies about Dr Burns selling you drugs? What about you accusing Dimple of killing Throot or accusing me of having sexual relations with a man after he'd been murdered by Grub and his gang?'

She was twisting everything. I had to fight back. 'I was ill, suffering terrible hallucinations. You operated on me a week ago after Grub's attack. You kept me sedated and took out a brain tumor.'

Her laugh sounded like a cackle. 'Miracle worker I may be, but brain tumor patients aren't normally well enough to ravish their cooks within a few days of surgery.'

My anger erupted. 'This is all claptrap!' I bellowed. 'I don't know your game yet, but I'll be—'

'Quiet, Ronald,' Charity said, firmly killing my verbal assault. 'It's not for me to punish you – not now – and not for me to judge you. You demanded this event because of your wounded pride. You wanted public recognition. Now you have it.'

I gaped. There had to be more to it than that. As I steeled myself, Susie crept up behind me. She waited for my head to turn before speaking. 'Enjoy your triumph, Ronald. If anyone deserves it, you do.' Before I could rouse a response, she had strolled off along the processional aisle towards the exit.

I gritted my teeth, expecting Dimple to come up next. She did, her nakedness covered with a robe. Her look aimed straight for my eyes. 'Shame on you, sweetie,' was all she said before heading down the red carpet after Susie.

As I braced ready for Charity, her voice rang out to the crowd. 'Go, all of you. Our aim is to make a difference. We must never forget those who depend on us. We must always guard against those who would have us fail.'

I stayed tense after her resonating rallying call, thinking she would soon be beside me. When it was obvious she wasn't coming, I turned the best I could. 'Release me, damn you. I'm in agony in this chair.'

Nothing came back. Having told everyone to go, she forced me to wait. I could sense her hovering as time stretched away. Repeatedly, I complained, each repetition more vitriolic and frequent. I should have saved my energy. Not until the auditorium had cleared did I so much as glimpse her. By then, enforced immobility and frustration had reduced my appeals to forlorn whimpers.

The shock when she eventually reversed my chair stole my breath, not least with surprise at her strength. My own giant on-stage picture faced me, making me feel like a midget. After all that had happened, it sickened my stomach.

She stood imperiously. 'You don't deserve an explanation, Ronald.'

Rising anger mustered my reserves. 'I don't need one! You've just been a clever bitch and turned the tables.'

She sighed, grossly unimpressed. 'What a simpleton you are. All this was pure theater. You wanted glory and, for a while, you had it. I also promised that you'd be treated as you fully deserve ... and on that I believe I've delivered.'

My retaliation was swift. 'You believed that lying bitch Dimple. You should—'

'Enough, Ronald,' she commanded. 'Your ignorance is showing. You think you know Dimple? I assure you, you don't. If she so much as fancied a snack, she'd cheerfully carve out her mother's heart.' She smiled as my jaw dropped. 'Consider yourself lucky. Susie warned you not to upset my protégée, yet you ignored her advice, as you ignored my warning about being on guard against those who would have us fail.'

My head struggled to cope, as confused about what to believe as about what was real. Unexpectedly, the chair straps fell away, finally allowing me to rise. My aching limbs eagerly called out to be rubbed and stretched.

Charity spoke uncompromisingly. 'You've wantonly betrayed us by communing with our enemies, Ronald; once, face-to-face. But understand this, there'll be no more chances.'

I had no idea what she was talking about and cared even less. Glowering back, I said, 'I've had it with you and all your sycophants.' And I meant it. I was off that stage more keen to get away than a learner swimmer faced with a great white.

I'd hobbled to the tenth row of seats before she called after me. 'See this before you go.'

It was the last thing I wanted, yet I was powerless to resist. I turned. On stage, the huge display screens were showing the conference room as Grub made his murderous charge. I watched myself pull away from the table, my chair toppling, and I saw Grub become entangled before crashing down.

'Now see how brave you really were,' Charity said over the playback.

But I was already seeing: seeing myself paralyzed with fear, then keeling over; seeing Susie abruptly discard her tearful playacting and rush to pick up the fallen machete. Within seconds, she had viciously thrust the blade clear through Grub's heart and twisted it vindictively.

As the screens blanked, Charity smiled. 'Take comfort, Ronald. Grub did scratch your arm, but too superficially for you to feel truly heroic. Susie did a better job later, after she'd popped you with her little needle to prolong your ignominious faint.'

Only empty bravado made me blurt something like, 'I don't believe it.'

I heard her laugh. It made her words blister like acid. 'Do believe, Ronald, and do be in my conference room at 10 o'clock tomorrow morning.'

'N-not in a million years,' I stammered like a drunk attempting to contrive a dignified exit.

Another laugh. 'You can keep the apartment and servants.'

The offer sobered me. It sounded like a consolation prize. Grimacing bitterly, I recalled how I'd demanded my pound of flesh. What a fool, I'd been. Any flesh on offer had been snatched by Charity and swallowed whole; and enough was enough. No way was I in the game of letting her steal anything more.

'I'm not panting to your doggy whistle,' I seethed like a fool who thought he had choice. 'Not for an apartment or servants or any other damn thing.'

She came straight back. 'Dimple particularly asked that you be kept on.'

'Dimple!' I gasped, astounded.

Charity looked beautiful again, her features beguiling. 'Go home, Ronald. Let James and Adelia look after you.'

'No,' I began, but her soft voice cut in, playing havoc with my battered nerves. I fell to silence.

'It's all right,' she said. 'Adelia has been rehired. We're paying her generously so you can gawk and pet all you please.' My jaw quivered. 'Thank Dimple, not me. She explained it all ... told her that you're pathetically ineffectual.'

I stared back, mortified by my undeserved abasement. I don't recall saying anything. Don't suppose there was anything I could say. All I remember is staggering along the carpet, her chilling warning in my wake.

'Don't be late tomorrow or Dimple will collect you, or maybe I'll send Susie with her machete.'

Chapter Fourteen

My limousine was waiting when I careened like a stricken ship out of the auditorium, its door held open, the chauffeur standing smart. I fell in like a mentally deficient zombie, as eager to get away as I'd been to arrive; but not without a final bemused backwards squint. They must have anticipated it. My unmissable facial image over the entrance had been hatefully shredded.

As the car drove off, I couldn't avoid the display screens still active along the route. No traces of Charity's pictures remained, only mine as large as would fit. Emblazoned across them all was the same caption: *Ronald Foster disgraced. Impotent woman-beater proved coward and liar.*

The road trip might have passed in a morose haze had those images not kept leaping out. Their continual assault felt like vicious hammer blows mercilessly thumping home Charity's revelations. Already shriveled by my public humiliation, I withered to nothing in the back of that limousine, yet I shrank still more when I spied masses of people gathered at the gates of my exclusive apartment building. Not until then had I realized the sidewalks had been deserted. The sound of spiteful jeering soon demolished that crumb of comfort.

The chauffeur cut across whatever I was mumbling. 'Be through in a sec, sir. They'll not touch the car.'

To my amazement, and intense relief, no one in the intimidating mob laid a finger on the limousine despite our agonizing slowness. That was their only concession. None held back from attacking me verbally, their unanimous condemnation screaming out, searing into the underbelly of my soul like white-hot razor wires. I couldn't stop shaking. I was still shaking when James came to escort me inside.

With the apartment door safely closed, I stumbled into the sitting room and threw myself headlong onto an elegant flared-arm sofa.

James followed, I think as far as the threshold. I ignored his polite, 'Is there anything you'd like, sir?'

I suppose it was only seconds before I heard Susie's huff. 'It's rude not to answer when someone asks a question, Ronald, and very childish to lie flat out oozing self pity.' Then she said, 'James, be a dear and ask Adelia if she'll kindly make coffee and bring in some of her delicious pastries.'

'Right away, madam,' he answered like a turncoat.

I kept my eyes buried in the cushions hoping I'd only imagined her voice. Even if I hadn't, she was high among the people I least wanted to see, along with Adelia.

Susie confirmed her presence by mocking me. 'Could it be you're sulking because little-old-me stuck the blade in that oaf, not Ronald the modest hero?'

My breathing became heavier. I said nothing, not even when she laughed. Silence ensued until Adelia tapped and wheeled in coffee and cakes.

'Would you like me to pour, madam?'

I moved a cushion to peek, secretly. Susie had stood to admire the beautiful presentation on the silver trolley. She soon switched to looking Adelia up and down, just as I had that morning in the kitchen. The cook's vibrant auburn tresses flowed loose, covering the shoulders of the same silky blouse.

'You look enchanting,' Susie said. 'Easy to see why Ronald couldn't keep his hands off you.'

'Was a chunk of a surprise,' Adelia blurted as if nattering to her bosom pal. 'But now Dimple has explained everything and I'm being paid extra – and a big chunk extra I don't mind saying – he can ogle and paw me all he likes.'

That was it. 'Stop yacking as if I'm not here!' I told them, the pith mostly lost in the sofa.

It was my turn to be ignored. Susie beckoned Adelia

close.

'I like the lowness of this,' she said, stroking the cook's blouse, 'but undoing a couple more buttons and not wearing a bra should really shake him up.'

Adelia's enthusiasm was unbelievable. 'Shall I do it now?'

Susie responded just as eagerly, keen to help Adelia with her buttons. 'Why not! I'm sure Ronald is far too much of a gentleman to gawk while you're topless.'

Her attempt to ridicule me still further rang like a clarion warning. 'I want you out of here!' I yelled, sitting up, feeling unsteadiness cling to my legs. 'I know what you're doing. You're trying to—' I didn't bother to finish. When neither took any notice, I crushed everything into a glare and wobbled out, fearful of getting caught in another of their schemes.

Once in the bedroom, I collapsed, flat out again. Seconds later I was up, locking the door. 'And stay out,' I hollered as if they were poised and listening.

No way could I settle. Too many acidic memories were blighting my mind, festering. I'd really believed everything was going well for me. I still couldn't grasp how Charity and her duplicitous whores had so ruthlessly turned it all on its head. Neither could I accept the playback of Grub's fateful attack as truly authentic. After all I'd seen, it could easily have been faked, or so I told myself.

I tried sprawling on a black velvet chaise lounge. All the switch did was bring on bleak realizations. Until that moment, I'd not appreciated how merciful total shock had been in blunting my reactions to their malevolence. I'd not really soaked in its true force or ugly implications. From that moment it was different. It felt as if hordes of savage barbs had ensnared me, every one intent on dragging me back to the fear I feared most; the nebulous fear that had sparked off my original catastrophic panic.

Though flying on the brink of hysteria, a memory of nonentity woman squirmed into my head like an insidious snake and wrenched me down. Crazy, I know, but all I could think was that she knew I was hunting the person who had thrown my life into chaos – she *knew!* Even in my state, I picked up that she couldn't have plucked the idea from inside my head. That was impossible, yet I eagerly seized her flaky confirmation like a lifeline. It renewed my conviction that the *someone* who had triggered my panic had in no way let go. They were still in malevolent control. That shows the state I was in. Talk about having a blinding epiphany of the obvious!

'Knew it all along,' I brayed sanctimoniously into the empty room. 'Bet whoever it is, is laughing their head off, especially after all they've just put me through.'

I was behaving like a self-indulgent half-wit, doling out meaningless scorn instead of seriously pondering nonentity woman's freakish interference. I'd not even realized how unquestioningly I'd been accepting impossibilities, how deaf I'd become to the cries from deep within my soul. Yet, at that time, it was all too hard. Far easier for me to focus on the people I knew to be treacherous. Stamping on all my better instincts, I bent the knee to vengeance: how I might get even and with whom.

Grimly, I set to the task. Tossing the two-faced Susie straight onto the payback heap was a clear no-brainer. Yet, no matter her alleged machete wielding antics, I still saw her as just the help. The same with Dimple – a real bitch-queen: lying, cheating and sadistic in equal measures – but an also-ran nonetheless.

Charity was something else, definitely, especially after she'd so glutinously contrived her own public exaltation and my public denouncement. So many people! Yet stamping her as my tormenting *someone* didn't feel right. It never had. It felt altogether too pat.

Like a hungry cat scampering after rodents, my brain darted in all directions. Then it settled on the apparently obvious: Charity knew more than she was telling; much more than she'd leaked in the auditorium. But I had a tag-on thought: why had she explicitly accused *me* of betrayal. I agonized over that. Why accuse me unless she was in some way vulnerable, or paranoid? She certainly had a habit of harping on about *guarding against those who would have us fail.*

I caught myself pacing. Another thought – an insight – wafted teasingly in the air. Though I could sense it, my concentration was as rickety as a rotted out staircase in a derelict house. Annoyingly, it drifted away, leaving me piled high with frustration. I needed to get a grip.

Forcing myself, I dragged out my own first principle as if it were a comfort blanket. But clarifying the task wasn't easy, especially with my mind all over the place. Took quite an effort to hit on any rational task to clarify. When I did, I sat with a jolt.

I'd settled on Charity's charity. Not sure why. It had just popped up like a road-block premonition. None too confidently, I bit the bullet and thought round its function: its support for the partially blind *and* partially deaf, no one else. Made me puzzle how such a relatively limited client group could possibly generate the unbelievable crowd gathered in the auditorium. It didn't add up. Either Charity was lying about the charity itself, or the vast majority who had turned up were members of rent-a-rabble.

I began pacing again, not sure if I was crawling out or sinking deeper into quicksand. Yet the numbers weren't imaginary. For her own reasons, Charity had beefed up my humiliation beyond every sensible limit. After another three turns, I halted abruptly, confounded. I was looking directly into the face of nonentity woman.

'H-how the hell did you get in here?' I stammered, instantly fearful, instantly hating everything about her.

'I've come to encourage you,' she said quietly.

'Encourage!' I yelled back. 'Have you any idea—'

'Shush,' she whispered. 'Say no more. Think more.'

Insistent raps, followed by the sound of the door being rapidly unlocked, stopped me telling her precisely where she could stick her encouragement. Within a breath, Susie had burst in.

'What are you doing in here?' she demanded hotly. 'Who's with you?'

I swung round and round again: shocked my interloper had gone, shocked she'd managed to get in anyway, and shocked at Susie. I sat down, fixated on Susie. In the living room, on the worst ever day of my life, her outfit had been the last thing on my mind. Even so, I couldn't believe the attractively dressed, if flustered, woman in my doorway was actually her; until she scowled in her own special way.

I expected her to blast me for eyeballing her stylish cerise dress, but she was interested in only one thing. 'I asked who's been in here with you?'

I can't explain it. I felt a stirring of my usual self. I could almost feel the ordeal they had so maliciously orchestrated being set aside. One thought dominated. Susie was worried. She didn't just want information, she needed it.

'An hallucination,' I answered. 'Mine or yours? Who knows?'

She didn't like it. 'Very amusing, but I doubt Charity will be laughing if you've had more dealings with those who would have us fail.'

She'd used that same expression. Made me wonder if it lay behind the wafting thought I'd lost earlier. Unsure, I stiffened my chin to give nothing away, then tried grim sarcasm in monotone. 'I've had a roughish kind of day so, do me a favor, run along and murder someone or whatever else you do when you're not pretending to do brain surgery.'

I hadn't expected her to soften. 'All right, Ronald, maybe I was mistaken, but you've been up here for hours and Adelia has cooked you something special.'

'Naturally,' I said heavily. 'It's my special day. It's tell everyone everything day. The whole world now knows I'm impotent, that I beat women, and who knows what else.' I shrugged, not finding it hard to look defeated, yet Susie's angst had lit a steady flame.

'I'll stay to dinner if you like,' she volunteered. 'From tomorrow we'll be back working together so we might as well draw a line and start afresh.'

'Forgive and forget, kind of thing?'

'Best for—'

I was quick to cut in. 'Good bye, Susie. I'd sooner wrestle a starving shark over a tasty fish than have dinner with you.'

'Be careful,' she said coldly, 'and get your head straight for the morning.' She waved her arms around the bedroom. 'You'll have to start earning all this if you want to keep it. So be warned – and make no mistake – you'll be accountable to me.'

To make sure she'd gone, I trailed her out of the apartment and slammed the door. James appeared.

'Are you intending to dress for dinner, sir?'

I almost laughed. My life had become a living nightmare. Other men with half my troubles would have slit their throats long since. Yet the biggest issue for James was whether I wanted to dress for dinner.

'No,' I said. 'I'll eat as soon as Adelia can serve.'

Having decided to wait in the dining room, I arbitrarily picked a chair around the magnificently inlaid walnut table and sat, propping up my chin. My mind soon resurrected the sheer malevolence behind Charity's elaborate jamboree. She – they – had really gone all out to humiliate me, which was spectacularly ripe considering their own blood-curdling shenanigans. That was when I fell in. It felt as if a blob of insight had leaked out of nowhere and smeared my brain. Humiliating me had only been the sideshow. What they'd really wanted was to break me – break my spirit. But why?

After several calming breaths, I came back to the nervy link between the charity and whoever lurked behind *those who would have us fail*. For sure Susie had been nigh on desperate to get into the bedroom when she thought someone was with me. She'd spat accusations like a real she-wolf and virtually arraigned me for being up close and personal with the *would-have-us-fail* merchants.

I stood and wandered round the table, not registering its craftsmanship or the equally skillful work exhibited in the sideboard and cabinets. It wasn't a great leap to reason that nonentity woman might be an ally after all, in some half-cock haunting-my-hallucinations sort of way. After all, she did say she'd come to encourage me, and she'd told me to think more.

It wasn't much. I sat down again and had a mental conversation: Well, ally, reckon Charity and Susie would love to get their hands round your neck, if you exist outside my head. Either way, stop bugging me. I'm doing what you want.

As I grimaced at my own lightheadedness, Adelia grabbed my attention. She had come in with a trolley loaded with terrines. Far more compelling was her blouse. It was barely fastened. Though I knew she was baiting me, I couldn't resist. Every time she came in with a new trolley-load, my eyes tracked her. After bringing in more food than ten could eat she stood beside me.

'Would you like to help yourself, sir?'

I sighed, entranced. To be honest, despite our history, it was hard to contain myself. Only the fear of repeating my mistake and plunging into deeper trouble kept my hands down.

'I'll sample everything,' I said, not intending to be ambiguous. 'When you've served, go and dress properly. You're here to cook and dish up. That means ignoring any advice you get from Susie. Understand?'

She smiled. 'Whatever you say, sir.'

After overloading my plate, she bowed revealingly and swayed to the door a little too provocatively. It was strangely sobering to observe the legacy of Susie's brazen sitting-room guidance; how she'd fueled Adelia's desire to perform for extra pay. Plain little Susie, full of venom; my boss-bitch.

I surprised myself by eating heartily. Maybe it was being cocooned in comfort away from the malice that had been unleashed against me. Definitely Adelia's cooking helped, and so did my embryonic optimism, though I still felt decidedly fragile and rudderless. Three thoughts rumbled in my head: Adelia had a magic touch with food; her dress sense would embarrass a street-girl; she could be bought.

The promise of extra cash had turned the frightened woman of the morning into the rousing temptress of the evening. It seemed entirely reasonable that she might prostitute herself a little further and become my mole, for the right price. The possibility put me on my feet, mentally replaying the scene I'd glimpsed in the living room.

Even in my damaged state, I'd mentally registered the way Susie had so eagerly explored Adelia's blouse. True, I'd not seen much, but I still reckoned my boss-bitch had overly enjoyed her touching-up experience. Made me wonder if her public prudishness might be an exploitable sham.

Chapter Fifteen

By morning I'd managed to rationalize my degrading experience. I awoke feeling remarkably at ease. I'd have done better to ditch my smugness and be more questioning; and there were some mighty nagging questions. Why, for instance, had Charity volunteered such damning and distinctly graphic disclosures about Dimple; and what was the trail behind Grub's out-of-the-blue arrival in the conference room? As it was, I challenged nothing. I merely lay in bed, arms like wings either side of my head.

As far as I was concerned, I was my own pole-star. All I saw was how Charity and her side-kicks had overcooked the goose. They had delivered one doozy of a performance in smashing me down, but hadn't been smart enough to keep their mouths shut. Both Charity and Susie had showed nervousness about betrayal; about how vulnerable they were. To me that meant they were scared of something, specifically something I might do if I joined those who would have them fail.

But I wasn't that dumb. Having already been caught out by a secret camera in the kitchen, I'd cottoned on that other rooms could be similarly equipped, but maybe not all. Susie had only been able to hear me in the bedroom, otherwise she'd have known for sure about nonentity woman, or she would have if my enigmatic visitor hadn't been a figment of my imagination, probably.

Rolling over, I hid a rueful grin. Though I'd vowed never again to play their games, I really had no choice.

They were my only footholds to my goal. Besides, after the way they had dug their claws in, they owed me, and I had to get close to get even.

When James knocked ready to be of service, I was careful to appear deflated and kept up the act as I wandered into the kitchen. As if tempting fate a second time, I surprised Adelia.

Recovering quickly, she smiled. 'Good morning, sir. I've done like you told me.'

I was oddly disappointed. She had taken me at my word and ousted the previous day's revealing outfit for a short sleeved, button-to-the-neck blouse and knee-length black skirt. I wanted to touch her everywhere just to make her earn her money. I didn't.

By the time she had prepared breakfast, the notion of using her as a potential spy had become less appealing. It made more sense to use their technology first. Better to manipulate them through their own monitoring devices, assuming I was right and things said in the apartment were being recorded, evaluated and furtively revealed to Charity, Susie or Dimple, or all three.

I decided to test Adelia. 'Guess you know I threw Susie out yesterday. Bad thing to do. I was upset and didn't want her tasting your excellent cooking.'

Her expression swam between delight and shock. After a thinking delay, she said, 'There was plenty in case you had a guest.'

'Would you have liked Susie to stay?'

She began to get ruffled. 'That's not for me, sir. Are you happy with this blouse?'

I played clever. 'Do you think Susie would like it?'

My cleverness stumped her. 'She liked the other one, said so.'

'All right,' I said without emphasis. 'Maybe we should make a pact: you wear what Susie likes and I'll do what she wants. How's that?'

Confusion danced across her face. When she thought she understood, she relaxed. 'Want me to change now, sir; right here, right now?'

All my desires joined in silent crescendo, yelling, *yes, yes, yes; take everything o and get over here*. Too much was at stake. I shook my head and capped the conversation.

'You're fine, Adelia, thanks. Just help me make things right with Susie. I'm inviting her for dinner so wear something really sexy. Buy whatever you need.' Her confusion returned so I added, 'If Susie sees how well you're pleasing me, she'll be pleased too, then we'll all get along.'

I reviewed my plan on the way to the 10 o'clock meeting with Charity. It was thin, not really a plan at all, yet if Susie had heard and believed my kitchen conversation, I stood to regain her trust and win the freedom to set my own traps.

'Speed up,' I told the chauffeur, impatient to get to the conference room and assess Susie's mood.

It was the first time I'd been in that room since Grub had died there, possibly at Susie's hands, though I still didn't want to accept it. To my astonishment, nothing had been cleared up, except the corpse had been removed. Remaining, was a sickening puddle of blood on the carpet like an ensanguined backdrop to the armchairs strewn around where I'd been sitting. Made me cringe, particularly with memories of that day so close to the surface, and memories of all that had happened since even closer.

Must be honest, it took all my grit to sit and wait. I hadn't expected Dimple to arrive first or to see her in a crimson halter dress, a dress that scooped so low it fully displayed the diamond orbital in her navel. Her back was completely bare, the dress so short it was more like a skimpy valance. I couldn't help gawking at the generous measure of skin so unashamedly revealed, every inch absolutely flawless.

'IIi, Ronnie,' she cooed, moving to stand within touching distance. It was obvious she wanted to show off her absence of bruising. 'Think I did pretty well yesterday.'

I floundered, unsure if she was congratulating herself or asking my opinion, but I'd endured more than enough first-hand experiences to know that Dimple was entirely beyond redemption: a dangerous, treacherous and scheming bitch-queen. On top of that, my ears were still burning with the lurid character reference Charity had given in the auditorium. I kept quiet. It felt safer.

Unsurprisingly, my thoughts chucked me straight back to the on-stage climax of Dimple's lying betrayal and my judgment that she deserved to die. I rubbed my forehead as if reliving my attempt to rub away her made-up bruises, and came to the same conclusion. She did deserve to die, and she wasn't the only one.

'Stop touching your forehead,' she complained, her mood taking a dip. The down-beat didn't last. Pouting, she teased, 'Nothing to say? Too chewed up because I got the better of you yesterday?'

I planted a counterfeit smile. 'You got me all right. Made everyone in the audience believe you.'

'Don't sell me short, sweetie. I did more than that. Was me who told The Blades to slice up Frank, and me who told the cops about them. Me again who led Grubby here by the whiskers.' She laughed mockingly. 'And his whiskers sure turned you to jelly, didn't they?' Another mocking laugh. 'And I told Susie that she'd have to do the killing for you. Let's face it, you never finish anything – and as for your idea of girl bashing ... pathetic! One puny slap then off you ran, sobbing like a—'

'Okay,' I interrupted, burying the urge to stand and throttle her. 'I've heard it and I get it. All right?'

Susie swept in, her hair combed back extra tight. Making no attempt to sit, she sandwiched me between herself and Dimple. 'Forgive and forget. Is that you today, Ronald?'

Dimple answered before I could. '*Forgetting* is his middle name.'

'And forgiving, Ronald, what about that?'

I looked at Susie, trying to work out if my conversation with Adelia had been relayed. All I saw was a new harshness in her eyes, a grim severity that contradicted the lively floral pattern on her light pink two-piece.

'No choice,' I said thickly. 'Got to move on.'

She ignored me. 'Great dress, Dimple. Love your style.'

Dimple moved seductively to stand closer to Susie, then pirouetted gracefully. I watched, easily spotting the change in Susie's hard expression. Instantly, my head filled with memories of Susie with Adelia, their eagerness. I almost laughed. I'd been so right, or so I figured: my boss-bitch did have a thing for girls and, for sure, Dimple knew all about it.

I couldn't believe it when their flirtatious encounter suddenly erupted into intimate cuddles and caresses, or the astonishing abruptness that ended it. Within a breath, they were again framing me between them like a squatting meerkat, both standing and behaving as if nothing had happened.

Brusquely, Susie said, 'You want to forgive, forget and move on, is that right?'

Her humorless smile rattled me. It took a second for my qualms to adjust, not least because she'd infected my words with her own. Cautiously, I nodded.

'Well I want my pound of flesh,' she announced, icily throwing back the gauntlet I'd thrown at the hospital. 'And I'll take it now.'

Dimple's bout of loud giggling did nothing for my unsettled nerves. I'd not anticipated this kind of game and hoped it was nothing more than Susie wanting her own back after I'd thrown her out of my apartment.

'You want me to apologize?' I asked, doubting it would be enough. 'I do. I'm sorry. After what happened, I was feeling damned raw. I lashed out. I'm sorry.'

'Know what?' Dimple declared. 'He still apologizes like a habit.'

'You feel it lacks genuineness,' Susie mused with phony yet disturbing solemnity.

It warned me that they weren't convinced I was beaten – and they had to be – and I was the only one who could do the convincing. My thin plan of using Adelia as an information pump depended on Susie being tempted back into friendship. Kowtowing to her was always going to be the price.

Dimple dragged back my attention. 'Wouldn't accept his verbal trash if I were you.'

I leaped in, hoping to forestall any reprisals they might be brewing. 'No. I am sorry. I mean it.'

Susie took no notice. 'You're right, Dimple. He's like a spring, all coiled and ready to let rip. Bad temper is in his eyes. He could lose control at any time. What would we poor maidens do then!'

They were ragging me. Between clenched teeth, I said, 'I'm not in a temper.'

'You are, sweetie,' Dimple goaded.

'No,' I said, glancing at Susie. 'I'm calm. I'm here waiting for Charity. You all floored me yesterday. There's no point—'

'Be quiet, Ronald,' Susie said before pausing ominously. 'So you're floored, calm, sorry and just waiting like a good boy for Charity's orders so you can fly off obediently?'

I had to say, 'Yes.'

'He should prove how obedient he is,' Dimple said cheerily. 'A personal demonstration.'

A vicious claw hooked into my stomach. Their ragging had twisted up a notch. Unless Charity came in and saved me, I knew I'd have to save myself. In the hope of her arrival, I craned towards the doors, each in turn. No sign. Charity was late, unforgivably late. No matter my best intentions, my hackles were rising. Though I fought to deny them, deep down I feared there would be blood on the carpet, female blood to join Grub's. If that happened, my softly-softly plan would be as dead as Frank's sliced up carcase.

Dimple laughed. 'He should dance on the table. That should do it.'

Whether it was her laugh or stupid idea that tipped me over the edge, I don't know. Either way, my self-control ducked out. I stood slowly, shaking with rage. 'Enough of this—'

The point of a machete stopped me, yet Susie still gave it an extra prod before swishing the blade through the air at high speed.

'We told you, didn't we?' she scoffed lightly. 'We said you were losing your temper.'

I had no idea where the weapon had come from, and it didn't matter. My delusional doubts about Susie being Grub's killer fizzled. My entire concern centered on not being her next victim. Like a dilatory snail, I caught on. I'd been dumb, unbelievably dumb. They'd played me like a hackneyed tune and sucked me into their manipulation. My plan to lull them had foundered. I scarcely breathed. A deathly pallor betrayed my sick fear, laying my soul bare.

'Like I said,' Dimple prompted, 'he should dance for us.'

When I didn't move, Susie again sliced the air.

'All right,' I gasped. 'I'll dance.'

'On the table, sweetie,' Dimple insisted.

I had to do it. Gripping my chair, I stepped up before crawling on wobbly knees onto the highly polished surface. A *get up* reminder came when cold steel slapped my buttocks. I got the message and hurriedly stood to face them.

Dimple sighed. 'Not exactly graceful, is he?'

Susie nodded. 'And he's not dancing.'

I took the hint and began lifting my feet and swinging my arms monkey-style. They watched, their silence like a menacing denunciation. All I could do was hope for their swift boredom, or salvation from Charity's arrival. How little I understood.

The first hope-puncturing harpoon came when Susie testily shook her head. 'Try harder, Ronald, or you'll be dancing with one leg.'

That fired me up. I jiggled the best I could, all the time conscious of their conspicuous disapproval. At the least sign of me slowing, the machete smacked the table.

'Look, he's as rigid as an effigy,' Dimple complained after a while. 'It's only his chicken-heart making him do anything at all. He'd be shouting and harassing us poor girls if you didn't have that machete.'

'Suppose so,' Susie answered, pretending to be on the bright side of a deep revelation.

'And that's not good enough to prove obedience,' Dimple decreed, toying with her dress straps. 'He's always ogling us girls. He should do a striptease so we can ogle him.'

Hearing that brought me to an abrupt standstill. My mouth stretched. My breaths came hard and fast. My brain bristled with abrasive scorn then lurched into a tangle. Like a dolt, I clung to the notion that they were only amusing themselves. 'No way!' I yelled.

Susie's blade instantly changed my mind. Its first slice slashed through both legs of my pants, catching my skin. The second attack was more of a flurry, ripping my jacket, nicking flesh and making me howl. Within seconds, I'd been brought to my knees.

Alarm contorted my face as Susie came close. 'You know what we want, Ronald, so be a good boy and do it.'

I really don't know how, but I managed to stand. My whole body shook. Amidst a fluster of inelegant gyrations, I struggled to remove my ruined clothes, one item at a time until I was cavorting naked.

'Don't stop on my account,' Charity said from behind

me. 'I like to see people enjoying themselves.'

In knee-jerk reaction, I swung to her voice. About fifteen strangers were with her. When I saw them, my surviving crumb of delusional self respect dropped like garbage into a bottomless gutter. I crashed down into an inelegant squat. The cacophony of their derisory laughter wounded far deeper than the blade of steel.

Allowing me no respite, Susie slapped the machete across my back. 'Charity doesn't want you to stop, Ronald. Neither does Dimple, and neither do I.'

Chapter Sixteen

I had no choice. I had to continue sordidly exhibiting myself as people took their places around the table. None seemed to notice Grub's blood. A few began clapping to give me a beat. Others soon joined in, sneering at my increasingly shambolic movements. I thought Charity would intervene once everyone had settled but she clapped along with the rest, until I hit my physical limits and dropped to my haunches.

'Stand and face me,' she demanded.

I dragged up the strength from somewhere. All eyes were on me, no one speaking. I tried telling myself it was just a bad dream, another inexplicably weird experience, yet my skin felt chilly and convincingly exposed. I couldn't doubt it. It *was* happening. Due to some freakish chain of irrational events, I'd been led to this moment. Against all the laws of reason, I'd come before a swarm of pitiless individuals as an object of derision; a naked dullard fit only to cavort on a polished conference table.

Charity sat back and held my unstable gaze. 'We'll deal with you as first business, Ronald.'

My breathing faltered. I felt defenseless, like a succulent child among cannibals. I know it sounds ridiculous, but I couldn't resist admiring her dress. It was vivid claret, its V-neck plunging into a softly tied bow, its waist cut away as daringly as the neckline.

For the first time, she acknowledged my compulsive appraisal. 'I hope you approve.' There was no hint of affectation. 'I hope so because the approval of others matters. It's why I'm so disappointed in you, Ronald.' Her comment did nothing to reassure. 'I'm particularly disappointed after all the trouble I went to yesterday; the great pains I took to fulfill my obligations and demonstrate that lust, pride, insatiable greed, vengeful intentions, anger, deceit and all your other faults can only lead to your downfall. Yet you ignored the lesson. You've been wasting your time scheming against this charity ... against Susie, against Dimple, and against me.'

I shook my head, mumbling, 'No.'

She contradicted immediately. 'Yes. Who do you take me for? Do you deny your presumptuous attempts to be clever? Do you deny your audacity in making false assumptions about the numbers involved in this charity and the numbers in the auditorium? Deny if you dare. Speak!'

Astounded, I stood motionless. In some mind-blowing way she had harvested my private thoughts.

'Very disappointing,' she scorned. 'And as if that isn't bad enough, you then scheme to bribe your cook into spying for you.'

'No,' I said, shivering at the ominous accuracy of her indictments.

'Yes, Ronald. I've no idea what gave you the idea that Susie is lesbian or bisexual, even less about what possessed you to ensnare Adelia into acting for you as seducer. Did you not know that Adelia used to be Susie's cook? Did you not understand that it was Susie who asked her to work for you until someone permanent could be found? Speak!'

I couldn't speak. Everything I'd planned had been plucked from my brain and stretched out like a barbed string of reckless fantasies. I felt utterly crushed, a transparent fool.

She slammed me with a frightening stare. 'You are here now, standing fully exposed, because I ordered it. To me, you were always fully exposed, always. I know you've had flirtations with those who would have us fail, and I know it's happened again despite my serious warning.' She paused, but I was in no state to respond.

Her manner inexplicably changed. 'But I understand how it can happen, I really do. I know how one thought can lead to another and, before you know it, you can believe I'm vulnerable. You can believe that this supposed vulnerability can be exploited ... if only you could meet more of those who would have us fail. But I did warn you. I said there would be no more chances if you defied me. Yet you persisted, as doubtlessly you would have persisted in your other deranged fabrications. You might even have gone so far as to imagine that Dimple here deserves to die, or that killing Susie or me would be a good thing.'

'N-never,' I lied shakily.

'Silence, Ronald,' she flared, standing as she spoke. 'I've told you before, it's not for me to judge you; but now I do have the power to punish. Before I decide if your disloyalty and contemptible deceit deserve leniency, I'll give you a chance to openly admit your faults ... your one and only chance to ask for mercy and join us with an open heart.'

My heart was open, openly pounding as if it were about to explode. She knew everything. Denial was as pointless as it was dangerous. At that moment, I believed my fate depended on her alone and, like a fool, I was blind to what she was really asking. 'Mercy,' I said. 'Mercy please.'

'Do you admit your faults and genuinely want to join us?'

My nod wasn't good enough. She told me so, emphatically.

I blurted it out. 'Sorry, yes. I admit my faults. Everything you said. I want to join you.'

Not for a second did I consider the consequences of what I was saying. Yet I did – at least subconsciously – kind of expect a brief delay while she graciously chewed over my plea. It didn't happen. As I finished speaking, she turned to leave.

To my horror, she said, 'No mercy. Let punishment begin.'

At once, almost everyone leaped from their seats and attacked. Don't ask me to explain, but I specifically watched Dimple follow Charity out. I didn't notice Susie. All hell was breaking loose: fists pummeling, fingers dragging, bodies raining down on me. I remember multiple hands, elbows and feet – nothing more until an unnervingly jovial voice floated my way.

It was Dr Burns. 'Back again!' he said. 'Just as well you bought a season ticket.'

I kept quiet. My eyes were closed, the way I wanted

them. None of my recent experiences had encouraged me to accept that I'd simply been carted off to hospital. It had to be worse than that.

Nurse Bridget, the doctor's wife, spoke next. 'You'll be fine with us, Mr Foster.'

After all I'd suffered at her hands, I could almost taste her nauseating lie. I tensed mentally, kidding myself that I'd soon fall asleep and reawaken at home; if I still had one.

'Do you remember what happened?' Burns asked.

That was no problem. Being pulverized by a crowd of cretins who enjoyed a mob-handed thump-up was singularly unforgettable, especially as I'd been stark naked on a table at the time. I recall thinking it odd that nothing hurt. I stayed zipped.

'We know you're awake, Mr Foster,' Bridget said. 'We know you can hear us. We only want to check how you're feeling.'

Burns chimed in as well. 'You took quite a bashing, but you're perfectly safe here ... for the moment.'

A tickle in my throat made me choke. When I gasped, my eyes automatically flew open. Unable to pretend any longer, I looked first at the ceiling. It seemed like an ordinary hospital ceiling; the little I could see of the headboard looked like a hospital headboard; the faces peering down at me peered from hospital uniforms. When I pushed my eyes sideways, I could make out the edges of medical equipment.

'That's better,' Burns said. 'So tell me, do you remember what happened?'

I wasn't interested in answering questions. The absence of feeling in my body had started to wind me up. 'What have you done to me?'

'What do you think we've done?' Bridget asked with a smile.

I tried closing my eyes again, frustrated I couldn't get a straight answer. It was either riddles from nonentity women or run around blabber from sadistic nurses. 'Tell me!' I demanded, glaring at each in turn.

Burns came back swiftly. 'No need for attitude, Ronald, but if you want it straight from the shoulder, you're paralyzed. Early days, but things aren't looking too hopeful. Doubt you're feeling much from the neck down and, to be fair, doubt you ever will again.'

'Not to worry,' Bridget said, refreshing her smile.

I gaped, figuring it had to be a sick joke. I guessed they had pumped something into me to smother sensation. 'That's humbug,' I said, hoping I was right.

'Okay,' Burns answered. 'Whatever you say.'

When his face disappeared, I called out, 'Hey! Where are you going?' All that came back was a door click. The only face still visible belonged to the caustic nurse.

'Reckon you've upset him,' she said.

Too frightened to risk upsetting her as well, I fought the urge to scream and murmured, 'Please help me. I need to understand.'

'You said it was humbug, Mr Foster, so I guess – since bugs bite– you've really been chewed.'

'No, please. Be honest. What happened?'

She sighed and took a long time to decide what, if anything, to tell me. 'Let's just say you'd be dead if the girl you bashed hadn't intervened and saved you.'

'Dimple!'

'So you admit it now. On stage you said you'd only slapped her. You accused her of having someone else do it.'

I didn't care that Dimple had been faking. I was desperate. 'I'll admit to anything you want, just tell me what happened.'

'That smacks of coercion, Mr Foster, and we don't want our patients believing they're under pressure.'

I shrank inside, fearing her skills in mental torture. Gruesome memories warned that she was about to lead me in circles. Even so, I had to press on. 'Please tell me what's wrong with me.' When her face pulled away, my neck refused to track her. Doubly alarmed, I whispered, 'Please don't go.'

It seemed an age before her face reappeared on the opposite side of the bed. 'Make up your mind, Mr Foster. Do you want to know what happened or what's wrong with you?' She gave me no chance to answer. 'Anyway, I'm sure you know what happened. You're pretending, aren't you?'

I had to concede and say what she wanted. 'All right, yes, I know. I think I know. I was set upon by a plague of morons in Charity's conference room.' I searched her eyes for confirmation.

'*Set upon*, eh,' she mimicked. 'I'd say they beat the meat out of you, but then I don't have your education.' She paused to smile. 'Mind you, I'm sure morons don't come in plagues. That's locusts; other insects too, and obviously diseases; and you can get plagues of rats. Dare say other things come in plagues too, but not morons.'

Despite her sarcasm, I felt relieved. Her version matched mine. I didn't have to wrestle with some other factious version. Seconds later, her face dipped from view. 'Wait, please,' I said. 'Tell me what they did to me.'

'I just told you. Weren't you listening?'

I was on her merry-go-round. 'Sorry, yes, I mean, what damage did they do?'

'I'm not a doctor, Mr Foster. You'll have to ask a doctor about that if you want more info. Shame you upset Peter when he was here … Dr Burns, I should say.'

I mustered as much control as I could. 'Please apologize for me and ask if he'll come back.'

'Sorry. Passing messages isn't in my job description.' Moments later, the door clicked.

I felt empty, gutted. She'd gone. She'd cold-heartedly left me helpless. She and that no-good doctor had crammed my head with the bleakest of news then left me alone to wallow in profound misery. I heard a sound.

'I thought you'd gone,' I said, my voice bloated with dread as much as hope. When nothing came back, my jaw quivered. It was too much. The awful reality of my situation came crashing home. All my battened down emotions overflowed. Tears I'd been holding back rushed out. My wailing sobs filled the room, echoing, bellowing out my unquenchable grief.

I've no idea how long I cried. What I remember is another noise cutting through. Not that I cared. I was in no state, yet that didn't stop my imagination thumping me with the worst of torments. As much as I could fathom anything, I feared the appearance of nonentity woman, her coming to scorch my wounds with acid.

Hatred overcame me. With my words whirling like dust in a storm, I screeched, 'Go away. I'm not interested. You brought all this on me with your riddles and rubbish. Charity knew about you all along. She knows you're out to harm her. You're one of *those* and you can go to hell.'

Whatever the noise had been, it became footsteps walking slowly to my bed. Certain it was nonentity woman, I squeezed my eyes to exclude her.

'It's time we talked, Ronald. I think you're ready now.'

Against my will, my eyelids flicked open. Susie's hair was softly groomed, not scraped back. Her light blue dress was so modern it wouldn't have looked out of place on Dimple, except for its high neck. Though I ached to say something, I could only sob.

Chapter Seventeen

I'd set out that morning intending to con them into believing I'd been broken, and ended up truly broken. Time weighed heavy in that hospital room, my tears streaming while Susie kept silent, sitting and waiting.

Only when my pent up fears, confusions, and passions had all been sobbed out, did I regain some control. Even then I was feeble, far too fragile to feel proper disgust at the way I'd crumpled. Right then, my horizon barely went as far as flicking my eyes sideways to gaze at Susie.

'I'm so s-sorry,' I stammered.

'I believe you are,' she said indifferently.

I'd hoped for more compassion. No chance. Her softer attire had done nothing to soften her harsh expression.

Crisply, she said, 'Charity would have let you be killed. You do understand that?'

Only my physical incapacity stopped me shuddering. I could have been torn limb from limb in that conference room. Unable to nod, I whispered, 'Yes.'

She looked me straight in the eyes. 'I can arrange euthanasia if you wish.'

'No!' I choked, stung by her damning proposal.

She seemed disappointed. 'So you think your present condition is better than being dead?'

'Yes.'

'Even though it's of no use to Charity?'

'Suppose not.'

'Yes or no, Ronald. It's a simple judgment call.'

'No.'

A flicker of satisfaction crossed her face. 'Charity agrees.'

I wanted more. I sensed there was more, maybe some kind of redemption. 'I didn't mean to—'

She butted in like a predator with toothache. 'Whatever you meant or didn't mean is of no significance, Ronald. You've had endless chances to do the right thing and you've betrayed every trust put in you. You deserve to be stricken down.' When my tears welled again, she spoke severely. 'Start that again and I'll leave.' Her pause left me on tenterhooks until she was ready. 'You can't stay here and Charity definitely won't provide a place for you. The Asylum seems the best option.'

'A-asylum,' I gasped. 'Surely there's some—'

She reacted badly to being challenged. 'Are you questioning my judgment?'

I looked away. Every sinew in my useless body was questioning her judgment. I was being written off without anyone lifting a finger. I still said, 'No.'

It was a while before she spoke again. 'What did the nurse tell you about what happened in the conference room?'

The subject change wrenched Bridget to mind and stirred up old anger. Submerging it, I said, 'She told me Dimple intervened, saved me.'

'Do you believe her?'

Susie's unfeeling aggression fueled my fire. Not trusting myself, I dawdled over my reply. 'I have to accept what she says.'

'Do you think it's likely that Dimple saved you?'

This time, my frustrated anger cracked. 'Where's this going?'

Susie stood up. 'You've learned nothing, have you? You're still the same self-centered, pig-headed braggart you've always been.'

Though still exasperated, I closed my eyes, fearing what might be coming.

She was in no hurry to extinguish my misery. Eventually, she said, 'I told Peter and Bridget Burns precisely what to say and do. It was a test of your temper. Once again you've failed to control it.'

I said, 'Pardon?' I think shock had put me on autopilot.

She shook her head as if to a naughty child. 'For your information, I was the one who stopped your beating. By the time Charity and Dimple had left, you were already well on the way out, most likely cued by a panic attack after all your oafish exertions. You fainted. Whatever you think, you were hardly touched, mostly noise and slaps. If I'd let them get serious, you would be dead.'

I stared, completely thrown about what to believe.

She hadn't finished. 'I hope this last lesson has hit home, Ronald, or else it really will be your last lesson. Do you understand what I saying?' I nodded, not realizing my neck had moved. 'Use the rest of today to think and we'll talk tomorrow.' She half-turned. 'Come to my house in the morning and make absolutely sure you leave every scrap of your old self behind. If I catch so much as a whiff of temper or anything else I don't like, I will deliver you to Charity.' She stepped away. 'And make no mistake, being delivered to Charity and being dead are less than a shadow apart.'

My mouth fell open as she left. Relief at not being paralyzed surged through me, yet it soon waned. I felt as if I'd been thrashed with a bullwhip, its braided leather poisoned with malignant revelations. Dark and rampaging doubts stole any joy from the fresh tingles in my extremities that promised freedom from immobility. Within seconds, my blissful taste of reprieve had withered like an isolated grain swamped by sheaves of despair.

Thoughts of the loathsome Burns' duo reared in my mind, yet Susie had made them out to be little more than pawns in her own ruthless scheming. She may – or may not – have rescued me from the conference room attack, but it was she who had so cruelly enforced my ignominious table dance; she who had sliced me with a machete; and she who had promised death for disobedience. By every conceivable standard, the whole situation was nth degree deranged. In the context of a charity supposedly existing only to support the sight and hearing impaired, all was full-on raging madness.

Took me a while to calm down. When I did, I focused on my body. Escape was uppermost in my mind and, for that, I needed limbs that moved. Since I wasn't clock-watching, I can't say how many hours passed before I was able to shuffle about the room. I think, a lot. During the whole time, no one came in either to see if I was alive or to gloat.

The main difference an extra couple of hours made was an almost normal walk and realization about how lucky I'd been. Although Susie's machete swinging had given me some nasty cuts, none was anything like deep enough to thwart my plan. Same with the bumps and bruises from the mob assault: enough to make a point, but nothing too serious.

I was about to cheer, when I had a double-take. Susie would never have blatantly defied Charity. She wouldn't have dragged off my attackers unless told to do so. More than that: I wouldn't have survived her machete-slashing unless it had all been for show. That meant my boss-bitch had been inflating her status. She'd probably had about as much control in that conference room as a hogtied donkey. Whoever had been issuing the orders, had also set limits.

Inevitably, my suspicions returned to Charity. She was far too on the pulse not to have full knowledge. Yet I still doubted her ultimate control. In fact, I more than ever suspected she didn't have it, especially given her disclosures about fulfilling *obligations* and only just getting the power to punish me.

I sat somberly on the bed. Apparently, the real bastard-in-chief – my sadistic nemesis – had realized that the auditorium fiasco hadn't been enough to break me. My mortifying conference room dance and the ensuing fake paralysis amounted to their second attempt. Quite obviously, they wanted me broken, but equally, they wanted to keep me alive. For me, this presented an intriguing conclusion. Not only were they nervous of me joining *those would have them fail,* they could actually need me for something, maybe something I alone could do. Whatever their game, it definitely was nowhere near over.

I caught myself going in circles again and stopped. Nothing had fundamentally changed. I still had my own primary task, and priority one was getting far away from the nefarious Burns' dyad. Snags instantly lined up. No clothes, a firmly locked *unlockable* door, and windows too high in the medical block to be usable. With nothing for my feet and only an open-back gown for covering, I was reduced to festering with frustrated anger.

Right then – had I the capacity to pick out an extra full blown bummer to wind me up – an uninvited appearance from nonentity woman would have trumped it. Yet there she stood on the far side of the bed, patiently waiting to be noticed. When I saw her, blood drained from my face. Nonsensically, I scrambled off the bed and squeezed deep into the side chair.

'Hello, Ronald,' she said as if she'd known me for years.

I couldn't grasp what scared me most. The way she had materialized in a sealed room – a room I certainly couldn't get out of – or the fact she'd simply popped in for a chat. Having had Susie burst into my bedroom last time, I was well wary, especially with the likelihood of hospital surveillance cameras spying for the enemy. Gesticulating like a frightened child, I waved her to silence. Then I remembered she probably wasn't real.

To be honest, after the initial shock of her appearance, her questionable existence didn't seem to count for much. I suppose that contradictory metaphysics had started to become merely incidental in my life – not that putting her in a philosophical pigeon-hole did anything to stop my imagination running riot. Among the most rational of my impulses was the urge to grab hold and force her to transport me out of the hospital.

It was a while before my mental hysteria cooled and I sat normally. By then I'd shot my bolt about not inviting unwanted attention from the nursing station.

Nonentity woman ignored my confused entreaties. 'It's good you've thought more, Ronald. Now accept this warning: the person you're looking for runs headlong into traps. He only sees what he wants to see and hears what he wants to hear.'

I'd never encountered anyone who so inexplicably riled and scared me. Her doling out more riddles roused anger out of all proportion. Only self-preservation forced me to mask it. I just wanted her to go and never come back. Not for a second did I remember she could actually be an ally.

As I'd feared, my reaction to nonentity woman's appearance triggered Bridget. She dashed in faster than a ravenous vulture smelling fresh carcass. 'You're behaving strangely. Tell me why?'

My mind cleared. Why, I'm not sure, but I sorely needed

the boost. Relying on past experiences, I assumed that nonentity woman would have vanished, but I checked anyway. Relieved, I studied the nurse who had so callously crammed my head with lies before leaving me broken. 'Well, let me see,' I snarled. 'Could be that I was told I was paralyzed only to find it was a fib. Could be I'm locked in this torture chamber with no one bothering to check if I'm dead, alive or climbing the walls. Could be—'

I didn't hesitate. The door had been left ajar and I wasn't about to waste the chance. I bolted, and promptly discovered my legs to be less reliable than matchsticks supporting a mansion. Desperation kept me upright, lumbering not very fast and not very steadily, but scurrying for all I was worth.

She called after me, 'Mr Foster, I've brought your discharge papers.'

The double-dealing cow had obviously pegged me as dripping, let alone wet behind the ears. No way was I stopping. My speed increased as I headed down the passageway to the lobby. Not the elevator, I told myself, not wanting to be grabbed at the bottom. It had to be the stairs and I had to find something less conspicuous to wear.

One level down, I diverted into a main corridor. After a few embarrassing encounters, I'd filched enough clothes to look like a visitor. Once on the ground floor, I pitched my walk at blend-in pace. My gaze dodged direct eye contact as I headed for the main entrance.

To me, the final thirty yards to the doors never seemed to shorten. My vision was glazing over, I guess from the strain. My pores were leaking sweat. I didn't see the wheelchair coming the opposite way, not until I'd piled into it. The clash sent me sprawling.

'Are you blind, idiot!' the outraged woman shouted, her bulk formidable, her complexion already florid. 'You could have killed me.'

I struggled to get up. Although my shins and palms had taken the brunt, the impact had provoked a mass reaction from the cuts and blows I'd suffered in the conference room. A crowd sprang from nowhere.

'S-sorry,' I muttered, keen to get away.

She glowered, then her eyebrows shot up and she squawked at the top of her voice. 'You're a thief. That's my husband's jacket.'

I couldn't believe my luck. 'No,' I said, fighting alarm. 'I assure you—'

'Thief!' she barked again. 'You think I don't know my own husband's best jacket. I sewed that badge on special.'

Security Officer Baines picked his way through the pack, his uniform smart. 'What's the trouble here?'

The woman plunged straight in. 'He stole my husband's jacket.'

I had to deny it. Shaking my head, I said, 'I didn't! But I don't care, really I don't. Take it, lady, if it'll make you happy.' It was a stupid thing to say.

Baines noticed my facial bruises and watched me slide off the jacket. As I handed it over, he said, 'You wait here. Let her check.'

The woman was already rifling the pockets and soon yanked out a wallet with her picture in it. 'Told you,' she yowled triumphantly. 'Thief, thief, thief!' She turned to the officer. 'I want to press charges. People like him should be locked up. We're not safe with murderers like him about.'

I'd had enough. 'I'm not a murderer, you stupid gasbag! Your husband's coat must have got muddled with mine, that's all.'

Baines tensed. 'No need for offensive language, sir. If what you say is true, we'll go together and collect your jacket.'

'He's lying!' the woman bellowed. 'Don't you start messing with me. Arrest him. Stick him in a pit. He deserves death, stealing from my poor sick husband. Amounts to murder in my book.'

'Well it's not murder, madam,' Baines corrected. 'But the circumstances do require explanation.'

'How dare you take his side, you jackass,' she squealed. 'You're both villains, picking on a poor handicapped woman and her dying husband. Should be ashamed of yourselves. He's probably dead up there, beaten to death for his jacket.'

My temper broke loose. 'This is ridiculous!' I began, but Baines cut me off.

'But easily sorted, sir.' He took a firm grip on my arm. 'Show me where you muddled the jackets and—'

'What about me?' she screeched. 'You talk about jackets,

what about my murdered husband?'

Baines sighed. 'I'm sure he's not been murd—'

A new voice stopped him. 'Ronnie. Oh, Ronnie.'

Everyone looked to where the voice had come from. Most gaped, me included. Dimple was strolling towards the group, unhurried and looking spectacular in a flared primrose dress. Decorating its sweetheart neckline was a dazzling diamond studded gold necklace. Her wrists displayed matching bracelets; her fingers bristled with gemstone rings.

'Silly old you, Ronnie,' she said, walking through the gap that appeared for her. 'You picked up the wrong coat. This is yours.'

I gawked at the jacket she was offering. It looked exactly the same, even to the badge. No words came.

'Take it then, sweetie,' she said. 'I'm late and you're supposed to—'

'One minute, miss,' Baines interrupted. 'How did you come by this jacket?'

She stepped close to him. 'Do you like your job?'

Baines blinked in surprise. 'Are you threatening me, miss?'

The chief security officer rushed over, clearly flustered, already calling out. 'Enough, Baines. Move on.'

'But, sir!'

'*No buts*,' the chief snapped. 'This woman now has her husband's jacket and Mr Foster has his. Simple mistake, as this charming lady has pointed out.'

The wheelchaired woman was having none of it. 'No mistake!' she erupted, her fury beyond reason. 'T-this jacket was in my husband's private room. He's been murdered for it!'

'We could go and see,' Dimple suggested, smiling innocently as she withdrew slightly. 'But if I'm delayed any longer, I fear Mr Baines will lose more than his job.'

'Correct,' the chief echoed, astounding Baines.

'So, sweetie,' Dimple cooed at the flabbergasted officer. 'Do you really want to push?'

Baines turned to his chief. 'How did you know Mr Foster's name? How could you hear and—'

'Enough! Your job is on the line here.'

'You're all in it together!' the woman screamed, her

florid face sweating profusely. 'You—'

For a few seconds, no one realized she was having a heart attack. When we did, none of us attempted to call a crash team. We just watched the shudders until her head lolled forward, saliva dripping onto her lap.

'Come on, Ronnie,' Dimple announced indifferently. 'You can walk me to my car.'

I glanced at Baines, expecting something, not sure what. His face looked as if a demon had claimed his soul. I felt that look. I'd seen it in my own mirror. The man was in his own living hell.

Chapter Eighteen

I didn't speak as Dimple ambled to her open-topped sports car. It was the same red as her hair with flashes of the same yellow.

'Don't get in, sweetie,' she said when we stopped. 'Just because I saved your ass doesn't mean I want it in my car.'

Should have known she'd spring one on me. I still had to ask. 'I don't understand what happened in there.'

'I understand, sweetie. That's all that matters, isn't it?'

As ever, she was being a bitch-queen. 'No, it isn't.'

'Now, Ronnie, if you start getting feisty I'll drive off and not tell you where you're to go.'

I persisted. 'But how did you— how did anyone—'

'You're being a bore, sweetie,' she huffed.

I huffed straight back, yet I was too achy and weary to keep on. Feeling like a chicken faced with a skewer, I nose-dived for the least painful option. 'All right. Am I to go back to my apartment or what?'

'It's more the *or what* for you, Ron, and you can't complain. You've done nothing to earn the apartment Charity lavished on you.' She paused to pluck a card from her jeweled purse. 'Try here.'

I read the address. 'It says *Asylum*. I thought—'

Her labored grin stopped me. 'You're not clever enough to think, Ronnie. Settle for doing what you're told.' Without another glance, she sped away.

I gazed after her, maybe in the hope she'd come back. She didn't. Oddly, I felt no anger. Should be damned angry, I told myself. Then I fell in. Getting angry was futile, especially all alone in a parking lot having just witnessed another barrel-load of mind warping impossibilities. Something bizarre always seemed to happen when I sensed a thin ray of hope. There was always some new twist to blast me sideways into yet more rampaging uncertainty.

I began walking, not thinking where, just walking. For the first time, the idea I might actually be mad crawled to the top. I figured, why else would I let a few pernicious people stamp all over my life? All they did was cram my waking hours with bile and vindictive contradictions.

Maybe, I wondered, I was getting random nudges towards a nut-case hospital because I really was under treatment in a unit somewhere and being looked after by proper doctors and nurses. Maybe the haze of insanity had stopped me seeing the whole truth. At that moment, the harrowing idea seemed naggingly plausible. Even Susie had said it was important for me to face up to reality and that the asylum was my best option.

Those last thoughts brought me to an abrupt halt. In the state I was in, I wasn't sure if Susie really existed any more than nonentity woman, let alone whether anything she said had any actual validity. As far as I knew, she – along with Charity and Dimple, Dr Burns and Bridget – was part of a vile pastiche generated by my sick brain.

I glanced about expecting to see the abnormal, but found only the disconcertingly normal. Unsure if I should laugh or cry, I checked back at the hospital. It lay behind me like an accusation, kept at bay by its parking lot. It was a similar story with the surrounding streets. They all played host to cars and people and houses and shops exactly as common sense, not insanity, said they should. What I didn't expect was a car to pull up, two youngish men to jump out, and for them to whack home a few hefty punches.

'That's for girl bashing,' one of them said before they zoomed off, leaving me folded double and gasping for air.

Got to tell you, there was nothing imaginary about those thumps. Both men had powered in as if releasing a mountain of compressed rage. Took me a minute to realize how hurt and shaken I was. Spotting a low garden wall, I stumbled over and eased down to recover. Moments later, a broom handle smacked across my back.

'Clear off, you scum. Pity them boys didn't knife yer!'

I bounced off that wall like a spring-loaded rabbit, my arms flapping uselessly. When I glanced back, I couldn't believe my attacker to be a middled aged woman in a green dress suit.

'Told you to git,' she snarled, her broom jabbing in my direction. 'So git!'

It was pointless to argue. With no idea where to go, I chewed through the pain, made an arbitrary choice, and lurched away. To be honest, I felt chopped, pommeled and pretty sorry for myself. None of it was my fault. My faceless *someone* had twisted the knife, again.

That thought bit deep and became entwined with nonentity woman's warning. Guess the combination gave me a eureka moment. I saw clearly that my tormentors had changed tack. Having so far failed to break me, they had switched to trying to convince me I was mad. It was just another maneuver, but it brought me up short. With so much else going on, I'd almost forgotten my real quest. I had forgotten it. I'd let it slide. It had taken nonentity woman's remembered warning to get me back on track.

My thoughts bounced all over the jacket incident and the attacks outside the hospital. 'Couldn't resist those extra prods, could you,' I said aloud to the empty street. 'Had me thinking I really might be mad.'

Satisfied to be refocused again, my walk became stronger and straighter. But I was deluding myself. The more I trawled for ideas to expose my enemy, the more lost and trapped I became. When I could take no more brain knotting, I belatedly resorted to my task-clarifying first principle.

Easier said than done. In the end I was happy to grab at any straw. I never expected to pick an offering from nonentity woman; from her riddles. She had told me *he* runs headlong into traps and only sees and hears what *he* wants. If she was to be believed, I had to believe my *someone* was a man. That meant my three super bitches had to be second tier, as I'd always suspected. And there was something else. It meant that all three were expendable. I could cheerfully squeeze each one till a name oozed out. Then it would be payback time; his turn to scream.

My thoughts quickly turned to Susie. She was expecting

me at her house in the morning. How very convenient, I decided, blindly setting aside images of her killing Grub. I only needed a simple plan: pacify her first then, when she'd accepted my surrender, turn on her. She'd soon wish she'd never been born.

A flashing sign distracted me, bright orange. It read: *Asylum.* I gaped. The odds of this particular place popping up like a salving blessing in a good-luck drought, were millions to one. At once, the thought I least wanted surged back like a tidal wave. Insanity answered so many questions. Maybe I'd been right about being under treatment. Maybe a haze of insanity had stopped me seeing the truth, for here was the asylum, the place I was supposed to go. In a torrent of emotion, my hardcore plans panicked and fled.

I recollect shuffling towards the yellow brick building. Absurdly, I noticed its elegant facade and magnificent portico. Its grandeur seemed to confirm the fragility of my madness and smash through my last flickering attempts to hide from the glaring truth. I felt crushed.

The weight of realization slumped my shoulders. I trekked through the fluted stone columns to a revolving door, its panels dark wood, partially glazed. Inside, thick carpet made me think I was treading air. From the distance, a mirror-polished reception counter beckoned, no one in attendance. I recall glancing left and right, expecting something, seeing only the generously proportioned vestibule. I accepted at face value its abundance of rich leather chairs grouped around low tables and its imposing sofa-encircled floral displays.

A receptionist quickly appeared, the collar of her white blouse graced by a neat ruby cravat, the same color as her skirt and waisted jacket. 'Good afternoon, sir,' she said, her chestnut hair swaying free above her shoulders. 'I'm Carol. Welcome to the Asylum. How may I help?'

I kept my gaze low, not really wanting to see her or talk. More than anything, I didn't want to be welcomed.

Although she must have noticed my bruised face, her smile never faltered. When I kept silent, she merely checked her information screen. 'You must be Mr Foster. We've been expecting you, sir.'

'Tell me where to go,' I slurred at her.

'Certainly, sir. Clarence will take you.' As she spoke, a

bellboy in ruby uniform hurried to the counter and touched his hat respectfully. 'Suite 707 for Mr Foster, Clarence.'

He really wasn't much more than a boy. 'This way, sir,' he said, arm outstretched.

I trailed him like a condemned villain en route to the gallows and flopped out on the bed once he'd gone. My mind kept rehearsing a solitary connected thought: I'm mad. Nothing is what it seems. Somehow, I fell asleep.

The sound of rattling woke me, a deliberate sound. 'Good morning, sir,' James said, his attire impeccable. 'Would you care for coffee or prefer tea?'

Hearing his familiar voice jarred me and goaded my body into taking painful revenge. I winced, struggling to remember where I was. When I did, I squeezed my eyes shut, unwilling to face anything.

'Are you all right, sir?' James asked. 'Shall I call a doctor?'

I was having none of that. 'No doctors, ever!'

Rawness forced me to swing up and sit on the bed, eyes reluctantly open. My stolen clothes had been replaced with neat pajamas. It was all familiar territory, or so I figured. I'd had another memory lapse or hallucination. This time, I didn't care. I told myself I didn't care. The fates, real or imaginary, had tossed me another reality, maybe. Either way, I pointedly avoided looking round. I preferred to believe that, somehow, I'd jumped back into my confiscated apartment complete with the admirably toadying James. It didn't matter that my scenario was at odds with Susie and Dimple's story of eviction. They could easily have lied.

James punctured my thoughts. 'Miss Susie is expecting you at 10 o'clock, sir. Would you—'

'Miss Susie!' I echoed, stung by the unwelcome link to the previous day. I decided to play dumb. 'It's morning, is it?'

'Shortly after eight, sir. I came to the hotel so—'

'Hotel?'

'The Asylum, sir. You arrived yesterday after your discharge from—'

I cut in again, getting angry. 'Discharge!' Despite my reluctance, I had no choice. I had to scan the room. Too many obnoxious connections were knitting together.

James patiently smoothed over my heavy-tongued interruptions. 'You came to the hotel from hospital, sir, and now I've brought a selection of clothes for you. We'll do our best to make you look utterly splendid.'

Considering how I felt, my grunted response was remarkably polite. I didn't feel like looking splendid, utterly or otherwise, at least not at that precise moment. Having gone to sleep believing myself insane, it was under-skin aggravating to wake up in a hotbed of semi-continuity and mixed up truth.

'Who's paying for this place,' I asked, not that I cared. It was impulsive, a hair-brained urge to learn something.

'As with all your expenses, sir, it'll be charged to your account.'

'How much is in this account?'

James wasn't the least flustered. 'I really don't kn—'

'What about the apartment?' I challenged, wanting him flustered. 'Why was I booked in here?'

He was too good. 'Sorry, sir, these matters are outside my remit. Might I suggest you inquire of Miss Susie.'

I'll sure do something to Miss Susie, I thought. The idea of squeezing her for information was once more firm in my head. 'Get me ready.'

Susie answered her front door in the same red satin tunic she had worn on my first disputed visit. Her choice wasn't lost on me. Allegedly Frank had been dead at the time, yet I still believed otherwise. Far as I was concerned, he'd been plenty lively enough to float Susie's passion boat, indisputably so. I closed my eyes for a few seconds, half expecting Frank to appear and make the deja vu complete. On opening them, I noticed Susie's hair. It was hanging loose, just as it had that day. As intriguing, her tunic was significantly unbuttoned.

'You're early,' she said coldly.

I ached to say, *and you're ugly*, but I needed to get over the threshold with her believing me bruised and broken; not furious, scheming and in a mental war zone. Making unnecessary adjustments to my fine silk tie, I said, 'Sorry.'

She shook her head as if to a delinquent urchin, then stepped back leaving me to follow inside. When I joined her in the living room, everything was exactly as I remembered.

Wisely or not, I said, 'I've been here before.'

She chose not to answer. 'You're staying at the Asylum.'

She could have been asking or making a statement. Her lack of inflection made it an evens bet. I jumped in anyway. 'My apartment has been stolen from me.'

She took a long breath. 'I was very specific about how you were to behave, Ronald, so I suggest you withdraw that remark and apologize.'

I mentally kicked myself. I'd not been there five minutes and had already put her back up. I blamed our sparring history. Taunting her was like a habit. 'Apologies. Yesterday was ... traumatic. I now understand how wrong headed I've been.'

'Mmm. We'll see,' she said unconvinced, moving to adjust her cushion. The shift caused her tunic to gape, drawing my eyes like wanton bees spotting forbidden nectar. She saw. 'I told you to leave every scrap of your old self behind, Ronald. That includes treating me like a sex object.'

Things weren't exactly going to plan. I was about to ladle out another apology when I heard the unmistakable sound of footsteps from the bedroom. Immediately, our eyes clashed. She moved faster, but I caught up and pushed her aside. After clambering upstairs, I threw open the door.

My shock matched Adelia's. The cook stood immobile, staring back, too stunned to do anything about her nakedness. Susie was on my heels. She ruthlessly elbowed me aside before rushing in and slamming the door. I was left like a clod on the landing.

Chapter Nineteen

It took a few moments for me to regroup after being elbowed, but it was Susie's violent door slam that really singed my imagination. Her memorable tunic had already rekindled my belief that Frank had shaken her sheets, no matter his alleged murder. To have found Adelia in the same bedroom – and as bare skinned as a freshly sheared lamb – was a whopping bonus topped with the finest whipped cream.

And how differently Susie had reacted! This time there had been no brazening it out, no parading nude and gleefully tormenting me. Instead, she was skulking away with her not-so-innocent ex-cook. And to think that Charity claimed to have no idea why I'd suspected Susie of being lesbian or bisexual. What a joke! More like a full blown farce. Dimple had been fanning Susie's sensual appetites only minutes before my dance ordeal, and only minutes before Charity had arrived in the conference room. How I wished that, at the time, I'd been in a better state to speak out and burst Charity's bubble. The question was: how could I exploit my boss-bitch's pseudo-closet sexuality and cook her goose with Charity?

Smelling blood, I ignored prudence and kicked in the door. Susie's shot missed, but not by much. The loud report anchored me in the frame, dumbfounded, too astonished even to twitch. If I hadn't stepped sideways in anticipation of the door's possible recoil, the bullet would have hit. I could have been killed.

'How could you?' she panted, face flushed, tunic ripped.

'I really had to fight to get you a last chance and this is how you repay me.'

Leaving no gap for thinking, I blurted, 'I-I'll say nothing to Charity. I didn't see Adelia. I saw nothing. I'll just go.'

She fired again, this time at the ceiling over my head. As fragments spat on my shoulders, she said, 'Don't playact with me, Ronald. You tried to rape me. Charity will definitely hear about it, and so will the police.'

My heart thumped like a doped-up boxer. 'Don't pull that one, Susie,' I pleaded. 'There's no need. I promise I'll never breathe a word about Adelia being here.'

She aimed unswervingly at my head. 'Adelia is not here. She's never been here. She doesn't even know where I live.'

I couldn't believe she'd resorted to such pitiful lies. Neither could I let her get away with it. 'For crying out loud, Susie! She used to be your cook.'

The gun didn't move. 'At a different house, never here.'

I sagged. She was tossing out piffle and expecting me to gulp it down. Keeping half an eye on her, I peered round. To be fair, I didn't expect to spot any Adelia bits sticking out like colorful flags in a breeze. They wouldn't be that sloppy. I had to push. 'Easy, Susie, but I know Adelia is under the bed or in the closet. She's hiding in here somewhere, just as you're trying to hide your true sexuality ... as if anyone cares.'

Her face reddened. 'Swap places with me, and do it slowly or I will shoot.'

Didn't like the sound of that. Moving as she'd demanded would trap me in the room with her controlling the door. Even so I didn't argue. She had the gun and it was still pointing at my head. Taking care not to provoke her, I stepped cautiously and she did the same.

With the shift complete, she said, 'Now look for Adelia yourself, you horrible— just look.'

Figuring she would have shot me by then if she was going to, I checked every possible nook. It was a bit galling to find no trace, but that meant nothing. Shrugging, I glanced through the windows and pointed. 'Wouldn't be hard for her to climb down that—'

'Shut up, Ronald,' Susie snapped, mingling disappointment with anger. 'Face the truth for your own sake. Stop sheltering behind all this nonsense about memory and time lapses.'

It was obvious then. She was trying to bamboozle me. 'I've said nothing about any lapses. That's you—'

She chopped across me. 'What time did you arrive? Tell me that.'

'Just before ten. You told me I was early.'

'And how long do you think you've been here?'

My eyes narrowed. She was up to something. 'Not long,' I said cagily. 'Less than fifteen minutes.'

'You're sure, Ronald, completely sure?' She waited for my nod. 'All right. Look at your watch, your own watch that's been on your wrist the whole time.'

I didn't trust her ill-boding instruction or like the ominous way she spoke.

'Go on, Ronald. Look. See for yourself.'

Boss-bitch had unsettled me, made me nervous. Like a recalcitrant, I fought her control, yet she had the power. Grudgingly, I peeked, then took a harder look. 'Can't be,' I mumbled, my legs letting me down, feeling wobbly. Two hours had passed.

She kept quiet as I sank onto the bed, then said, 'You're a danger to yourself and others.'

She didn't expect me to leap up and snatch the gun. Neither did I. It was lunacy to jump her. She could easily have pulled the trigger. Breathing heavily, I leveled the weapon at her chest, not sure what to say or do next. I resorted to bravado. 'Clever trick with the watch, I'll grant you that.'

She stood her ground. 'No trick.'

I smirked like a preening adolescent, yet inside I was stuffed with chilling qualms. Too many weird experiences had already rung my bell for me to be sure of anything. Of all times, this was when nonentity woman's words slithered back like oozing toxic waste.

I couldn't escape them. I became locked on her warning about my enemy's please-himself perception and blindness to traps. She'd warned me. But why a *warning*? By my reckoning, these characteristics showed weakness; and weakness was to be exploited not warned against.

Without realizing, I said, 'Should have picked up that contradiction.'

Susie didn't like it. I guessed I'd blanked her. I knew I had, and she was well miffed. 'What contradiction?' she hissed at me. 'You're a mess, Ronald, and this nonsense has to stop and stop at once.'

Feeling strangely cocky, I shook my head. 'You'd like me belly-up, wouldn't you. Well it's not going to happen. Move. I want you on the bed, hands where I can see them.'

'No.'

I should have known she'd be difficult. 'Sit or I'll shoot. I have the gun now.'

'Then shoot, you ungrateful oaf. I'm going downstairs.' She didn't so much as glance back on her way out.

That left me feeling a right chump and damned annoyed with myself. After glaring at the gun to offload the blame, I shoved it in my jacket pocket and trailed her downstairs. She was sitting in her living room waiting, her tunic refastened, the tear pinned.

Barely glancing my way, she said, 'Sit.' I did and she carried on. 'I'm not convinced it's wise, but I'm prepared to forget about your violent assault and move on. I'll put it down to stress since you're clearly on another planet.' She paused. 'You should thank me, Ronald.'

I wanted to throttle more than thank her. I'd had my chance to shoot and fluffed it. A decent sized wound would have had her talking in no time. Instead I'd let myself be outmaneuvered and exposed as a inept four-flusher.

Petulantly, I asked, 'Why?'

She understood well enough that I wanted real answers, but that didn't stop her sidestepping. 'It's good manners to thank people who help you.'

I felt anger stir, impatient to get out, the kind of anger I wasn't supposed to show; and I had fine cause. She'd adopted Dimple level tactics. Firing off rape accusations and guns was classic Dimple, and all to conceal her sexuality. I recalled Charity's indignation at the mere thought of Susie being anything other than heterosexual. There had to be something behind it. For sure, Susie was red hot keen to stop Charity discovering the truth.

Despite the provocation, I managed to plaster a lid on my anger. I even grudgingly conceded that Susie had pulled off an impressive time trick. But, bottom line, it was just another trick in another set-up to break me down; and I'd had enough, more than enough. Only one thing kept me bottled: a frustratingly unanswerable question. Would I learn more by playing nice or by reverting to plan and squeezing Susie till she sweated a name?

'Where are you, Ronald?' she demanded, piqued at being shut out. 'You're certainly not here.'

'I am here,' I said, eyes down, deciding to bide my time.

She huffed, not satisfied, but let it go. 'You've alienated everyone you've come into contact with, including me.'

When she stalled, I looked up. 'Is that a statement or a question?'

'Don't be clever, because you're not. I've already said how I had to fight to get you this last chance. Now it's your turn to fight for me. I need an answer now.'

Dimple tactics again, I thought as I scratched a non-existent tickle. In the parking lot, the bitch-queen had rejoiced in telling me I wasn't clever and here was Susie having her own spiteful claw at my mental prowess. That said, I had no real handle on what she was talking about. Rubbing my forehead, I said, 'I'm not writing any blank checks.'

'Don't do that!' she yelped, upset.

No way was she referring to blank checks. I felt like saying: don't do what, you stupid unreasonable bitch? But I dug at her another way. 'You give nothing and expect everything.'

To my surprise, she said, 'Yes.'

I asked straight out. 'What do you want, Susie?'

'I've told you,' she countered as if I were dim. 'Your commitment to fight for me.'

That set off a few alarm bells. I spoke before I'd thought. 'What about Charity? Have you two fallen out? And what about Dimple? She knew to send me to the Asylum where *you* wanted me, so you two must be in cahoots. Are you trying to trounce Charity, is that it?'

Her reply was loaded with contempt. 'Your mind is a sewer, Ronald. Your *yes* or *no* is all I require.'

I had to make a stand. 'Then answer my questions.'

'No.'

She really was an exasperating bitch! I'd pushed deep into my chair, about to lose my cool when, like an epiphany, I saw the light. At the hospital, she'd threatened to deliver me to Charity if I showed a whiff of temper or anything else she didn't like, yet she'd not stopped needling since my arrival. All I could think was that she needed guarantees, especially now I'd caught her with Adelia. She wanted me either docile or dead, and maybe making me dead needed Charity's say-so. All the nonsense about me fighting for her was a reserve ploy in case her trumped-up rape allegation turned sour.

'Let me think a minute,' I said, glancing her way.

Her eyes found mine. Hers showed no emotion. She'd been so different when we'd first met, but a lot of malice had been thrown each way since then. Maybe enough for her to want me dead more than docile.

I looked away, not liking my precarious options. Every instinct told me to walk off into the proverbial sunset. I didn't. I sat there and stewed over Charity and her charity. Not for the first time, I pondered why everything and everyone connected with it was so dangerous. It was a labyrinth of deceit, an unmitigated sham. Charities weren't in the business of threatening let alone killing people, yet I'd been a continual target. Worse, my nemesis was somehow using it as his conduit.

'You've thought long enough,' Susie said impatiently. 'All you're doing is ferreting for ways to avoid your responsibilities, and that makes me worry.'

Her tone adamantly signaled decision time. My plan to squeeze her for information suddenly seemed risky and probably futile. Anyone could be in the house, with or without clothes, with or without a machete. And anyone could be poised outside. Dimple's remarkably opportune appearance at the hospital had proved in a particularly mind-blowing style that my *someone* had people constantly on the case. He could be lurking outside himself, watching, ready to shoot me straight back to hospital for torture, like a rat in a far from gilded cage. I needed to make only one wrong decision to reap a gruesome whirlwind.

'I'm still waiting,' Susie said tersely.

I resisted her stare, but couldn't resist the inevitable. No matter how much I wanted to escape, I was stuck in the charity's clutches, trapped until I could find something to loosen their grip. Grudgingly, I said, 'All right.'

'What's all right?'

It was a shove too far. My mouth shot-blasted what I was thinking. 'Stop being a bitch. You know full well what I mean.'

She said nothing, yet her stare was enough to freeze burning coals. I had to recant right then or seize her throat and squeeze.

'Sorry,' I said before it was too late. 'It's like you said. I'm stressed, on another planet.' Her icy silence persisted. 'What do you want me to say, Susie? I'll fight for you if that's what you want.'

As ever, she was ungracious. 'You're a man of straw, Ronald. A worm has more balls.'

As my face tightened in a surge of anger, she rushed from the room and up the stairs. Confused and defused, I gaped at the door as it closed rapidly behind her. At once my thoughts bolted to the gun in my jacket, wishing I knew how many bullets remained. I would have checked, except someone was already coming down. Not sure if it was Susie, I cautiously dipped into my pocket and aimed the still concealed weapon towards the doorway.

When Susie called out from the hall, it settled half the question, but was she alone? 'Come on, Ronald,' she coaxed. 'Emergency. One of our clients is about to commit suicide.'

Immediately suspicious, I asked, 'How do you know?'

'Phone. Didn't you hear the ring from the bedroom?'

I had to award her points for quick thinking, not that I believed her. The alleged conversation had been far too brief. Playing for time, I said, 'You don't need me. A worm has more balls.'

The door began to open.

Chapter Twenty

With Susie's door opening like a portal to a mausoleum, I felt my body tense. Anyone could be coming in. My finger stiffened on the trigger.

'Stop sulking,' Susie scolded, still out of view. 'And stop being selfish. Someone needs our help right now.'

She was pedaling the same implausible story. I gave it the same mistrust. 'Show yourself.'

I hadn't expected it, but she stepped into the door frame, her tunic replaced by a boring brown dress. 'What exactly do you mean: show myself?'

I couldn't understand how she'd found time to change, yet my relief at seeing only her caused me to relax the gun. Even so, I reckoned she well deserved a slap down. Snorting, I said, 'Some emergency if you've dressed for it!'

'Come with me,' she huffed. 'I've no patience for your offensive humor.'

I don't remember leaving or getting into her car, but I recall her driving as if life and death meant nothing. I held tight to my seat. I may have closed my eyes. When our pace slowed, I peeked to find we were in a bright part of town, modern and bustling, not at all the setting I'd imagined for a potential suicide.

I tried to get more information but she would only tell me the client was male and in crisis. When pushed, she added that he was around forty, though she claimed not to be sure.

The building at which we stopped was the ugliest in town, least it seemed that way to me. For no good reason the architect had festooned idiotic concrete drapes across the glazing, each styled to clash with its patterned surroundings. Not that it mattered.

'So where is this loser?' I asked. 'Has he a name or do we say, *hey you?*'

She didn't answer. Neither did she move. Though predictability wasn't exactly her middle name, I fancied I could hear her thoughts. *What an ungrateful person you are, Ronald; how rude and uncooperative, and after all I've done for you.* At that moment, I really wished I had squeezed her for information, not taken the easy route and bowed to her demands.

'His name is Simon,' she said after a long delay. 'Simon Hudson. He could jump.'

I wasn't feeling massively sympathetic. 'Yeah well, suppose it's pretty tough when someone nabs your pencil.'

She didn't rise to my bait. 'Go to him, Ronald. We need to nurture his potential. He's a valuable asset. He's special.'

I squinted, puzzled by the peculiar label. 'Asset?' When she didn't respond, I shook my head and tried to wriggle out of the task she was ditching on me. 'Look, I know nothing about jumpers. I'm—'

'A man of straw?' she interrupted harshly. 'But this time you'll see the job through. I'll not tolerate another Mrs Bessel episode. I'm halfway to thinking you deliberately electrocuted yourself that day just to get attention.'

The bitch knew precisely how to get under my skin. 'That's hogwash and you know it!'

'Then take responsibility for once. Go and do your job.'

My head began to hurt. She was talking circular drivel. I wanted to yell: *how can my job have anything to do with stopping jumpers?* The words wouldn't come.

'Reception is in there,' she told me, pointing. 'Tell them your name and ask to see Simon Hudson.'

Though I'd not have believed any answer she gave, I had to ask, 'Why is the charity involved? Is there bad news about his hearing and sight? You've told me nothing.'

She was having none of it. 'Go, Ronald, before I take that gun from your pocket and put a bullet through your kneecap.'

Her unexpectedly extreme reaction galvanized my spine. I checked my jacket. To my relief, the weapon was still there, and I intended to keep things that way. Susie had no business keeping guns. Innocent charity workers didn't need guns. One second-hand machete was quite enough.

'I won't tell you again, Ronald,' she threatened.

I had to go. Memories of that machete had freaked me, making me want to get out, fast. Self-consciously I stalked to reception. Oddly, that walk restored a few grains of confidence. More came when I caught my reflection in a pane of black glass. I was decently dressed, very smart indeed, thanks to James' foresight in bringing clothes to the Asylum.

The brunette behind the desk was a few years passed being a sex kitten but hadn't caught on. I didn't like her. Everything spilled over a bit too much: her mouth too big for her face; her bust too big for her plunging dress.

Forgetting to identify myself, I came straight out with it. 'I've come to see Simon Hudson. He's about to jump off the roof.'

She laughed and stretched over to nudge me, blind to my bruising. 'That's a good one,' she beamed, sitting back to check her screen. 'You must be Mr Foster.'

That shook me. Couldn't understand how she had my name on-screen. 'Did someone tell you I was coming?'

She shrugged, making her bosom wobble distractingly. 'Not me personally, sir, but you're down to see Mr Hudson so someone did something.' She giggled. 'He's on the twenty-eighth floor. Use elevator three. Jessica will meet you and take you directly to his office.'

That sounded a bit strange. 'He's not on the roof?'

She laughed again, but I didn't share her amusement. I'd had it all before with Susie: her saying one thing and me falling into an itchily different situation; not to mention her cobbling together lies and distortions to dribble out afterwards, the bitch. I hesitated. It made no difference to me whether the guy jumped or sat with a beer and wrote nice letters to his mum. I just wanted to get done and go.

Elevator three was empty when I stepped in – definitely – and no one came in via the doors. Quite how nonentity woman managed another of her appearing acts was beyond me. As always when she came close, my nerves and anger clashed, swirling in confusion, egging me to escape through the compartment walls.

'You've stopped thinking, Ronald,' she said sternly. 'I warned you about traps. You mustn't get distracted.'

'T-that's not what you said,' I niggled pedantically, 'You said—'

'Hush now,' she whispered. 'Be at peace. Simon is one of us. It would be wrong for him to jump, just as it's wrong for you to be here.'

Her words were easy enough to understand, yet my brain felt as if it had been hooked out and doused with glue. Burbling, I mumbled, 'Why can't you—' I couldn't say any more.

The elevator had opened and nonentity woman was nowhere to be seen. She'd vanished. From the lobby, a slim young woman in a cream uniform was peering at me, plainly conscious of my clobbered features. She looked around the same age as Dimple, yet had none of her confidence. The opposite; she appeared visibly nervous.

Shakily, she said, 'A-are you Mr err Mr—'

'Yes I am,' I volunteered, intrigued by her excessive timidity. Oddly, it smothered my own agitation like a salving patch. 'You must be Jessica.'

She nodded and tried again. 'I'm to take you to Mr err Mr—'

'Hudson,' I said, feeling moved to rescue her.

She smiled faintly, then set off, me trailing a couple of paces behind. I remember thinking she had good legs, that she could be a real peach if she stamped on her butterflies.

When she stopped, her lips trembled as if she wanted to say something, but I was losing patience. Her ongoing jitters were unsettling me and I didn't need unsettling. It was enough that I had to face a suicide situation with a complete stranger. Only then did I realize her stage fright was probably down to Simon Hudson and his lethal intentions. Relenting, I pouted ready to utter something appropriately patronizing. She got in first.

'Make sure he jumps,' she said as if ordering a cheeseburger, her angst gone. 'Otherwise Susie really will shoot out your knees.'

I gaped in horrified surprise as she held my gaze, presumably to be sure her message had found its mark. She then strolled off, my eyes in tow until she turned from sight. I felt as if a dredger had gouged into my stomach and clawed out its fill. Made me reach for the wall to steady myself.

Jessica's astonishing about-face had spectacularly flat-footed me and sent my head into woolly mode. What she'd said was beyond belief. Was I actually expected to cheer Simon onto, and then off the roof? Try as I might, I couldn't accept that Susie meant for him to jump. That couldn't be what the charity wanted.

As I struggled for mental grip, it dawned on me why every move I made was either known or anticipated. The charity clearly had tentacles everywhere. The packed auditorium had been no exaggeration of Charity's empire as I'd assumed. It had been affirmation. For sure, Charity had her own vengeful reasons for putting on that show, but she'd actually kept her promise and gathered everyone connected with the charity.

Couldn't help shuddering. The duplicitous Jessica could easily have been there. She could have witnessed my public humiliation. My guess was that, after leaving me outside Simon's office, she'd gone swanning off to her friends to hoot about how cleverly she'd hoodwinked me, the disgraced hero. Made me sick, especially given the bellyful of hassle I'd already had dumped on me.

On top of Susie's ludicrous instructions, I'd endured a tacky experience with a rambunctious receptionist, and a confounding elevator encounter. Nonentity woman telling me I'd stopped thinking was something I'd not needed. Neither had I taken kindly to her jibe about traps. She'd not warned me about them. If she had, I might have been spared the mind contorting mess surrounding Simon Hudson.

Jessica's unexpected return bucked me from my self-centered carousel of woes. Still at a distance, she said, 'Susie told me to shoot you myself unless you're in that office within one minute.'

I stared, refocused and, this time, not in disbelief. I was finally on their page. She was another Dimple. Maybe not so favored, yet of the same breed of conscienceless vixen who would blindly do anything, whose soul was a cauldron of poison.

The sound of someone else walking the corridor made me turn. It was a woman, mature years. She looked as hard as diamond and just as expensive in her black suit. Acting as if I wasn't there, she swept into Simon Hudson's office and held the door momentarily. Unsure what to do, I checked for Jessica's reaction. From somewhere, she had magicked up a gun and was pointing it straight at me. That was enough. I was inside before the door had clicked shut.

'Mrs Dunstan,' Simon said, half-rising, clearly dismayed. 'This is—'

'A complete mash-up,' she cut in. 'And I'll not have it.'

I stayed mute and watched the formidable lady stride to one of two visitor armchairs in front of Simon's congested desk. It didn't need a diagram to explain who was who's boss or that Simon was in the proverbial. Neither paid me any attention.

She eyed him as if he were a pile of worthless scrap tossed out by a junk shop. 'Well?' she said.

I looked too. Susie had been right about his age. He was around forty. But she'd been wrong about him being poised to jump. He didn't even look the suicide type, if there was a type. I think I sighed. I know I fought the nausea of being pulled every which way against the middle.

Simon took a deep breath. 'You've read my report?'

Mrs Dunstan was domineering. 'Do you imagine I'd be here if I hadn't?'

'Suppose not,' he conceded.

'Well?'

I saw him gulp. 'It's all in the report: our objectives, the impact study, the—'

'I told you I've read it,' she interrupted. 'And now I'm telling you to rewrite it with a lot more attention to who pays your salary and a lot less to producing wishy-washy trash. Got that?'

He tried. 'I understand that you're—'

'You understand nothing,' she snapped. 'If you did, you wouldn't have written that garbage you call a report.' She stood to go. 'Change it.'

He sucked in another deep breath. 'Can't do that.'

Her face clouded as she dropped back in her chair, the pace deliberately slow. 'Tell me I misheard you.'

'Can't do that either,' he said, shaking his head. 'I know a lot of money is at stake, but the—'

She barged in. 'Stop there! Just tell me: after all these

years have you suddenly seen a mystic light? Have you heard an inner voice?' She grunted dismissively. 'No need to tell me. It's written between every line of your garbage-ridden report.' When he didn't answer, she went on, 'You weren't employed for your conscience, Simon, or your principles and most assuredly not for your pretty face. You get things done. You overcome. You find the loopholes and you make us money. Right?'

He wriggled uncomfortably. 'I'm not sure any more. It's not as simple as that.'

'Spare me your bleeding heart,' she sneered, folding her arms.

Up till then, I'd just stood there like a spare part. It was all I could do. She was obviously trying to crack him, but what, if anything, was I expected to do? I'd no idea whose side I was supposed to be on.

Struggling for inspiration – and with nothing much to go on – I made a superficial appraisal and mentally squeezed into his shoes. I'd be pragmatic, I decided. Give a little to keep a lot. From what I'd gathered, the rejected report sounded pretty much like stuff he'd been doing before, only he'd caught *conscience* this time. There couldn't be any real harm in bending the knee just once more. Take my advice, Simon, I said in my head, do what you usually do. That way you keep your job and get this old witch off your back.

Mrs Dunstan distracted me, her voice unexpectedly conciliatory. 'Just rewrite the report, Simon. It's not exactly the first time you've polished the truth to disguise a few awkward lumps. You're very good at it. That's why you have this executive office all to yourself. It's thinking space.' She smiled. 'So think, Simon, think very carefully. All I need is a *yes* and you keep your job ... and I'll be off your back.'

A shiver swooped down my spine. My silent counseling had been seized and paraphrased just as it had at Mrs Bessel's with that so-called financial consultant. Back then, no one had acknowledged my presence either, yet Mrs Bessel in particular had relayed my thoughts as if telepathically linked. Unnervingly, Mrs Dunstan was doing much the same, elbowing in and stealing my psychic entreaties. I felt strangely violated.

Simon didn't like it any more than me. As I gawked at Mrs Dunstan, he twitched and hedged. 'As I said, it's not as simple as that.'

'Don't push me,' the lady threatened. 'You can't bury your head, pretend you're blind, deaf, and dumb. If this deal falters, you go down. A few words in the right ears and you won't just be unemployable, you'll be serving time.'

I straightened as if a pole had been shoved down my throat. Simon wasn't dumb, and neither was he blind or deaf, partially or otherwise. There was no discernible reason for him to be a client of the charity, yet Susie had specifically said: *one of our clients is about to commit suicide.* Worrying me most was her desire for his suicide to succeed, if Jessica was to be believed.

Simon distracted me this time. Head lowered, he seemed defeated, yet his tone declared the opposite. 'You're right. I have manipulated the truth in the past, worse than manipulated, but not this time. I have seen the light, you're right about that as well. Nothing massively dramatic, no inner voice, but realization nonetheless. Enough for me to wise up to what I've been doing here and doing to myself. I've stopped laughing at religion and started listening. I've also—'

'Shut it, Simon, before I throw up,' Mrs Dunstan scorned, stiffening angrily. 'You sound more sick inducing than a Sunday school teacher.'

I shuddered as nonentity woman's words suddenly bludgeoned my brain: *Simon is one of us. It would be wrong for him to jump.* Belatedly, I caught up. I saw that, at the core of the yarn Susie had spun, lay the single grain of truth that mattered. Simon was special. He was among those who would have the charity fail. In some way, his report had triggered alarm bells and marked him out as an enemy. Why else would Susie have manipulated me into encouraging his demise?

Though my emotions roared into overdrive, they soon became ensnared in a labyrinth of deceit and double-dealing. So many contradictory stories had been pitched my way that anything could be the truth. Yet one thought topped out. The time for skulking in the shadows had passed. I had to get through to Simon. I owed it to myself. If he really was an enemy of the charity, I needed him. He could be the one to show me how to destroy from within. With his help, my own scheming *someone* could soon be exposed and laid out on a slab ready to be carved up.

Resolutely, I stepped up to the desk. 'We need to get out of here, Simon. We need to talk.'

He stared directly at me, frowning. Then all was darkness.

Chapter Twenty-one

Sheer frustration made me yell out. I hated that I'd been robbed of my best chance of a potential ally, unfairly robbed. Unwilling to give up, I struggled with all my mental energy, desperate to recapture the one reality that had given me hope.

Despite my concentrated efforts, other sensations rapidly overran me: debilitating sensations of floating as if encased in a black cocoon of soothing waters. Immediately, terror gripped my heart. I'd experienced exactly the same blackness moments before being ejected in the place where Grub and his gang had held sway. As if poised for a cue, strange noises began to infiltrate, soft initially, then louder until my brain was awash in an agonizing flood. I screamed and clamped my hands over my ears. It made no difference. All the noise was inside. I must have passed out.

As I stirred, heart-gripping terror returned and pushed everything else aside, including my bitter resentment. Like a child clamping shut its eyes to block out monsters, I pretended nothing was there. But I couldn't cling to childhood any more than I could wrap myself in a self-generated cloak of delusion. Fear honed my instincts. I became alert to every tiny sound, every wisp of possible danger. Yet my eyes remained stubbornly closed, steadfastly refusing to confront what could so easily be another unknown and dangerous reality.

A single thought gradually surfaced. The black cocoon heralded trouble. By instinct more than anything I knew it was special. Even though I didn't understand, I'd suffered more than enough memory lapses and reality swaps to recognize its distinctive qualities. It had engulfed me after the Mrs Bessel assignment and now again after seeing Simon, both encounters ordered by Susie.

Inevitably, my resolve weakened. I had to know where I was. Self preservation demanded it. My eyes flipped open. The room was small with red painted walls, no furniture, no windows, and no carpet on its cement floor. An unadorned lamp hung from the clashing blue ceiling. It gave off only modest light. The door had a spy-hole, a straight through job, just like an antiquated prison cell. Not until I stood did I realize I was naked.

Hurriedly, I checked every corner. I was alone. Perversely, that's why I began talking aloud. 'What's going on?' I asked. 'Why take my clothes?' When no one answered, I wasn't sure whether to be relieved or disappointed. 'Suppose it could be worse,' I said louder, explicitly recalling how Dimple had commanded Throot to beat me. Still no answer.

Getting angrier, I hollered, 'You've given me nothing. Is it day or night?' Then I held off, listening in case anyone had heard. Seconds later I was kicking myself for being so cretinous. The last thing I needed was some moron to hear me and get bright ideas about stepping up my torment.

After pacing anxiously and getting nowhere, it dawned on me that I'd been thrown a waiting game. There was no point in wearing myself out. Grudgingly, I nestled in the corner on my haunches waiting for someone or something to come in. Nothing. Finally, the pressure became intolerable. Leaping up, I darted for the door and twisted the cheap knob. It turned and the door yielded. I didn't like it. It was too easy. My luck wasn't that good. I swiftly closed up, not yet ready to face whatever lay beyond. I began pacing again. I figured it had to be a trap. There was no other reason to throw me into a virtual cell with an unlocked door.

More time passed, no idea how long. It both calmed and forced me to think. The black cocoon had been the same, but that was about all. There had been no feelings of intense heat before it grabbed me, and I could remember striving to stay with Simon, not like last time when everything rapidly blanked.

My thoughts rambled on and hit nonentity woman – disturbingly contradictory thoughts. I loathed any prospect of seeing her, yet she had pulled off some damned impressive appearing–disappearing stunts. I wouldn't have minded if she'd turned up right then and there and whisked me off somewhere safe. It would definitely have proved she wanted to help.

'I'm here, girl,' I said quietly. 'Door's not locked, as if you care.'

I'll admit I did wait and I did hope. No one and nothing was my reward. When I could stall no longer, I returned to the door. The knob again turned easily, the door eager to swing open. I held it, only cracking a gap wide enough to peer out. I saw a stubby corridor in the same inane decorative style. At its far end hung another door, purple. That's the locked one, I guessed. With no choice, I padded along the concrete to find out. I was wrong. It opened directly onto cobblestones.

It was night, unnervingly dark at first, courtesy of no lamps, but more penetrable as my eyes adjusted. Steeling myself, I headed out in the first direction impulse led me. As far as I could make out, I'd come into a small courtyard. The building I'd left seemed nothing out of the ordinary, merely one of a series of single story structures with no obvious purpose.

My nakedness reasserted itself, reminding me of my battering in the conference room. It also brought memories of my impromptu foray for clothes in the hospital and how that had turned out. Dismissing the flashbacks, I tried a random door, heart pounding. It was secured. After another three, I found one that opened. Inside, a pair of dirty overalls lay draped over a busted chair. They were horrible, nothing like the fine attire I normally wore. Reluctantly, I scrambled into them and rushed out, annoyed there were no shoes. My speed increased in line with my keenness to get far away.

I'd covered only a few yards when a male voice called out. 'Is that you, Ron?'

I kept moving, sure it was my imagination.

He called again. 'P-please don't leave me here.'

Believe me, I didn't want to stop, but whoever it was knew me well enough to recognize me in odd garb in the gloom, or so it seemed. I slowed a notch. For me too there had been a stir of recognition, something in his voice. Warily I halted and turned.

'It's me, Ron ... F-Frank,' he said. Then he collapsed.

I stood motionless, watching him crumple to the cobblestones. He could have been anyone. His calling my name and claiming to be Frank meant nothing. Most testing was a simple fact: Frank was dead – supposedly – cut to ribbons by machetes with *Throot lives* carved on his chest. People didn't make comebacks from deaths like that. They stayed dead, normally, unless recalled by a certain bitch-lady in need of deniable sexual gratification.

A self-congratulatory *told you so* swept into my head. All along, I'd doggedly clung to disbelief when it came to Frank's murder and, apparently, the proof I'd been right lay just a few yards away.

I advanced slowly. Frank, if it was him, wore overalls like my own. Naively, I dismissed it as coincidence and crouched beside him. He stayed motionless with only shallow breaths hinting at continued life. His face was filthy, but it was Frank's face; or that of his twin brother.

I asked the obvious question. 'What happened?'

Frank twitched minutely but was in no state to answer. I stood up, plagued with new irritation. It promptly spawned anger. He had no business turning up in my freaked out reality. I hardly knew him anyway and he definitely wasn't my responsibility. Besides, I was in enough trouble without him as an extra liability.

I peered down. By the look of him, he was as good as dead, and for the second time around. I stepped back, intending to run off as originally planned. Only an afterthought kept me hovering: Frank might know something. There was a slim chance of dragging out a few useful snippets before he finally croaked, maybe more than snippets.

On my haunches again, I said, 'Listen, Frank, it's me, Ronald. You need to tell me what's going on.' He didn't stir. 'Waste of time,' I snorted, suddenly nervous, worried others might be lurking in the dark.

As I stood and began checking, he gasped, 'R-Ron—'

To be honest, I nearly didn't bother. He'd always been an idiot. Only the outside possibility of learning something made me kneel again. 'What can you tell me?'

'I'm c-cold.'

That took the biscuit. I huffed long and loud. Who did he think I was! For sure, I wasn't his carer. And what did he expect? I couldn't conjure up warmer clothes or a blanket. Best I could do was get him into the nearest building. But that required effort, which meant it had to be worth my while.

Still don't really understand why I helped him up. His weight was almost beyond me. If he hadn't made some effort by staggering along, I would have left him to it, whatever *it* was. Fortunately, the closest building was unlocked, but that didn't mean I trusted it. Far from it. I carefully positioned Frank as a shield in case we walked into a rat's nest and shoved open the door. Then I held back, listening. Nothing. I had to chance it. With him in front and me propping him up, we slid inside like refugee snails. Still nothing. Not a sound. After a nervous pause, I somehow managed to grope for a light switch, close the door, and not lose my grip on Frank. Can't claim we were bathed in light, but I could see we'd entered a gaudily painted windowless room. And there was furniture: a couple of chairs, a bed frame and, against the wall, a mattress topped by a folded blanket.

It was everything we needed and all way too convenient. I didn't like it. Regardless, I lowered Frank into a chair, but he was too unsteady. I had to swing over the mattress so he could lie down.

'T-thanks, Ron,' he murmured once I'd manhandled him onto the bed.

'What can you tell me?' I said. All I got was a wheeze and a look that told me he was overwhelmed. I'd asked too big a question. 'Okay, Frank. Tell me what happened to you?'

'M-machetes,' he mouthed.

I knew all about machete wielding gangs, emphatically I did, but hearing him name the weapon gave it extra nastiness, an added dose of brutality. I don't need this, I thought, but I had to be practical, and I'd already brought him in from the cold. It was ridiculous not to check out his story and take a better look at him. Sure enough, there was blood amidst the filth on his skin, plenty of it, caked on.

Made me wonder if Charity had only falsified the timing of the gang attack.

Frowning, I said, 'I did see you at Susie's house, didn't I? You were playing humpity-bumpity with her, yeah?'

He nodded none too convincingly. 'I made c-coffee.'

Right on, I thought. Frank had slammed down proof that my version of Susie's far from platonic exploits was right. Okay he wasn't exactly slamming it down, but he was oozing out the dots for me to join up, and it matched what I'd always believed. They had tried to palm me off with a mountain of lies. Vindicated, I could finally wallow in a deep glow of self satisfaction. Made me feel slightly warmer towards Frank.

'How did you end up here?' I asked. 'Matter of fact, where is here?' When he attempted a shrug, I persisted. 'Did they dump you here after the attack? Did they think they'd killed you?' Another shrug. Annoyingly, he seemed as clueless as I was. 'So what can you tell me?'

With an effort, he said, 'T-they cut something into my chest.'

I sagged. I'd already heard about that and didn't fancy a first-hand slice by slice account. After dallying a while, I figured he was too damaged to be of any more use and decided to cut my losses. As I turned away, a nasty thought reared in my head. I could be tomorrow's Frank. Charity and her bitches had probably kept him on until he'd served their purpose, then cast him adrift, leaving him alone to die.

Along the line somewhere, Frank had tipped over a pivotal point and fallen from grace; and it had been quite a fall. He'd dropped from being Susie's horizontal refreshment to being live meat for machete wielding-thugs. Most worrying was the vacancy his nose dive had created; a vacancy I most definitely did not want to fill.

With new anxieties spurring me, I tried again. 'Did they ask you to see people?' Frank nodded. 'Did they want you to go—' I stopped short. How could I possibly ask if he'd been sent to nudge some old lady into wasting her money or prod someone into suicide? I settled for a more open question. 'What did they want you to do?' His reply was a slow head shake. I needed another tack. 'Okay. I'll tell you what happened to me. You say if it rings any bells.'

For the next few minutes, I ran through my experiences – the lowlights – especially those involving Susie since she seemed the most tangible link between us. As I spoke, his eyes widened, particularly at the mention of memory lapses and shifting realities. When he grimaced, wanting me closer, I bent to listen.

'Touching your f-forehead,' he panted, then he dried up.

Was that it? I thought, drawing back. Had I put myself out and risked capture just to be fobbed off with some bilge about foreheads? I hadn't even touched my forehead: not to scratch it, sooth it, or give it a dose of snake oil.

'You're rambling, Frank,' I told him. 'You're talking twaddle.'

I'd hit the spot. To my surprise, he rallied, his voice fleetingly strong. 'No! Our foreheads are marked ... powerfully marked. That's why they want us.'

He was still talking twaddle. 'Listen, Frank, there's no mark on my forehead, never has been.' I checked his. 'None on yours either.'

He became agitated. 'It's there. It scares them. Rubbing it is the key. D-don't let them know you know.'

Not sure why I bothered, but I said, 'You're contradicting yourself. If they want us *because* of this mark, why does it scare them ... and what does rubbing it have to do with anything?' He didn't answer. 'Whatever,' I puffed dismissively. 'What about the reality shifts and memory—'

I broke off. There was no point. Blotches of gray were fast spreading over his skin. Moments later he was dead, incontrovertibly this time.

After double checking for a pulse, I stood, galled at having wasted so much time. 'So no fine words to finish on, Frank,' I sneered. 'Just mumblings about marks and who knows what other gibberish. Frankly, *Frank*, if I'd known you were off your trolley, I'd have left you on the cobbles.' I'd straightened ready to leave when one final insult splashed into my head. 'Got to tell you, Frank: you sure clocked out on a low ... for a one-time Susie-bedding woopie-maker.'

Had I'd known – had I'd understood anything – I would never have delivered such a savage and unpitying verdict. But I didn't know and I didn't understand. Angry frustration was all that drove me as I stomped contemptuously to the door. But I didn't exit. Macabre curiosity had caught me. Frank had said about something being carved on his chest. According to Charity, *Throot lives* had been written: and it was Throot who had beaten me and Throot who had lost his head. It was only right that, before I left, I spat my vengeance on Throot's name.

Heart racing, I edged back to the bed and lowered the zip on Franks overalls. As it rolled down, cuts – some like gouges – peeped out. They looked raw, grimly fresh. For several seconds, my stomach churned for me to quit. I couldn't. I needed to see.

'What a mess,' I gasped when the zip had spread fully open. My face contorted as I tried to make the slashes read what they were supposed to. 'Knew it was lies,' I said when I failed.

Without troubling to refasten the overalls, I traipsed to the door feeling oddly disappointed. Something made me turn to give Frank one last glance. What I saw, bludgeoned me like a steam-hammer to the nose.

I crashed against the wall, mouth gaping, heaving for breath. Before, I'd been too close. From the doorway, the writing was screamingly legible. But Throot's name wasn't there and neither was the word *lives*.

I ran.

Chapter Twenty-two

Really spooked, I didn't stop running till my feet were too grazed and bruised to go on. Even then my brain insisted I keep going, forcing me to stumble forward. By the time my body finally rebelled, I was thoroughly exhausted, too feeble to care where I was or what might happen.

Despite the state I was in, the illumination of nearby street lamps gradually penetrated my skull and I saw a low wall wide enough to lay on. Using the last of my strength, I staggered over. It was still night, still dark except for pools of light from the lamps. I lay flat, eyes too weary to stay open, brain indifferent to my reckless vulnerability. Anybody could bury a knife in my chest for the fun of it, or kick my head in. Either or neither, it didn't matter. Within moments, deep sleep had engulfed me.

'Reckon you'd do well to come with us, sir,' a man said gently. 'Get them feet of yours cleaned and patched up. Could do with a spot of TLC all over if you ask me.'

Yanked from sleep, I threw open my eyes and tried to move. I was no longer on the wall. I'd fallen and landed at the edge of a narrow road, no footpath. I coughed, as much to clear my head as my throat. Two blue-uniformed ambulance crew were crouching close, facing me. I recall thinking that dawn was breaking, a new dawn that promised nothing to cheer me.

The same man spoke. 'We'll help you up, sir, when you're ready.' Turning to his partner, he added, 'No rush though, is there, Dan?'

Dan hastened to reassure, his hairy eyebrows arching like mutant caterpillars. 'No rush at all, Tom. You take your time, sir.'

Although it felt as if I was fighting through fog, I managed to speak. My voice sounded weak, reminiscent of Frank's. 'I w-won't go to hospital.'

Tom smiled encouragingly. 'Not to stay, sir. They won't keep you in. Not to worry about that.'

I winced as pain from my abused feet joined with all my other aches and demanded I submit. I resisted and glanced round. I was in a village, the outskirts by the look of it. The smell of agriculture was in the air. 'Where is this?' I asked, thinking only of escape.

'Quiet little place, sir, very rural,' Tom answered. 'Doubt you've heard of it seeing how you're not from these parts.'

As I began to feel relatively normal, a thousand questions flew to mind. I started with the worst. 'There's a courtyard near here, single story buildings. Abandoned maybe. Ever seen it?'

Tom looked knowingly at Dan. Both men shared a smile. 'Sounds like you mean Ditchcoop Yard,' Tom answered, still smiling. 'Get a few strangers wander out from there. That where you came from?'

No words would come. Thoughts of that yard had broken loose the horror of Frank's chest. There was no denying I'd panicked. What I needed was rationalization to obliterate the memory. I hit on stress. Being whisked away from Simon Hudson and finding Frank like that was enough to stress angels. All I'd seen was a jumble of cuts on a dead man's chest, nothing more.

'What goes on at Ditch-whatever?' I asked, not in the least tempted to mention anything I'd seen or the corpse I'd left behind.

Dan was quicker to reply than Tom, '*Ditchcoop*, sir. Don't rightly know; private property see. Belongs to the Overlord of the District. Should say *Overlordess*.'

'No, Dan,' Tom corrected. 'It's *Lady* of the District.'

I rubbed my hair, making it more of a mess. 'What did you mean about strangers wandering out of there?'

'Plain enough, sir,' Tom jumped in quickly, pleased to get in before Dan. 'Strangers in overalls, sir, just like you, barefoot and all. Reckon we should be asking you what goes on there, not other way round.'

Dan checked his watch. 'Better get you sorted now, sir.'

My face set squarely. 'No hospitals.'

'Lots of them say that, sir,' Tom advised amicably. 'That's why we have instructions.'

I frowned, picking up a dark undertone. 'Instructions?'

'Simple really,' Dan hurriedly answered. 'Can't have folks with bloody feet and no shoes going about frightening the natives, so to speak. We give them a choice. They either come with us to get sorted or they get put back.'

My frown deepened. 'You mean put back in Ditch-whatever?'

Dan looked pleased. '*Ditchcoop*, sir. Spot on. You got it in one.'

'So what's it to be?' Tom asked, winking at Dan as if he already knew the answer.

I grunted, irritated, then scrambled up to sit on the wall. To my annoyance, the effort spitefully reminded me how much my body had been mangled and sapped. 'What happens to the people you put back?'

'Don't know, sir,' Dan said with a shrug. 'Never seen any a second time.'

Immediately, my mind leaped to Frank: how he'd looked, how he'd died. I shuddered. Even without his pitifully brief appearance, Ditchcoop Yard sounded a top place to avoid. I nodded slowly. 'All right, if I can't stay in the village I'll walk away from it. No one will see my bloody feet so no one need get frightened.'

'You can't walk with those feet, sir,' Tom said, pointing. 'Not with no shoes either. You wouldn't get far and we'd end up rescuing you again.'

I held back my temper. 'I won't need rescuing.'

'If you fancy a walk, sir,' Dan suggested, 'why not walk back to Ditchcoop?'

This pair was really getting on my nerves. Tightly, I said, 'I don't want to go to Ditchcoop any more than I want to go to hospital. I just want to go.'

Tom looked puzzled. 'Then why did you come to the village at all, sir?'

That was it. I'd had enough. Standing resolutely, I said, 'Thanks for the wakeup call. I'm off now. Give my regards to the *Overlordess* of the District.'

I could feel Tom and Dan watching me hobble away, their eyes like daggers in my back. After a few yards, I had to glance back. They were looking at each other, but oddly. When Dan arched his caterpillar eyebrows, Tom took the gesture as his cue.

'You're going the wrong way, sir,' he yelled at me. 'Keep going that way and we'll have to shoot you. Instructions see, nothing personal.'

His words sent a river of ice flowing down my spine. Though I wandered on a couple more paces, I had to turn and double check. 'What did you say?'

'Don't be difficult, sir,' Dan coaxed. 'A flea sucking blood in the next village could hear Tom.'

He was probably right. 'Tell me,' I said, 'what happens to the people you take to hospital?'

'Don't know, sir,' Tom said, echoing Dan. 'Never seen any a second time.'

I squeezed my eyes to make sure I wasn't dreaming. I wasn't. Having laid out my choices, the two uniformed men were waiting patiently for my answer. So that was it, I thought: the hospital, Ditchcoop Yard, or get shot. I made a break for it. The hard road punished my feet with every wobbly stride. When a bullet smacked into a tree only yards ahead, the message seized my lungs and crushed them empty. I staggered like a drunk, no pace left.

'Next one won't be a warning, sir,' Dan said, his rifle steadily aimed.

I knew I was done for. No matter where they drove me, I'd never get out alive. Defeated, I hunkered down, head lowered, waiting to be scooped up.

With Dan driving the ambulance, Tom sat cheerfully in the back with me. 'Glad you saw sense, sir,' he said. 'You wouldn't believe the paperwork when we have to shoot someone ... and it's so unnecessary. Don't understand what gets into some folks.'

He didn't deserve an answer. Besides, I was miserably preoccupied reflecting on the bleakness of my luck, especially as getting away had seemed vaguely achievable at first. By my reckoning, Frank was to blame. After he'd suckered me into helping him, it was all wasted time; time wasted when I should have been running for freedom. And as for those cuts of his! They spelled nothing, no words. They were just random and meaningless slashes. I'd been over sensitized by all the rubbish he and the bitches had been feeding me. The vehicle slowed.

Tom spotted my unease. 'We're crossing the ford, sir. Village gets its name from it, part of its name leastwise.'

I studied his face. I had to try. 'Listen, Tom, you're taking me to die, to be butchered like a spring lamb. Don't you get it? No one ever comes out of your hospital. Once I'm in there, they'll kill me.'

His face creased with genuine concern. 'Never thought of it like that, sir. You don't suppose same thing happens at Ditchcoop Yard, do you? ... seeing how they never come out of there, not a second time leastwise.'

It was my chance and I pounced. 'I saw a man die when I was in that yard. He'd been cut to ribbons with machetes.'

Tom pouted quizzically. 'You didn't do it, did you, sir?'

'Course not,' I baulked, swallowing down my temper. 'You see now, don't you? You understand why I need to get away. I've nothing at all against your village, no desire to interfere with anything. All I ask is to be dropped off before we get to the hospital. I'll vanish. You'll never see or hear from me again. Promise.'

Tom scratched his chin. 'What about Dan? He's seen you. He knows you've been here.'

I man-touched his upper arm. 'You're a decent bloke; Dan is too. Ask him to pull up and I'll talk to him.'

'He's driving.'

I slapped down my hackles. 'I know, but he can pull over.'

Tom pondered, then searched through the windows, both sides. 'There's no incident here, sir. Can't pull over unless there's an incident requiring our services.'

I trod cautiously. 'Normally, yes, I'm sure that's right but—'

'It is right,' he said with the confidence of experience. 'That's the instruction. Once we're on the move we don't stop till we reach the destination entered in the log.'

'Unless there's an incident,' I said.

He frowned. 'But there isn't. I told you that.'

'You could pretend.'

He winced as if I'd hurt him. 'You mean make a false log

entry?'

I closed my eyes. My temper was whirling in eagerness to get out and strangle the dim-witted crewman. I stole a precious minute to calm down. 'I appreciate you're a guy with integrity – Dan too – but you don't have to be slaves to a log.'

He took umbrage. 'You're making your troubles our fault, sir. If you'd explained your ideas before we'd logged the hospital as our destination, we might have *pretended* you'd gone back to Ditchcoop Yard and made a different log entry. As it is, we must go to the hospital, as per the log.'

I couldn't help it. I exploded. 'This is madness! I'm to die because you won't change a couple of words in a log!'

Dan surprised me by opening the back doors. Eyebrows on the twitch, he said, 'Who's to die?'

I collapsed inside. We were at the hospital. My conversation with Tom had been so intense, I'd not noticed. My options were stark. I could either risk running away and probably get a bullet, or go inside and accept any death they cared to dish out.

'You can have a wheelchair if you want,' Tom said.

'You know what I want,' I shot back. 'And it's not too late. Get Dan to close the doors and drive off. Your log entry is correct now. You can't be responsible once you've dropped me off.'

Dan looked puzzled. 'You've got to get out, sir, otherwise you're not dropped off. That's right, isn't it, Tom?'

'Quite right,' Tom said, then I guess he noticed my head drooping. 'You all right, sir?'

I sighed. My life depended on convincing the crewmen to release me, yet I could hardly bear to go through it all again. With no alternative, I roused myself, took a deep breath, and smiled at each in turn. I hadn't realized a nurse had joined us: an attractive lady in her mid-twenties, a natural looking blond, emphatically not the sadistic Bridget Burns.

From a quick assessment, she looked amenable, so I gratefully ditched the chore of repeating everything I'd said to Tom, and went for a charm offensive.

'Sorry about all this fuss, nurse,' I began. 'These gentlemen have very kindly brought me in, but there's really no need to do anything. I'll nip to the washroom, give my feet a wipe, then be on my way.'

Smiling, I set about leaving the ambulance. Almost before I'd twitched, the nurse had pulled forward a wheelchair strong enough to support an ox.

'In you get, Mr Foster. I'm Chloe, and it looks to me as if your poor feet deserve a smitch more than a casual wipe. What's more, I think you need a thorough check-over.'

I didn't care if her name was Chloe or Old Mother Hubbard. She was fast becoming a pain. Managing to sound polite, I said, 'Really, there's no—'

'Mr Foster,' she interrupted briskly, 'are you hospital phobic? Shall I give you an injection to—'

'No!' I flared. 'No injection.'

'Then come quietly,' she said.

I calculated the odds of my feet taking the strain of running with Chloe, Tom, Dan, and a rifle intent on stopping me. Grudgingly, I slipped into the chair.

'There. That wasn't so bad, was it?' She laughed lightly. 'Can't imagine what you think is going to happen.'

As she spoke, the ambulance men waved me a jaunty *goodbye*. I pointedly ignored them. 'Do you have any doctors here called Burns?' I asked sourly.

'Don't know all the names,' she said as she wheeled me towards the entrance. 'But we've no Dr Burns in my unit.'

I didn't respond. My grip on the wheelchair had become so tight my knuckles had turned white.

As if through a tunnel, I heard her voice. 'Mr Foster, what's wrong?'

I think she crouched beside me. She may even have followed my fixed stare to the huge sign that proclaimed the name of the hospital. It read: *Dimplesford General.*

Chapter Twenty-three

When Chloe accelerated my wheelchair into the building, my eyes rolled back as if stuck to the hospital sign. Yet the sudden surge jerked me from my stupefied state.

'Stop!' I yelled, leaning forward, readying myself for a dash to freedom.

She stubbornly kept up the pace. 'It's for your own good, Mr Foster.'

I growled, but she kept scurrying along the sanitized corridor, speeding passed a stream of closed doors. I knew that leaping out would be too hazardous. An awkward tumble could easily lumber me with an extra injury and turn me into ripe meat for recapture. All I could do was calculate the best point to jump, and that point was looming a few yards ahead at a cross-corridor intersection. I figured the nurse would have to slow or risk a damaging collision.

She must have read my body language. With no warning, she kicked on the wheelchair's brakes. Poised though I was, I stood no chance. The rapid deceleration shot me forward onto the easy-clean floor. My head whacked down. As I lay dazed, she pricked me with her syringe.

For me, the next thing was a mercilessly throbbing head. To be honest, the pain really got to me. It was more than pain. It was torment. I almost cried, thinking of all the escape opportunities I'd not been able to grasp. They tortured like golden nuggets set too high on a greasy pole. I'd missed out big time and ended up in bed in Dimplesford

General, a death-dealing charade of a place.

It didn't take much for me to link the nefarious Dimple to the instruction-setting Lady of the District. It completely explained why the village people I'd come across had acted like automatons, and why strangers appeared only to disappear.

I groaned, fighting despair, and tried to move onto my side. I couldn't. My wrists and ankles were held fast. Frightened, I struggled hard to free myself. All that did was toss my covers onto the floor and expose the leather cuffs pinning me down.

Chloe rushed in. 'What's all this fuss?'

'Fuss!' I yelled. 'You've chained me down. Laid me out like a sacrificial lamb!'

She shook her head as if chiding a nitwit. 'They're not chains, merely restraints for your safety, nothing more. We have to follow instructions.'

'Yeah!' I scorned. 'Ever heard of bed rails? You're a lying bitch!'

'And you're very rude, Mr Foster,' she countered. 'However—'

'Hang on,' I barged in. 'You know my name. Matter of fact you called me by name when I arrived.' I glared. 'Those idiots in the ambulance didn't know it and I've not told you, so what the devil is going on?'

Her eyes answered first; a look that revealed I'd degenerated from nitwit to dork. 'This is a hospital,' she patronized. 'Of course we know your name. Do you imagine we stamp numbers on our patients' foreheads?'

My jaw dropped. The hairs at the back of my neck had become cold and stiff. It wasn't that her argument made no sense. My mind had dragged up Frank's ramble about marks on foreheads and how *they* were scared of them.

'That's better,' she said, seeing me apparently calmer. 'Since I'm here, I might as well tell you some good news.'

Like a dork, I dismissed Frank's implausible advice along with her sarcasm and said, 'You're letting me go?'

She stood on her dignity. 'I've been to a lot of trouble for you, Mr Foster. You might at least appreciate it.' She paused, but I didn't react. 'I've searched the staff lists of several hospitals. A number of doctors have the same name but after a few calls I tracked him down.'

I sighed. 'What are you blabbering about, you empty headed bimbo?'

She flinched, then became condescending. 'You won't shock or offend me, Mr Foster, so don't bother to try. I make allowances for patients who are clearly ... very tense.'

'Bully for you,' I sagged. 'So what is this stupendous news?'

She made me wait before saying, 'I've spoken to the Dr Burns you mentioned. When I told him you were here, he promised to come as soon as he could.'

I felt my life drain into an enfeebled squelch. Any glimmers of hope I'd subconsciously tucked away, spontaneously died. But Chloe hadn't finished.

After straightening my covers, she said, 'One more thing. We're very privileged. The Lady of the District is visiting later today. It's a great honor. I've heard she's really great at cheering people up.' She smiled proudly. 'I've requested that your name be put on her list.'

I couldn't help it. Tears filled my eyes, bitter tears that stung as they rolled down to soak the pillow. 'Please let me go,' I whimpered, sucked dry of all fight. But Chloe was busy unloading a sedative into my arm. I remember jolting when her needle stabbed me. My last thought before the numbing juice took effect was a hope that I'd never wake up.

The hope failed. I awoke with a start. Bleak memories scrambled to outdo each other and turn my waking moment into absolute misery. A rapid check confirmed I was still anchored down. A clear message: my death would not be made easy. When the door opened, I closed my eyes, not wanting to know.

Chloe spoke, sounding distinctly nervous. 'L-look who's come to see you.'

Dimple's confident voice soared by comparison. 'Hello, Ronald. What a delight to see you again.'

I heard Chloe gasp. It made me look. All her self assurance had vanished. 'S-so s-sorry,' she stammered. 'Didn't realize you knew each other. I would have—'

'We go back a long way,' Dimple cut in. 'Run along now. Let me chat with my old friend.'

The nurse couldn't get out fast enough. Made me bitter. The least she could have done was unfasten my straps, not leave me alone and helpless. Yet seeing Dimple in the flesh resurrected my belligerence. Defiantly, I resolved to resist, not pathetically roll over and let her smash me into gibbering pulp.

Noticing my gaze hard upon her, she said, 'Still ogling us girls, I see.'

I hardly heard but she was right. I'd seen her looking elegant before but, this time, she'd excelled herself in a flowing red and yellow sun-ray gown topped with a flamboyant hat.

'So tell me,' she prodded. 'What do you think of my hospital-visiting come Overlordess of the District outfit?'

Her words grabbed my attention – and whistled the wind from my sails. She was telling me she knew everything, right down to crewman Dan's verbal idiosyncrasies.

I kept quiet as she sat in the armchair next to the bed. 'You don't seem very pleased to see me, sweetie.' I didn't answer. She pouted. 'I've been nice. I really have. I even sent Tom and Dan to give you a ride.' She leaned forward and yanked the covers off my feet. 'Seems to me your footsies aren't bad at all. Have you been making lots of fuss about nothing?'

'You've no idea what I've been through,' I croaked. 'You try—'

'You're whining, sweetie,' she interrupted. 'Whining and sulking.' She smiled. 'Dan's a crack shot, you know. He wouldn't have missed if I hadn't wanted you here all snug and warm.' I shuddered. 'And now you are here we need to talk.'

'I've nothing to say,' I retorted. 'Kill me and have done with it.'

She edged closer. 'We are in a negative mood, aren't we! Talk I said and talk we will ... and the first thing we'll talk about is Simon Hudson.' I turned away. 'Then we'll talk about you fraternizing with the enemy, those who would have us fail. Then, well, we'll see.' She sat back. 'Your turn to talk now, sweetie. Why did you defy Susie?'

I tightened my lips symbolically, much to her amusement.

'No problem, Ronnie,' she said softly. 'However, as Lady of the District – and Medical Director of this hospital – it's my duty to ensure the best treatment for everyone, residents and visitors alike.'

I tightened again. This time it was my whole body and there was nothing symbolic about it. I watched mutely as she reached for the call button. Shortly afterwards, the nurse hurried in.

'He needs the new treatment now,' Dimple said without preliminaries.

'The n-new treatment?' Chloe echoed, her stance uncertain even after the Lady had nodded confirmation. Then she scuttled out, only to return moments later with a stout cane.

'Begin,' Dimple ordered.

Chloe gulped. 'T-this should stimulate your circulation, Mr Foster, h-help your feet to heal.'

I'd already spotted the cane and wasn't exactly lying there waiting for a picture book explanation. 'Don't listen to her,' I shouted. 'She wants you to beat me to death!'

'N-not at all, Mr Foster,' Chloe soothed, sounding as unconvinced as I was. 'It may hurt a little but it's really for y-your own good.'

Her first blow was timid. I howled anyway. Neither of us impressed Dimple. Chloe didn't need to be told to up her game, or else. Her next strike was harsher and managed to clobber both soles at once. I contorted, this time for real, and cursed her in the lull. She quickly came back with more punitive blows, all steadily spaced. No part of my feet escaped the hammering. Yelling made no difference. Like a child confused between fear and obedience, she gave her all, until Dimple stepped up and touched her arm.

'You're looking hot, darling,' she said. 'Slip off that uniform.' Chloe gaped, probably hoping she'd misheard. I knew better. Seeing the nurse's consternation, Dimple deigned to explain. 'Instructions. It'll keep you cool and increase your swing.'

I ached to laugh out loud at Chloe's fear. Only my own pain and open vulnerability stopped me. Sweating profusely, I scowled, red with pulsing blood, wanting Chloe to freak out so Dimple would vent her savagery on her, not me.

But Chloe didn't freak out. Albeit shakily, she began unbuttoning her tunic. I grimaced, well aware that Dimple was tugging both our strings.

Mind you, that didn't stop me clocking Chloe's delicate blue underwear. Thanks to Dimple, I could progressively see that facial beauty wasn't the only thing Chloe had going for her. What a simpleton I was. I took it all in, observing every moment as she self-consciously lay her uniform aside.

Dimple was unyielding. 'Ask the patient if he wants more treatment.'

'Do you want more treatment, Mr Foster?' she blurted.

'Not like that,' Dimple rebuked brusquely. 'You're forgetting your bedside manners. Go close. Show him you care.'

Using her arms to cover up as best she could, Chloe reluctantly came to the bed-head. Her words were whispered like a feather falling. 'M-more treatment, M-Mr Foster?'

I turned a deaf ear. She was only there to rack me – not the real me – but the me Dimple had seized on and blown out of proportion; the me who occasionally took an interest in women. I was stupid to get sidetracked by Chloe's enforced exposure, and even more stupid to try and forecast Dimple's intentions. Regardless of any answer I gave Chloe, it was obvious the Lady of the District would do precisely what she wanted – and I knew only too well that her Ladyship had no concept of mercy.

Chloe waited for my answer and while she waited, my stomach spawned enough anxious butterflies to start a clinic for neurotic flying insects.

Dimple broke the silence. 'You're still looking hot, darling,' she said to Chloe. 'Take off those other bits.'

The nurse flushed crimson, eyes locked, her pretty face twisted in alarm. Too scared to obey and too petrified not to, she stood limp with dread.

As an apparent afterthought, Dimple added, 'I could release the patient if you like. I'm sure he won't mind helping with those chic little undies.'

'No!' Chloe gasped, shivering.

Dimple smiled. 'As you wish.'

I shifted to more fully witness the nurse's well deserved comeuppance. She'd been a rule-bound tyrant to me from the start, only to behave like a miserable sycophant around Dimple. Maybe, I kidded myself, I might have looked the other way if she'd been half way reasonable. But she hadn't and I didn't. By my reckoning, she deserved everything she got, not that I could see much. Like some prissy vestal, she'd turned away as soon as she'd realized it was strip off or suffer something worse.

'You'll be more comfortable now,' Dimple declared when the nurse was naked. 'Undo his straps.'

Chloe's shivering faltered, then re-erupted at double strength. Silent tears streamed down her face.

'The straps,' Dimple insisted. 'No need to be shy. You've nothing we've not seen before.'

I met Chloe's eyes, haunted eyes like those of Baines at the other hospital, like my own in a mirror. Forlornly, she tried to hide herself as she came closer, finally halting at the bedside, unsure what to do.

'Ankles first,' Dimple suggested.

I guess Chloe decided to blitz her ordeal. In a flurry of exposure, she unfastened all my straps then dashed away to gather her clothes.

Dimple had other ideas. 'Of course he still needs to be held down, darling, and you don't need clothes for that.'

Chloe became immobile, her body bent slightly forward, her arms firmly clutching the items she had already picked up. From the way her back rose and fell, she was taking in huge lungfuls of air.

'Best if you sit on his chest,' Dimple advised. 'That will stop him getting up and ruining your excellent work.' She paused. 'I can't quite remember: what did he answer about wanting more treatment?'

I was about to wade in when Chloe's knees buckled and she dropped to the spotless vinyl floor. Dimple was having none of it.

After checking to confirm I was hooked, she said, 'No time for resting when a patient needs care, nurse. Up you get ... or a certain patient might grab the cane, beat you, and make you a patient in your own hospital.'

So that was it, I thought. Dimple wants to turn me into a fully fledged woman-beater. Scornfully, I shook my head. Don't get me wrong. The idea of getting my own back on Chloe for her wheelchair ambush and needle jabbing offered engrossing appeal, but far less with Dimple calling the shots.

The sounds of Chloe pushing up from the floor pinched

my attention. Sobbing openly, she tottered to the bed making no attempt to hide herself. Without a word, she climbed up and straddled my upper chest.

Beaming contentedly, Dimple ambled over. 'Very good, darling. That's real patient care. You're a credit to Dimplesford General.'

With Chloe on top and presenting herself like a gift from the gods, it was my turn to gulp in huge lungfuls of air. It would have taken no effort to grab any part of her, as Dimple knew full well. I had only to seize the moment. A tap on the door shattered my thoughts and shot a pole of rigidity clean up Chloe's spine.

'Lady of the District,' a man said courteously, only his head poking into the room. 'And my old friend Ronald.'

As I reeled, thunderstruck, Dimple smiled. 'Dr Burns! So convenient our nurse here contacted you. Saved me the trouble.'

Burns laughed as he came right in. 'No need of local nurses. I've brought my own.'

Bridget appeared seconds later, in uniform and wearing a smug grin. 'Hello, Dimple, Mr Foster. Looks like you're already having fun.'

Dimple nodded perfunctorily. 'Only just starting. The serious work can start now you're here.'

I'd been an idiot. Basking in Chloe's torments had lulled me into playing along with Dimple and her seductive ploys. With the Burns' arrival, the situation had changed ominously. I reared up like a sprung hinge, hardly aware I was tipping the nurse onto my legs.

'I'm not staying here to be killed,' I screeched, getting frantic.

'Dear me,' Bridget smirked, producing a cat o' nine tails from behind her back. 'With your permission, Dimple.'

The Lady of the District graciously waved her forward. I froze, terrified of being ripped to sheds. But it was the naked nurse who felt the barbed thongs. Her screams were harrowing, her skin instantly bloody and torn. I got it then. Bridget wasn't aiming for me. Still shrieking, Chloe slumped off the bed and began stumbling towards the door. Burns barred the way. Another ferocious lash flew out, sending the nurse face down onto the floor, her back multi-lacerated where the cruel strands had splayed.

'Wait,' Dimple said, turning to me, and turning my blood cold. 'Not entirely sure why, sweetie, but you've become preoccupied with sheep lately.'

I gaped like an empty bucket, not understanding. My nerves were in tatters at the thought of the whip being directed at me.

'You told Tom you didn't want to be butchered like a spring lamb,' she amplified patiently. 'And you accused Chloe of laying you out like a sacrificial lamb.' She smiled. 'See what I mean?' I didn't so much as twitch. 'Thing is, sweetie, you're no lamb, not in anyone's book. But the lovely little Chloe is.'

The breath blasted out of my body. 'W-wh-wh—'

'Shush, Ronnie, you sound like an imbecile.' When she moved still closer, I cringed away, gripping the headboard as if it had the power to save. 'I'm giving you a lamb, sweetie. All you have to do is sacrifice it. It's simple. She dies, you live.' On a glance from Dimple, Bridget tossed the whip onto the bed. 'There you are, sweetie. A little work and all your troubles and misdeeds disappear for ever and ever. What do you say?'

Chapter Twenty-four

I stared at Dimple. My mind somersaulted wildly, my heart pulsing at fever pitch. It took a while before I'd calmed enough to think. 'Give me a minute,' I panted eventually.

If I'd had any wits worth a dime, my suspicions would have squawked at the way Dimple so casually accepted my request.

'Of course, sweetie,' she said. 'You need time to man-up, but don't take too long. We don't want Chloe catching a chill or getting ideas of her own.'

The risk of the nurse getting ideas of her own was nowhere on my radar. I just wanted the world to stop for five minutes so I could catch my breath. Dimple's remark swung my gaze to the corner where Chloe was cowering, softly begging for pity. But I was all out of pity. My life was on the line and if slapping a whip across her back would get me off the hook, then tough on her. It was her worry not mine.

Problem was, no matter my decision, Dimple was less trustworthy than a homicidal maniac let loose in a three-ring circus. No way could I trust her even if Chloe were to play the role of sacrificial lamb. My head drooped.

'I'm waiting,' Dimple prompted. 'Want to nuzzle her first, have a little cuddle; is that it? You can, if you want. I know you're no use for anything else.'

Bridget and Dr Burns instantly joined with her taunting laughter, their fingers pointing derisively. My loathing of them bubbled to boiling point. I've no idea how I managed to keep the lid on my anger. Somehow I did. I didn't let fly.

I reasoned instead. Reacting blindly would only have made them laugh louder – so there was no point – and no point in trying to get away. Chloe had to go. Her dying would buy me time, hopefully enough to whistle up another reality, a better one.

Yet their raw mockery also did something else. It stepped me back to my tortured week in hospital under Bridget's sadistic heel. At the end, she and her drug pedaling husband had shamelessly ridiculed me. I'd craved escape then, just as I was again craving escape, and it had worked. I'd been tossed straight into a luxury apartment complete with James and the perplexing Adelia. I almost giggled. A freaky and impossible idea had suddenly become irresistibly appealing.

'I want to have a go with the nurse,' I said, deadpan.

'Then what?' Dimple asked.

'She's your sacrificial lamb.'

She frowned. 'Which means what, exactly?'

I had to say it. 'I'll whip her.'

'Till she's dead, sweetie,' she warned. 'Is that clear?'

As Dimple spoke, Chloe rushed to the bed, fresh tears in flood. 'Don't! Please. I—'

Bridget was just as fast. Her hand smacked over the nurse's mouth, silencing her. At the same time, she grabbed her hair and yanked her to the floor, finally squatting on her chest, holding her down.

Dimple took no notice. 'I asked you a question, Ronnie.'

'Yes,' I huffed. 'Till she's dead.'

'In that case you can have her.' She smiled.

'Alone. I want to be alone with her.'

She hesitated. 'You're pushing your luck, sweetie.'

'That's the deal,' I declared, the strength in my voice surprising me as much as her.

She was unamused. 'The deal is whatever I say.'

'Then go screw yourself!'

Dr Burns stepped forward. 'Want me to teach him manners?'

Dimple shook her head, still unsmiling. 'Every dog must have its day and this unheroic whimpering little mutt must have his.'

Bridget rose to her feet. 'Think he can manage her all by

himself?'

'Good point,' Dimple grinned. 'Strap our lamb to the bed.'

Chloe fought with all her power, but Burns and Bridget were implacable. They soon had her spread-eagled, wrists and ankles secured as mine had been.

Dimple ambled over to where I was standing to watch. Her approach made me shudder, my whole body churning inside.

After signaling the others to leave, she said, 'There you are, sweetie, she's all ready for you. I'll be generous and give you fifteen minutes. If you can't do what you want in that time—' She shrugged.

I stayed where I was until the door had clicked shut, then Chloe's entreaties eked through and belatedly registered. I glared, not the slightest bit interested in her appeals or in stealing a few furtive squeezes. On any other occasion, it might have been different – it would have been – but I needed time to sort out my rampaging head. I guess my abrupt detachment told her I was up to something; something that didn't involve molesting her.

'Please,' she whispered, 'if you can escape, take me with you.'

I gave her another glare, this time more condemning. 'Shut it, bitch. You insisted on dragging me into this place, you stay and enjoy it.'

She came back at me. 'How was I to know? I didn't understand.'

'But you do now, girly, don't you! Shame it's too late. You're—' I stopped short. To my intense annoyance, I realized I needed her. Stepping testily to the bed, I said, 'Listen. I'll not touch you. I just need you to yell as if I am. Got it?'

'Why?' she demanded.

Couldn't believe she'd challenged me so robustly. Suppose adrenalin was surging through her body as fast as it was in mine, dulling pain and sharpening obstinacy.

I tensed, getting mad. 'Are you daft as well as bitchy? If there's no noise they'll come in.'

Again she answered back. 'Take me with you.'

'Make a noise,' I ordered, slapping her face, more a touch really, no force behind it.

She knew it too. 'Not unless you promise to take me with you.'

Frustrated as well as worried someone might come in, I gripped her shoulders and fixed her eyes. 'Do me a favor. Make a noise. You trussed me up like a chicken for Dimple, so you owe me. Whatever happens, you're dead.'

Her eyes didn't flinch. 'No.'

I'd had enough. 'Okay, if you won't playact for me, I will play around with you.' And I did. My hands went to work as if all their birthdays had come at once, but she uttered not a single sound. I've no idea how long I kept it up, but the penny finally dropped. Angrily, I said, 'What in hell's name is the matter with you?'

'I don't want to die,' she hissed. 'That's the matter! If you've any ideas, share. I might be able to help.'

'Then make a noise,' I retorted.

She jerked her arms and legs pointedly. 'Undo me first.'

'You are a real ornery bitch, aren't you!'

Her scowl felt like knives in my eyes. 'Because I don't want to die!'

I groaned. She was sucking away valuable time. 'Whatever,' I said, hurriedly unfastening the straps. 'Now, noise.'

She began at once, at the same time scampering over to her clothes and throwing them on. 'Have you a plan?' she asked between screams.

I knew I'd sound deranged if I told her, but my mind went over it anyway. I must have been lightheaded. I actually whispered my thoughts. 'It'll sound crazy,' I said, 'but I was trapped somewhere before and it worked. Got taken to a different place, a different reality.'

Her screaming paused. 'A different reality? You're right. It does sound crazy.'

Time was hustling too fast for me to care. 'First, I think, I squeezed into a fetal position.'

Her eyes bore into me. After a gap, she said, 'We should do that then.'

'It only worked for me.'

She wasn't so easily put off. 'We can hold on to each other.'

To be honest, by this time I was convinced I'd completely cooked my last remnants of sanity. Flicking my head like a bad actor in eccentric pose, I said, 'All right, together on the bed.'

'What next?' she asked when we were entwined in place.

I wasn't sure. 'When it happened before, I was desperate, in a miserable state, crying in pain ... the works.'

'Speaking personally,' she said bitterly, 'I'm pretty desperate and in pain right now. I'll thump your feet if *you* feel the need for something extra.'

Sarcastic bitch, I thought. 'Make noise,' I said. 'Don't talk. I'm thinking.'

As she resumed her wailing, I tried to remember last time; if I'd done anything besides shrivel up and blubber. And remembering wasn't easy, not with her bawling and me clamped round her back watching blood ooze through her uniform.

I shuddered, freshly aware of the savage damage caused by just a couple of throws of the whip. An image of Frank's slashed body stampeded into my mind, a brutally vivid image. Now I'm as mad as you were, Frank, I thought. What a birdbrain! Why did you waste your last breaths telling me about invisible marks? Their supposed *power* didn't save you, did it?

Despite profound disbelief, I said, 'We need to concentrate on getting away from here, and we need to rub our foreheads.'

'Don't make this any crazier than it already is,' she said.

'You told me you didn't want to die,' I threw back. 'Neither do I. This is all I've got.'

'Then full concentration and hard rubbing it is. Let's go for it.'

We tried, but the sound of the door opening announced clearly that we'd failed. Even then, we clung together firmly, still rubbing our sore foreheads.

The Lady of the District led in, followed by Burns and Bridget, all three stone faced. 'I'm disappointed in you, Ronald,' Dimple announced choosing Charity's expression and sounding just as unimpressed. 'I gave you what you wanted, but apparently that wasn't enough. You had to try scheming behind my back as if I'm as birdbrained as Frank.' She paused to soak in my dejection. 'I can only assume that you were trying to make me cross, so I must show you how very silly you've been.' She glanced at

Bridget. 'Convince him. Leave no skin on the girl, only raw meat.'

Bridget relished her moment. She advanced swiftly, the barbed whip already in hand and primed to maximize its vicious potential. Her first strike clawed me more than Chloe. We both yowled, our blood aroused and keen to burst through the rents in our clothes. Again the whip lashed out and then again until our striving for a changed reality swallowed all our faithless skepticism. We were true believers, rubbing and conspicuously pleading for deliverance.

In a single moment, all my past and present torments – mental and physical – united in one utterly debilitating ensemble. Every atom in my body became consumed in unrestrained agony, the torture so extreme I couldn't even shriek out for mercy. Time stood still, the pain constant, all my senses ablaze. I felt I was suspended as nothing in the midst of nothing but the bleakest purgatory. Yet my mind was still functioning. Wherever I was, I was alive, still Ronald Foster.

When it came, change was gradual. I'd felt sensations of helpless falling before, but never like this, as if I'd been cast headlong into a bottomless pit. My eventual landing wrenched the air from my lungs and shook every sinew, joint and bone as if I'd smashed into solid rock. Not for a long time did I dare open my eyes.

In stark contradiction to my experience, I found myself deposited on a plain wooden chair. Nonentity woman sat a mere two yards away. I remember wondering how I stayed upright, how I managed to avoid sliding like a corpse to the floor. The room was as plain as the chair, as bland as the woman herself. She didn't speak, not even to greet me as when we'd met before.

There was no point shilly-shallying. 'What happened?' I gasped.

She didn't exactly hurry over her reply. 'You were touched.'

My temper found its legs. 'Why can't you ever give a straight answer? Touched by what?'

Again she kept me waiting. 'Would you like to know what happened to Chloe?'

I'd forgotten about her. I'd been through one hell of a

mill and not knowing what had happened to Chloe – or any other nurse – was fine by me. The look I was getting told me I'd better ask. 'Is she all right?'

It was then I sensed a change in myself. The anger I always felt around nonentity woman had ebbed after one solitary flare, and my usual fear had failed to bite. Needing justification, I swiftly put it down to overspill from my torturous arrival.

But there was no change in her. She was still just as calm; her tone placid, even when her words cut deeper than Bridget's whip. 'You used Chloe,' she said. 'You abused her as you abuse so many of those you meet.'

It was a strange moment. My normal reaction would have been to blast her, yet I accepted her censure meekly. For no reason I could grasp, all my senses had combined to tell me that this particular moment was unique; a critical point.

'You are real, aren't you?' I whispered. When she didn't answer, my unique moment fell apart and I became greedy to discover how I could use her. 'I've seen you get in and out of different places,' I said. 'I need you to—'

'Hush, Ronald,' she said so gently I felt a shiver. 'You've more important things to resolve.'

I choked on that. I reckoned I'd excelled myself and resolved things pretty well. Dimple and her medical assassins lay in my dust and they could stay there, eat it and be damned. I started to say so, but she chopped me off.

'Hush now, Ronald. Listen to the silence.'

I'd no idea what she was on about. 'All you do is dole out riddles and rubbish,' I complained. 'How can I listen to silence?'

No reaction, not for a long while. Then she said, 'Your time is running out and you're still not seeing or hearing. To understand, you must do both.' I huffed at that. Before I could say anything, she added, 'It seems this meeting is premature. I'll leave now to—'

'No,' I cut in hurriedly. 'Not till I get some answers.'

'Oh, Ronald,' she said softly. 'I've given you answers. I've told you the person you're looking for runs headlong into traps. He only sees and hears what he wants. You must try—'

'Riddles,' I tossed back, anger rising.

She looked sad. 'Does that description not remind you of someone? Can you not—'

I sliced into her sanctimonious piffle. 'No,' I said. 'Or yes. It reminds me of half the world.'

Her eyes pierced mine. 'Which world?' she asked. Then she was gone.

In truth, I was glad. All she ever did was dish out brain-twisters and make me feel like an undeserving slug. My hatred returned with a passion. I remember distinctly how the feeling welled inside, how my mind flipped once more and rejected all that had happened. Arrogantly, I dismissed her as no more real than a pink elephant in an alcoholic haze.

Still sitting, I scanned round. This time I noticed a door. Here we go again, I sagged. Is it locked or unlocked? Will Dimple be outside or will it be Susie? I even thought that Charity might put in an appearance or that I'd hit the jackpot and get all three super-bitches together.

I snorted to bolster myself, then pointedly fingered my forehead. 'Hey, Frank,' I mocked as if he were alive and tuned in. 'Looks like you knew something after all.'

'And now we know it too,' Chloe said.

I swung round. The nurse was standing in another doorway, one I'd not seen. She looked so different: no sign of injury, her uniform replaced by a short saffron dress. For a second, I squinted, unsure it was her, but the blond hair and stance convinced me. After looking her up and down, I liked what I saw, but couldn't think of anything to say. Right when I needed something clever, my mind had become a bucket of whitewash.

In uneasy silence, I watched her cross to sit in nonentity woman's chair. 'See you have new clothes too,' she said.

I'd not noticed, but I seized on her words and stood to give myself a thorough inspection. A smile nearly split my face. Every stitch was of the finest materials.

'How are your feet?' she asked.

That was something else I'd not noticed, and it wasn't only my feet that had healed. Despite all I'd suffered, I was unharmed, physically at least. In that moment, I realized the imprint of every inflicted torment had vanished as if it had never been.

Laughing, I stamped my feet. 'No pain,' I said

delightedly, 'which I guess means no bruises, whip marks or anything else.'

Her face lit up. 'I've been healed too. I feel so much better. It's fantastic.'

Not sure why, but her joyous naivety jolted me back to Dimple and her callous buddies. I sat again, my face as grim as hers was happy. 'It'll only be fantastic when I've evened the score.'

'Haven't you had enough?' she sighed, crestfallen. 'They were about to kill me. You could easily have been next. You still could be if you persist.'

'That's your fault,' I huffed, not making a lot of sense. 'If you'd not been so damned stubborn, I'd have had more time to get out of there!' I laughed sourly. 'Don't forget it was me who got us away, me who told you about hard concentration and—'

'About rubbing foreheads,' she threw in for me. 'I know. I was there. But I think we had help.'

'I did all the helping!' I scorned, nauseated by her attempt to scrape the shine off my achievement. 'And I went through agonies on my way here. It was excruciating. Apparently I was *touched*.'

She frowned. 'I didn't feel a thing. I was there, then here, in the next room.'

That sat me up. It was worse than a bellyful of bile to hear that she'd had such an easy passage; positively caustic to learn that she'd been somewhere I hadn't and possibly learned something useful. Between clenched teeth, I said, 'Did you see nonentity woman? What did she tell you?'

Her frown deepened. 'Nonentity woman? I met a kind lady. She was beautiful. I'm to go with her later after we've talked ... we two.'

I sneered dismissively. 'How very cozy, except the woman you met isn't real and you and me have nothing to talk about.' I had a double take. 'There's only one thing I want from you: payment for your life. You owe me everything, so you can watch my back. That'll give me twice the chance of—'

'It's not like that,' she protested. 'Let me help you understand.'

I was too wound up to see that she'd been sent in to offer a lifeline. I cut her short. 'I understand very well that you're letting me down big time.'

She stood slowly and faced me. 'Then I'm sorry for you. I really wanted to help, to make amends for so many things, but now it's up to you how safe it is outside.'

I stood too. 'Don't you start with the riddles!'

To my surprise, she reached out and touched my cheek. 'Meeting you and coming here has woken me up. I've realized things about myself and my past life; a lot of not very good things. But I understand now, and I'd hoped that we—'

'Enough of this hogwash!' I erupted, anger in control. 'I don't need your pathetic euphoria and I don't need you.'

I spun away, expecting her to cave in. In my head were plans to push her out in front of me. That way, she'd cop any nasties first. I waited, but all I heard was silence, heavy silence. When I turned, Chloe had gone.

Chapter Twenty-five

I'll admit that Chloe's cowardly runner shocked me. The sting of her face-slapping me with such selfish ingratitude kept me in that bland room feeling cruelly abandoned.

What does she know? I fumed. Telling me: *it's up to me how safe it is outside*. All she knows is how to grab onto a hero's coattails.

I did nothing, but inactivity built on my frustration. It finally swamped my guts with enough acidity to march me to Chloe's door and brazenly throw it open. I recoiled, unnerved. Instead of a room, a wall of blackness lay before me, a swiftly moving wall. I stared in awe, slowly realizing it wasn't the wall moving, but a flow over it, like a forbidding waterfall the consistency of blood.

It was mesmerizing. I became drowsy. I could hear my brain screaming for me to do something: to rub my forehead, kick the door shut, anything. I tried, yet I staggered forward regardless, helplessly drawn in, my legs powerless to resist, my arms unwillingly reaching out. The cascade of black blood was icy, freezing to my touch, its pull relentless, dragging me in. Bit at a time, the deluge engulfed me.

I can't remember too clearly, but I know I was shivering when the liquid darkness disappeared. My teeth chattered as if I were adrift stark naked in the extremes of an extreme winter. Seeing Simon Hudson came as a total shock. The executive sat alone, his face like a death mask. Unlike before, his desk was clear. The absence of the formidable Mrs Dunstan felt strangely palpable.

Though it was obvious where I was, I felt thoroughly disorientated. Somehow, I sank into a chair not knowing whether I'd been sucked forward or back in time. Either way, Frank's forehead tip had proved to be fickle at best. It had capriciously failed, denying me any chance of withstanding the black flow. My shivers soon changed from biting cold to biting resentment.

It felt surreal when Simon spoke to me. 'You,' he breathed so lightly it could have been a thought in the air. 'Come to gloat?'

I kept my mouth shut. Though this second meeting was completely unexpected, it doggedly resurrected my one-time hope of using Simon as an ally. But not for long. I'd endured too many other impossibilities since our first encounter, all capped by Chloe's betrayal. No one and no thing could be trusted. It was as simple as that.

Simon's prattling drew me back. 'I did what you said, wrote a whole new report.'

I didn't care. Whatever he had done or not done made no difference to me. I had no reason to stay. In fact, I had every reason to get out of there before something happened to spike my gooseberry.

He must have seen something in my reaction that angered him. 'I'm talking to you. You who made me cave in to that Dunstan woman. You who made me trade a report full of lies for a job, just so the company can make its billions.' His voice cracked as he added, 'What about me, my salvation?'

What a pathetic heap of horse manure, I thought. Whining about salvation as if I could influence his. 'Listen to yourself,' I sneered. 'I made you do this. I made you do that. I wasn't even here. I was—' I stopped, too indifferent to bother.

But he wasn't finished. 'Easy for you to wash your hands,' he spat back. 'I have to live with it, with myself. All because I listened to you.'

I didn't like the way he was gawking any more than I liked his driveling accusations. They weren't even true. I'd never said a word last time we'd met, not till the end. Mrs Dunstan had picked up my thoughts, that was all, and even that had been plain fluke. If anyone was to blame, she was.

Yet a light was dawning, a menacing glimmer that

made my soul lurch. Maybe I'd not been spared Susie's task despite all that had happened in between. Maybe it had been thrown straight back in my lap with the situation moved on, with Simon now at break point, jumping point.

I breathed heavily, well and truly aware that I'd been snared between festering jaws. *Make sure he jumps*, the cream uniformed vixen had told me with the backing of a gun. *Simon is one of us and mustn't jump*, nonentity woman had said. What a mess!

'It's none of my business,' I said, as much to bolster myself as to distract Simon's intense gaze.

When that gaze persisted, I thought about rubbing my forehead, not that I believed it would make any difference. Besides, I figured, even if by some freakish mystery it did work, there were no safety guarantees. I could be whisked away from one loathsome location and tossed like a hand-tied dummy into something worse, maybe back into Dimple's murderous clutches.

I caught myself thinking gibberish. It was just stupid prevarication to put off making a decision. Fear lay behind it: fear of denying Susie and her sneaky gun-toting sister-bitch in the corridor – if either was still around – and fear of trusting nonentity woman. It was pure madness to trust her, assuming she existed.

Again I caught myself. I was behaving like an idiot who believed that head butting steel spikes would bring triumphant enlightenment, not the hollowness of a fatally honeycombed brain. Nonentity woman did exist and it was crazy to keep bucking the truth. Even Chloe had seen her. For sure the bland woman's appearing and disappearing antics were impossible to fathom, but neither could I fathom my own jumps from one reality to another.

I shuddered, not because my rationale was irrational, but because my mind had spontaneously dumped a memory load of other obnoxious impossibilities. All were undeniable. All had occurred before my eyes. All made insanity look a very real possibility. Made me wonder if I'd really seen or just imagined those terrifying words on Frank's chest.

'Just cuts,' I said aloud, still stubborn. 'Nothing but random cuts.'

'That's what it feels like,' Simon chirped up, jolting me.

I'd been so preoccupied, I'd forgotten about him. The defeat in his voice surprised me.

'Cuts I've inflicted on myself over the years,' he added. 'Every one marking a terrible lie, like coffin nails in my soul.'

I snorted dismissively. He was being melodramatic as well as pathetic. Reluctantly, I gave him a moment's attention, but his troubles weren't mine. My business was finding a way to escape. Impulsively, I threw aside my plague of reservations and channeled my full concentration into forehead rubbing, and I rubbed for all I was worth.

'W-what's with you?' Simon spluttered, grimacing at my frantic behavior. Then he laughed. 'What's with me too? I'm sitting here talking as if you're real.'

I froze, my brain on fire. 'I am real,' I gasped, my strength leaking away as if he'd holed its reservoir. 'I've been sent to make you jump, maybe to stop you jumping.'

Simon shook his head. 'You're talking in riddles. Get out of my head. Get out of my life.'

I tried to linger, to speak, but bodily weakness was rapidly turning my legs into wayward reeds, my spine into slush. Enfeebled, I slid from chair to carpet, my muscles twitching like wannabe ripples. 'Listen,' I mouthed against the odds, 'I can tell you things.'

Simon took no notice. In retrospect, I guess he couldn't see me any more. But I could still see and hear him. He sat deep in his chair for a while, features blank, then spilled his thoughts. 'She never said a word, just grabbed the rewritten report and went off. She got her way and I got—' He didn't finish.

Though I struggled to keep them open, my eyes flickered shut. Moments later, the air-conditioned neutrality of Simon's office dissolved and I felt strong winds blasting my face. As if under independent control, my eyelids immediately sprang open, but nothing much else would move. I was virtually paralyzed. All I could see was Simon. He was dead ahead of me, taking slow pigeon steps along a low wall at the edge of an extensive flat roof.

I think I shouted, 'Don't jump!' I certainly tried. Simon didn't react. He'd become deaf to my voice.

To my amazement, a bullet whizzed through the air, its path ending in an explosion of brick fragments. 'Wrong instruction,' Jessica said, her aim pointedly shifting to my left knee. 'Try again.'

I stared, horrified. The sneaky vamp was still wearing the same cream uniform. 'H-he can't hear me. He doesn't even see me,' I stammered.

Susie stepped unhurriedly into view. She had replaced her boring brown dress with a shapeless lavender creation. 'Our charity has a job to do, Ronald,' she declared. 'Our exclusive mission is to help those who only partly hear and partly see. If you're to be of any use, you must get through to him, as you did in his office.'

I gaped, confused to my gills. She was right. I had got through to him, but that didn't mean I wanted him to jump, exactly the opposite.

When I didn't respond, Jessica became eager. 'Shall I take out his knee?'

That triggered my voice. 'No!' I yelled, still rooted.

Susie smiled at her keenness. 'No, Jess, not yet. He's a girl-gawker and girl-beater and would-be rapist. He likes to see exposed female flesh, not that he's capable of doing anything with it.'

Jessica laughed. 'Some hero,' she taunted.

I fought and failed to close my eyes. I'd been right. To deliver that taunt, Jessica had to have been at Charity's vengeful jamboree. I couldn't say anything.

'So you see,' Susie carried on, 'his own lust makes him pliable, and titivating his lust is a lot easier and less messy than shooting holes in him.'

Jessica got the message quicker than me. After nodding, she unzipped her uniform. As it dropped onto the roof, Susie reached out and touched the girl's shoulder. 'That's enough; or is it, Ronald?'

My voice coughed back to life, angry life. 'You think the sight of a half naked female will make me push Simon over the edge! How—'

'No one's asked you to push anyone,' Susie corrected. 'Talk to him. Make him see that jumping really is the best option ... for everyone.'

I couldn't believe what I was hearing. 'No,' I growled. 'And it would make no difference if the pair of you were cavorting in the buff around a dance pole. I'm not that shallow!'

Susie smiled. 'Pole dancing isn't for me, Ronald, though I dare say Jess would be marvelous at it.' The smile faded. 'But you are that shallow. That's why you have potential. It's why we're offering this once in a lifetime chance.'

As she spoke, I sensed the power of movement seeping back into my body. Relieved, I shouted, 'Don't jump, Simon.' To my frustration, everyone carried on as if I wasn't there.

Jessica turned to Susie. 'You want me to finish stripping off or shall I shoot him?'

Susie shook her head. 'Neither, Jess, not for the moment. He's too intent on judging Simon, which is ridiculous. Charity herself has told him more than once that we don't make judgments.'

'So he's lame brained on top of everything else?'

'Misguided, my dear. Too much contact with those who would have us fail.'

Jessica looked aghast. 'He's a traitor. Why are you still letting—'

'We mustn't forget those who depend on us,' Susie interrupted. 'He's lost his way, that's all. It's up to us to steer him through.'

I trembled, trying to shake free of all they were saying. When my strength finally approached normal, I was ready to do something, but nothing to help Simon. He was too deep in a screwball world of his own and, to be honest, he could damn well stay there. Without thinking, I fingered my forehead, my brain busy calculating the odds of getting to the roof door before Jessica could fire. At once, Susie and the girl cringed. I sensed their vibes and looked towards them. My forehead fingering had sized their attention. Both were steadily watching me.

I kept my gaze on Susie, belatedly realizing that I'd witlessly closed out my best hope of a quick escape. Her face looked strangely unsettled. When she laughed, it caught me off guard.

'You still don't know, do you,' she said. 'Despite everything, you're as clueless as the first time we met.'

'I know you need me,' I retaliated. 'You want me for something you can't do, something not even Charity can do.'

'What a clever chap you aren't,' she answered. 'How dare

you compare yourself with Charity!'

'Your lover, is she?' I sneered. 'Bet she doesn't know about Frank and Adelia, or Dimple come to think of it. You're two-timing her, aren't you! You're a puffed-up lying bitch who likes it any way you can get it ... and you've the barefaced gall to tear me down because I occasionally look at women. You're sick!'

Unfazed, she bit back. 'You've tried ranting at me before, Ronald, but it's different this time. So rant all you want. I'm staying to make sure you finish the job you started.'

Her unwelcome reminder about Simon struck a disturbing chord. I jerked round to the might-be suicide. He was still on the wall, stepping cautiously to and fro along the coping stones, oblivious to any of us.

As if hit by a thunderbolt, I finally got it. Simon *was* partly deaf and partly blind, but not in any conventional sense. He had the freedom to choose what he saw and heard just like the bastard who had stitched me up, the guy who allegedly ran headlong into traps.

I suppose Susie picked up my sudden remoteness. Coldly, she said, 'It's time to act.'

Something in her manner took me back to her arrival. She'd told me that, to be of use, I had to get through to Simon. She'd even spelled out the charity's exclusive mission. I knew for sure then. I'd been right all along. Despite her constant needling and denials, she was dead in the water without me, and so was Charity. Even Frank had latched on to them needing us, though I had to admit he'd also talked a load of other half-baked trash.

'I'll tell you about Simon,' Susie announced when I continued to ignore her. 'He's feeling sorry for himself now, but this is a new Simon, a Simon who has foolishly allowed himself to be sucked in by false promises. He's a hypocrite. For years he's been a fixer. He's repeatedly done everything he could to breathe life into his company's planet scourging projects ... and I don't mean puny maneuvers like hunting for loopholes, lying and common bribery. He's a world class operator whose efforts have blighted the lives of millions. So don't be misled. That feeble shadow you first saw with Mrs Dunstan is no more the real Simon than the pitiable specimen now pacing the wall. Look at him.'

Against my will, my eyes swung to the beleaguered executive. True, Susie might have been spinning a web of lies, yet I knew first hand of Mrs Dunstan's fury at Simon's change of heart. She'd even jeered about him seeing mystic lights and hearing inner voices. It wasn't a giant guess to conclude that something had happened, presumably the same something that had prompted nonentity woman to claim him as *one of us* and say he mustn't jump.

'I can see you're unconvinced,' Susie observed dryly, 'but I'll indulge you. Let's pretend you're right and imagine there are some things only you can do for the charity.' She paused for my defiance to cool. It didn't. Her voice was crisper when she spoke again. 'Make up your mind, Ronald. You're either with us or against us, and you really don't want to be against us. We can give you so much. Simply go over and speak to Simon. Make him see and hear you. Tell him his burden of guilt is too great to bear, too great for anyone to forgive. Tell him you understand. Tell him the voices that changed him – the voices that promised forgiveness – were malicious ramblings in his head. Tell him to jump and bring an end to the misery he's inflicted on himself and on the world.'

Alarmingly, Simon stopped walking as Susie stopped speaking. 'You again,' he said reproachfully, staring straight at me.

That stare held me rigid. I felt like a bit player in my own life, and in his too. Who was this man who, somehow, could see and hear only what he wanted? I was nothing to him, yet I'd ended up at the extreme butt of everything. For no reason I can justify, my brain went on a mindless bender. I experienced every conceivable emotion, every one marinated in jealousy. I figured that Simon had a gift. If I'd had it, I could have wiped out Susie and everyone else linked to Charity's deadly charity. How I thought I was making sense, I'll never know, but I did know that I wanted Simon out of my life.

Though it was the last thing I wanted to say, I blurted, 'They want you to jump, but you can escape. Rub your forehead and—'

'Cat got your tongue,' Susie mocked as if innocent of striking me dumb. 'And right when you were naughtily defying me and tossing aside Charity's lessons in humility.' She laughed and turned to Jessica. 'Dance for him, dear. Be his consolation while I show him how insignificant he really is.' I gaped as Jessica began to sway.

'I'm afraid we've no pole here for Jess,' Susie added, 'but you can't deny she's a beautiful mover.' Another laugh, then she said, 'So you think we're in some way incapable? You think you're special? Watch.'

Jessica's close and unashamedly provocative prancing melted away as Susie spoke. My attention was wrenched towards Simon. He was on the perimeter wall facing me, his eyes piercing. Moment's later, he held his arms high and stepped backwards from the building.

Chapter Twenty-six

I felt my knees buckle. It seemed impossible that after everything I'd endured, I'd been snatched back and forced to witness Simon's feeble cop out.

'Coward!' I shouted after him, my voice unlocked. 'What have you done to me!'

Susie preened. 'We won in the end. That's what counts.'

I gasped, as stunned by her cold hearted gloating as by my own ability to feel stunned at anything she said or did.

She smiled. 'Have Jess for the night if you want. She won't mind what you do ... or can't do. Isn't that right, dear?'

Jessica was still dancing, her body swaying, every movement burning with sensuality. She seemed as different from the nervous young woman I'd met at the elevator as it was ever possible to be. Her only acknowledgement of being clinically offered as a convenient bed mate was an indifferent nod.

Although I tore my eyes away, the ache to succumb gnawed like a hungry carnivore in the butcher's shop. Only the frightening prospect of snaring another Dimple-style feline shut me down. I shook my head, not trusting words.

Susie shrugged. 'Up to you. We'll leave you to it.'

Jessica took the comment as command and hastily dressed.

As they turned to go, Susie added, 'Of course this wasn't your success, Ronald. You had help from a friend. As far as the charity is concerned, you're still a failure ... and your time is running out.'

I flinched at that. Nonentity woman had also said about my time running out. Disturbed, I was about to speak when I noticed the daylight changing in a very unnatural way. It seemed to accelerate in jerky skips into darkness. My eyes flew to Susie. She was walking calmly away. Each of her steps brought forth greater gloom.

'Come to my house in the morning,' she said. 'There might be something you can do to make yourself useful.'

With my senses besieged, I lurched into defiance. 'And if I don't come?'

She didn't falter. 'Even you aren't that stupid.'

'Wait!' I said. 'I've nowhere to go.'

I heard her chuckle. 'You should have thought of that before rejecting a night with Jessica. I'll see you at 10 o'clock. Don't be late, or early.'

I'm not really sure what happened after that. One moment I was staring as they ambled away, arm in arm. The next, I was in a fury; an out of control frenzy. I remember charging, though my first strides were lost in a mental blur. When I caught up, I immediately lashed out at Susie, diving in with the full force of unbridled rage and smashing her down. Jessica tried to stop me, but my side-swipe sent her sprawling. I heard her head thump onto the roof's unforgiving surface.

I've no idea how many times I knuckle punched Susie. I'd been pushed beyond breaking point and wasn't interested in counting. To my mind, someone had to pay. It didn't matter that I was astride an unmoving body pommeling a face that was already turning to mush.

I glimpsed the last few seconds of Jessica's headlong return and realized my side-swipe hadn't been hard enough. She powered into my upper chest, bowling me over. She rolled too, but I was quicker to get up. Though she struggled like a six-armed monkey, she could do nothing to stop me pitching her off the roof. Unlike Simon, she shrieked as she went down. The shrill noise came to an abrupt end.

That was when my energy gave out. Exhausted, I plunked down, legs outstretched, my back against the low edging-wall. Slowly, the enormity of what I'd done seeped into my conscience, and out again. They had made me a killer, a twice over woman killer. I couldn't be blamed.

Under mountains of provocation, I'd cracked. I reckoned that, if insanity had skirted passed and missed me before, it had definitely hit me square-on this time. Perversely, I didn't care. Even being locked away in a madhouse seemed better than the living torment of Charity's confounding and malignant charity.

In retrospect, I wasn't particularly conscious of waiting for some do-gooders to spot the two fallen bodies and catch me like a launchpad assassin, but I guess that's what I did. Whatever, I took the time to calm down and glance around. There wasn't much to see, just a flat roof with its perimeter wall and a few housings for the building's services. The only other significant thing was the access door about thirty yards distant. Susie lay between it and me.

'They'll get here soon,' I said aloud, needing company from a voice, even it was just my own. 'Odd they're not here already. Simon jumped ages ago. Two flyers off one roof should have had people racing up here.' I glanced at Susie. 'She might as well go off too.'

I was in no rush. I'd assumed I'd be caught and that would be that. My thinking had changed by the time I reached her – and so had my attitude towards the appeal of a madhouse. No catchers had appeared. There was a chance I could dump her body and slip away. Moving purposefully, I picked her up and checked the blood leakage where she'd been lying. 'Not all that much,' I decided. 'Get rid of her first then—' Her eyes opened, stopping me dead.

'R-Ronald,' she gasped, mustering what must have been the dregs of her reserves.

I hesitated – obviously I did – but I'd already gone too far. I had nothing to lose. Resolutely, I started towards the wall. I was soon staggering, my strength proving weak. Her trembling struggles felt like butterfly wings within cupped hands, yet her battered eyes were sword points jabbing my soul. I tore away from those eyes and held tight, refusing to let her break free. Finally, I lay her on the coping stones ready to pitch her out of my life for good.

'R-Ronald,' she stuttered again. 'P-please—'

Not my finest hour, I'll admit, but I was fixed on delivering the shove that would launch her into oblivion. I should have expected her to grab my arm. Her desperate fingers were like steel jaws. Every time I wrenched them away, she clamped me with her other set. Anger provided my answer; anger and an awkward double fisted punch to her stomach. She convulsed uncontrollably, her grip gone. She made no sound when I bulldozed her off, open palmed. Neither did her accusing stare leave me until distance stole it away.

Exhausted again, I dropped down to lean against the wall, legs outstretched as before. It seemed inevitable that someone would be on their way. The grim prospect knee-jerked my fear of capture and loaded me onto my feet. I checked the wall for tell-tale blood spills. Nothing I could be bothered with.

It took an age for me to cover the few yards to where I'd first attacked her, and several minutes more to coax over enough dirt to camouflage the mess Susie had oozed onto the surface. It wasn't good enough, but I convinced myself it was. After all, why would anyone scour the whole roof on the off-chance of foul play?

Getting away had become the only thing that mattered and I couldn't afford to indulge my fatigue. Blanking everything but escape, I slipped through the roof door and down the stairs, all the while expecting to meet a herd coming the other way. To my astonishment, I made it to the highest occupied floor without seeing anyone. That gave me an energy boost and I quickly found an elevator.

As the doors opened on the ground floor, the reception desk loomed. Behind it sat the big mouthed brunette I'd seen before. I shuddered. She was wearing an unbefitting tart outfit that had no chance of containing her overspill. The last thing I needed was her to spot me in the wrong place at the wrong time.

As discreetly as I could, I turned out of direct view and waited for her to be distracted. To my relief, a visitor soon arrived and gifted me the chance to walk casually passed.

'Bye, Mr Foster,' she called out with a wave. 'There's a limo waiting for you.'

My eyes spread in conscience-stricken confusion. Half of me wanted to run the opposite way; the other half yearned to know more. Either way, I'd been uncloaked.

As I reeled, her oversize mouth curved into a hefty grin. 'Did Simon Hudson do it?'

I didn't think. 'Do what?'

When she sniggered, I figured it was due to my facial contortions as I kicked myself for speaking at all, let alone for asking such a dumb question.

'Did he jump, silly?' she amplified as if I were dim. 'You said he was thinking of jumping off the roof.' She laughed over loudly. 'Made me giggle, I can tell you.'

Despite my innocence of Simon's death, I felt as if *guilty* signs had spontaneously festooned around my neck, huge multi-colored signs that no one could possibly miss – and they were deserved, at least as far as Susie and Jessica were concerned. I mumbled something like, 'Got to go,' then scurried off, all my pretensions in tatters.

'Do come again,' she said brazenly, 'if you know what I mean.'

I didn't care what she meant and I didn't need her laughter following me like the bleats of an overcooked temptress. The disquieting noise stayed with me all the way to the main entrance. Outside, the premature darkness Susie had so preternaturally advanced was being held off by bright lights. I shook myself to ditch the memory. Deeper worries swiftly flooded in. Thanks to that coquette of a receptionist, the cops were bound to find out I'd been with Simon. Then they would be after me. I breathed heavily, my brain on the rummage for possible places to hide.

A stylish limousine pulled up very close, its coachwork gleaming, its rear-side window already sliding down. 'Ronald,' Charity said. 'You should get in.'

I'd forgotten about big mouth's mention of a limousine, very stupidly. There couldn't have been a clearer hint that the top bitch herself had found me. Despite everything, I was drawn to her strapless ruby gown, yet I fought to resist its allure, recalling the last time I'd seen her, how she'd denied me any mercy.

Bitterly I said, 'You set a pack of dogs on me.'

She seemed surprised. 'Not dogs, Ronald, though I could have ordered wolves.' Her smile scared me. 'You've shown promise since then.'

Maybe her unexpected concession sapped my wits. As if we were a couple of yarning buddies, I said, 'No one else thinks so.'

She seized my words. 'That's because no one knows you as I do. Our last conversation rather proves that, don't you think?'

I knew then. She was tying my strings in knots, tugging the ones she fancied, and she clearly fancied reminding me of my naked ordeal on her conference table. Like I needed a reminder! I could never have forgotten the way she'd ridiculed me in front of her cronies, let alone how she'd exposed my innermost thoughts with such frightening accuracy.

'You're a witch!' I accused hotly. 'You couldn't have known those things otherwise.'

She laughed. 'A witch! I eat witches for breakfast ... and the occasional ipsissimus.'

'You're mad,' I retaliated. 'Your whole charity is a—'

'Enough!' she said, no laughter. 'This isn't a negotiation. Get in or—' She fell silent.

I had to ask. 'Or what?'

She gave me another scary smile. 'I imagine that falling from a high building is quite exhilarating, until the landing of course. But nowhere near as exhilarating as throwing people off and watching them fall.'

My legs sagged like water-filled balloons. She knew. She knew everything. I should have been utterly astounded, but I wasn't. As she'd already demonstrated so indelibly, she knew things she couldn't possibly know.

I'm not sure how I made it into the car and don't recall the road trip. It seemed mere seconds before I was in an armchair, facing her from the opposite end of the conference room. All the tables and chairs were in place, no sign of Grub's blood on the carpet.

I still managed a flash of defiance. 'I want answers.'

Serenely she said, 'Answers have to be earned.'

My flash flared into determination. 'No! I refuse to get on any more of your merry-go-rounds. This has to be a dream ... a nightmare.'

'As you wish,' she conceded too easily. 'It's all a nightmare. Your sleeping imagination has dreamed up a wonderfully elaborate charade, a whole series of charades. Soon you'll wake up and be back— ah, but where? That really is a question.'

My mind galloped back to that first day in this same room with a whole bunch of strangers. Although I'd ransacked my gray matter endlessly, I was still no wiser about anything *before*. The only witness to something in the past remained my devastating echo of catastrophic panic.

'No answer?' she goaded, teasing me with a roll of her bare shoulders. 'This is no dream, Ronald. Your confusion is entirely due to your lack of commitment.'

My gaze dropped. I could have written that line for her. It was always my fault, never hers, or Dimple's, or the late and unlamented Susie's. Well aware that her enticing beauty hid very cold blood, I tried prodding for information. 'You said I was showing promise.'

She smiled faintly. 'I've already spoken of my high hopes for your partnership with Susie, yet you've fought against everything she's asked and failed two missions in the process, very basic missions. Worse, you've persisted in your association with those who would have us fail.'

I dived in. 'Why do they want us to fail? Who are they?'

She ignored my questions. 'However, your defining mulishness shows a certain strength of character. You need direction, that's all. It's just as Susie said earlier, you've lost your way.'

My eyes fell shut momentarily. Charity was quoting Susie's words to Jessica on the roof. She had to have been involved somehow. 'Were you the so-called friend who made Simon jump?'

Her expression didn't change. 'Simon was like you. He had free will. No one except Simon was responsible for his choices.'

I should have been more alert. I should have seized on the way she'd linked my free will to Simon's. Instead, I huffed, 'That doesn't answer my question.'

'I think it does,' she said unwaveringly.

I was on the merry-go-round again. 'Riddles and more riddles,' I seethed, exasperated.

'Then I'll be direct,' she retorted. 'How do you feel now you've murdered Susie and Jessica?'

She knew. That came as no surprise. In the limousine, her painfully transparent innuendos about people and high buildings had said it all. Even so, I tried flat denial.

She didn't flinch. Moments later, a huge wall screen appeared. A recording was already replaying. It showed all that had happened on the roof, everything captured in beautifully clear detail. I squirmed to turn away, but couldn't. A powerful force compelled me to relive each moment, each one of my heartless actions.

Her tone became sombre. 'Would you care to reconsider your claim to innocence?' I didn't respond. She let me stew a while, then added, 'Susie pleaded with you, Ronald, yet you still threw her off the building. So I ask again, how do you feel?'

I felt like a puppet, a helpless dummy suckered into a well orchestrated frame-up – into a pernicious trap. Relief came in a rush. The answer was obvious; it seemed obvious then. Susie really had been mounting a coup. Somehow, Charity had caught wind of it and used me to turn the tables.

Confidently I said, 'I feel as if I've done your dirty work.'

'No pity or regret?' she asked.

I was on a roll. 'You set the example.'

Her smile was enigmatic. 'Thank you, Ronald. I'll take that as a compliment.'

I pounced. 'Does that mean I've earned some answers?'

After a pause, she leaned forward, luring my hunger for her body. 'Wait here,' she said, startling me when she stood abruptly and left me alone.

As the door swung closed after her, the gentle click from the catch was more than enough to set my nerves jangling. As the seconds racked up, I pushed out of my chair and began pacing. The wait seemed interminable, every moment like an hour. When the door eventually twitched, my eyes were glued.

The numbing spectacle of Charity pushing in a gurney made me gasp. A sheet was draped over what could only be a corpse. In my mind, it had to be Susie. When the cover began to move, any composure I'd clung to crumpled away. Full of guilty fear, I stumbled back to the wall, horrified. My gape stretched ever wider as the body sat up and the cloth fell away.

'Short time, no see,' Dimple purred. The double shock drained the blood from my face. 'Who were you expecting?'

Another door slammed. The noise spun me round. 'Me, I suspect,' Susie said.

Immediately, my head filled with blazing cotton, my

brain alight with the wildest of thoughts. It was impossible to explain away Susie's survival, her total lack of injury. I retreated mentally, shriveled. Nonsensically, I noticed her bright orange dress, the way it hung like a misshapen sack – and her hair, the style looser but still wrong.

I yelled something. Whatever it was, it resounded in the room like the tormented wail of the undead. I remember my fingers flailing the air in the moments before I passed out.

Chapter Twenty-seven

I came round to hear Charity say, 'Too late for daydreaming, Ronald, or for concocting nightmares for that matter.'

My hands were tight against my cheeks. I pretended not to see or hear, which wasn't difficult. I felt deeply numb, inside and out. Every truth I'd relied on to give my life structure had been smashed and trashed. Impossibilities had become the norm. Even life and death had ceased to have rules.

Charity carried on regardless. 'Time for you to prove yourself and behave like the high caliber team player I know you to be.'

Yet another last chance, and with the same backhanded compliment she'd thrown at me right at the beginning. I sagged resentfully, remembering all my other last chances. Maybe for the first time, I really understood that everything was centered on a lie, on malignant cheating. No matter what I did or said, I'd always be brought back to start some fresh ordeal. I couldn't believe it when my mind looped round to Chloe.

'Do you intend to mope all day?' Charity asked.

That sounded wrong. By my reckoning, it had to be evening. You're off-beam, witch-eater, I spurned in my head, uneasy that memories of Chloe were still there, striking memories of the nurse in that austere room. I could hear myself scoffing at her sanctimonious drivel, yet her words kept repeating like pickax blows bludgeoning the thickest part of my skull: *it's up to you how safe it is outside.*

I shivered. Thinking back on her nonsense was as futile as it was skin-crawling. Everything to do with Chloe had happened a lifetime ago, before that freezing black cascade had taken me, before I became a murderer who couldn't keep his victims dead – well, at least one of them.

Chloe's disrupting words made me drop my hands, forcing me to notice change. I was no longer in a heap against the wall but sitting in a different spot. The unremembered move should have troubled me, but not this time. It virtually passed me by. Besides, I was more interested in Charity. She was standing clear of the tables, flanked by Susie and Dimple. All were wearing different clothes, all provocatively daring.

Why do I care? I berated myself, easily recalling Susie telling Jessica: *it's his own lust that makes him pliable.* The truth of my shallowness hit like a high speed train, making me nauseous, yet I couldn't resist soaking in their seductive apparel.

Susie noticed. With no hint of animosity, she said, 'Jessica is outside. If seeing us has excited you, I'll tell her to dance, naked if you like. She loves dancing almost as much as she hates being thrown off buildings.'

She wanted me to react. I didn't, not at first. I was still too boggled from her mystifying return from the dead – and there she was confirming that Jessica too had survived.

Instead of freaking out as every instinct insisted, I hit back. 'Guess Simon is out there as well. I'll get *him* to dance if seeing me has excited you.'

Charity picked up my taunt. 'Simon is no longer a client. Our years of painstaking support have been rewarded and he's moved on.'

'He committed suicide,' I rebutted curtly.

She smiled. 'A progression. He's joined others within our team of high caliber players.'

I could have gone back at her. I could have queried whether a thumping great mattress had miraculously appeared around the building and prevented Simon, Susie and Jessica from having their brains squashed into their feet. I could have sought clarification about what possible *progression* could have turned a suicide client into a star team player. I could have said a lot of things. What I did was huff and say, 'All I ever get is riddles.'

'And all you ever do is fail,' Dimple chimed in like the bitch-queen she was.

'Not entirely,' Susie corrected to my surprise. 'He never fails to be consistently predictable.'

I should have known I'd get acid not comfort, but Dimple hadn't finished.

'Ronnie, do tell. Why are you behaving as if you didn't read Frank's chest before you left him to the rats?'

That was one reminder too many. My palm flew to my forehead. From the way they grimaced, I guess I must have rubbed.

'Don't do that,' Susie said, retreating a pace.

Charity smiled. 'It is very rude to scratch at your forehead.'

'But it's okay to whip people and slice them with machetes!' I was about to say more when I realized I'd be daft not to exploit this chink in their communal armor. I rubbed my forehead again.

I'll give them this: they tried not to wince, but not well enough. That was when I knew they knew I'd finally cottoned on.

'You've nothing more to prove, Ronald,' Charity soothed. 'I completely understand your need for respect and your love of the finer things in life. Be assured of my generosity. I can provide everything you desire.'

I gulped at the spontaneous turnaround. They were on the defensive. I'd wrong footed them. Charity had changed tack and was unconditionally offering a key to the ultimate treasure chest. Mad Frank had been spot on: well, somewhere near the bullseye. For sure, there was some kind of invisible mark, and it did scare them. Yet even as I congratulated myself, I knew I was missing something. My previous forehead rubbing exploits had too often been damp squibs.

Annoyance quickly became my dominant emotion. I'd too easily forgotten the lesson of my conference room dance. Charity had the power to rake out my innermost thoughts, or maybe not. Truth was, she'd ignited fresh greed within me; a new and ravenous greed for all she could give. It compelled me to wash away the unexplainable and dub her *Illusionist-in-Chief*. I convinced myself that her previous insights could credibly be put down to fluke and damned good guesses. Stage performers and so-called psychics pulled off that brand of magic every day.

With avarice reassuring me of her abilities, I didn't want my next thought. Yet it yelled in my head: a warning that accepting her so-called generosity would put me firmly on her seductive hook – a hook I knew to be viciously barbed and frustratingly escape proof.

Disheartened, I snorted condemningly, 'You give but you always take more. How can I trust you?'

'We're not strangers, Ronald,' she said patiently. 'We go back a long way. We've been here your whole life, supporting you against those who would have us fail ... those who would have you fail.'

'I need to think,' I said, feeling perilously exposed. So many inexplicable things had happened that I knew I could easily have been wrong before, or wrong this time. Maybe she really could read me like a stretched out book. Either way, I was determined not to be manipulated.

'Think by all means,' she persisted. 'Think how powerless you've been feeling, how impotent. You only have to join us with a full heart to seize true power. The tests you've endured have shown your worthiness. The door is open for you to indulge your lust for life. Simply promise to help others come our way.'

'You mean the partly deaf and blind,' I scorned. 'Except they're not—' I faltered, wanting to say something about Simon. Before I could, Charity spoke again.

'The partly deaf and blind need help because they think they hear and see. The enemy has attacked them, shown them mere glimpses of truth only to leave them deserted and confused. Our task is to clear their paths, to loosen the chains that blind and deafen. And you can do it. You already have. You helped Simon through his crisis despite your inexperience.' Before I could say anything, she stiffened. 'I need your decision. Time is running out.'

My mind was gurgling, but I could still count, and this was the third time I'd been told about my time running out. I'd had enough. I needed space. I needed to be left alone. 'I'm leaving,' I said.

Charity challenged me at once. 'Because I told you your time is running out? That would be a mistake.'

I shrugged and started towards the nearest door. Dimple

spoke huskily, 'Don't go, Ronnie. I can show you things you've never dreamed of.'

'We all can,' Susie added. 'There's no limit to—'

'Quiet!' I roared. 'Stop treating me like a fool.'

Charity nodded. 'You're right, Ron—'

I cut her dead. 'It's up to me what happens outside.'

For once, I recognized my own bravado for what it was, yet I still made a move for the door. From nowhere, a lightning bolt struck the core of my brain; at least, that's what it felt like. All I could see was Frank's chest, the carved words screaming at me, tearing at my resolve. From that same nowhere, I found the strength to fight back and keep going.

There was an edge to Charity's voice when she spoke. 'You're wrong about what happens outside. We must never forget those who depend on us, those we serve. Going through that door will cost you everything. We've shown you how to embrace your true nature. Don't force us to hunt you down and—'

She broke off when I spun round. I'd never seen her look disturbed. That moment told me everything – it seemed to. I could escape. Why else had she talked of hunting me down? Feeling oddly lightheaded, I turned again for freedom.

Even then she wouldn't give up. 'Everything you desire, Ronald. You know how generous I can be.'

'I resign,' I shouted, glancing back to sneer, my fingers already poised on the handle.

Charity, Susie and Dimple were lined up, eyes glistening bright. It took all my mental strength to force my hand to throw open the door. A solid brick wall filled the frame, completely blocking my way. I gaped in profound disbelief. The wall was as impenetrable as my desolation.

'Disappointed?' Charity asked as if prompting an idiot child.

Instinctively, I knew she wanted me to face her, to face them. I wouldn't. Instead, I pounded the wall desperate for any sign of weakness.

'Try another,' she suggested, her voice gnawing at my brain.

I had to, as I had to bear their laughter as I chased round, finding each doorway the same, all totally blocked.

'What's the matter, sweetie?' Dimple cooed when I dropped into a chair, panting, head in hands. 'Did you really think we'd let you skip off after all we've done to keep you?'

'Shut up!' I screamed, tears dribbling.

'There goes his temper again,' Susie said. 'He's not changed a bit.'

'A little, I think,' Charity pondered conversationally. 'And for the better. You must have noticed the way he ignored my entreaties just now, as he ignored yours and Jessica's struggles on the roof. His aim was surely to punish.'

Susie mused over Charity's verdict as if I were an insect to be mulled over. I tried to shut them out, really tried. Yet I could still hear them joyfully crowing about how clever they'd been, and ridiculing me for taking so long to grasp anything. And they were right. I'd not grasped anything. Enlightenment was only just beginning to dawn; and it was a numbing enlightenment. I'd been so full of myself, I'd not seen my own naivety. Excuses immediately welled up to justify my failings, but there was no point.

As I withered in my seat, Chloe's words resounded once more, and I cursed her for them. She'd been wrong, disastrously wrong. I couldn't even get outside let alone control what happened out there. Charity had proved it.

What a defeatist dolt, I thought suddenly, more in desperation than faith. I'd not rubbed my forehead purposefully enough. I'd not assumed a fetal position or really focused on getting out.

As surreptitiously as possible, I checked their whereabouts. They seemed preoccupied so I dropped onto the carpet, legs squeezed up, fingers rubbing my forehead. After closing my eyes, I concentrated with all my might.

It wasn't long before I heard soft footsteps ambling over and standing round me. I could imagine their faces peering down, their smiles or frowns or grimaces. I didn't check which. Whatever, they didn't speak, not a word. I doggedly kept rubbing, time in a vacuum. I'd ceased to believe long before I finally stopped.

'Now then, Ronald,' Charity said kindly. 'I think we've had enough of your clowning.'

'Indeed,' Susie agreed. 'More than enough.'

'Up you get,' Charity ordered, her tone changed. 'Or

have you lost interest in getting your answers?'

What could I do? I'd tried. I'd failed. Not even nonentity woman had bothered to pop in with a frustrating little riddle. I scrambled to my feet and plunked into my chair. More accurately, I crawled up.

'You know,' Dimple said thoughtfully, 'I'm not convinced he knows even now.'

'Well Frank did tell him,' Charity sighed, 'and in a rather special way.'

I began shivering, the blood cold in my veins. They were at it again, patently taunting me. I yearned to plug up my ears and run headlong into one of their brick walls. That might at least crack open my skull and end my misery for good.

'I hope you're not considering suicide,' Charity scolded as if fused to my thoughts.

Stung, I looked at her directly. She showed no emotion, nothing at all.

'He can't be thinking that,' Susie huffed, 'not in his state.'

Dimple laughed. 'Maybe I should spell it out, just to be sure.'

'What?' I yelled, standing. Her pause stretched out interminably.

The three of them drew closer, stopping less than a yard away. Even then Dimple was in no hurry.

'It's like Charity said, sweetie,' she purred in her own time. 'Frank has already told you. It was written on his chest.'

I shook my head. I'd been fighting those words with every atom of my soul. They were a vile travesty, a perverted aberration.

'It's true, Ronnie,' she added with a grin. 'Think about your impotence. The dead can't eject the seed of life; and you're entirely dead, sweetie. Your mortal coil has done a bunk!'

Chapter Twenty-eight

It's strange to be told you're dead. It's a thing you never really expect. It's especially strange when you're standing up, hemmed in by three capable and alluring females. Granted, I'd been as gullible as a dehydrated sponge, but this was just too big a stretch.

Odd, I know, but after Dimple's singular announcement I felt exceptionally calm. Maybe it was because it had to be a lie – a huge one – far too paunchy to gulp down like a baleen whale swallowing plankton. Maybe it was because I'd been so caught up in a whirlwind of supreme inanity – possibly insanity – that calmness was the only emotion left to me; the surreal calmness of disbelief. No matter which, I felt remarkably able to toss aside Frank's apocalyptic message. I'd faced down the worst they could throw and survived their persistence.

Smugness soon overcame the calm. Unable to resist flaunting my new found confidence, I needled them, 'All right, ladies, if I'm dead, what about you?'

'Oh no,' Dimple said, still grinning. 'Not us. Just you.'

I should have guessed I'd get a glib brush-off like that. 'Okay,' I said, 'so who are you? Surely you can ditch your game playing now and tell me.'

Charity answered that one. 'We are stewards of the glorious Prince.'

'Right,' I said dismissively. 'That clears that up. And I guess this *Prince* of yours is partial to charities that encourage people to jump off roofs ... or are you just a trio of psychos on a day trip from fairyland?'

That hit Susie between the eyes. I was surprised when she bleated so defensively. 'He is supreme. He truly understands his people's needs.'

'Well he's not understood mine very well,' I shot at her. 'He plugged me through the mincing gates of hell.'

Sometimes when people look at each other, it's just a look; a place to rest their eyes. Not so with Charity, Susie and Dimple. When they locked on to each other, it was as if the whole room quaked.

Charity was first to look back at me. 'Those who would have us fail have poisoned your mind, Ronald. They serve an egomaniac who understands nothing and gives nothing. His slaves are dour and lifeless. Spite makes them sneak in and out of here and confuse with riddles; the riddles you hate. Joining them will gain you nothing, cost you everything.'

I had to ask. 'And this enemy is called?'

'We don't speak his name,' she countered acidly.

It was my turn to twist the knife. 'Course not, but I bet he's the reason you cringe when I touch my forehead.' No response, so I pushed. 'What is all that about, by the way? Why is your Prince so scared of—'

'Never scared!' Susie charged in hotly. 'You've no—'

'Easy now, Susie,' Charity cut in smoothly. 'His time is all but gone. We must help him see the light so that he makes the right decision.'

I puzzled at that. Since my first memories of the conference room, they had been forcing me into situations: giving me no choice, no explanations. It was a sea change to be offered help. I kept quiet.

It was Dimple who broke the silence. After getting a nod from Charity, she said, 'Thing is, sweetie, you *can* do some things we can't.'

'I knew it!' I jeered. 'You've been softening me up all along, ready for the big sell.' I was so worked up, I couldn't see that they were still lying and manipulating me. I plowed on, 'Do you seriously think that after all you've put me through I've the minutest intention of helping you? As far as I'm concerned, you and your Prince can go to—'

Something stopped me. I was in darkness, as if a dense cloud had swallowed me in an instant. There was nothing oppressive about it. I didn't hurt or feel alarmed. I waited. It was all I could do.

'When I first came to you, I warned that time is a strange thing, as much as it's anything at all.'

It was nonentity woman. I could hear, but not see her through the dark. 'Where am I?'

The cloud cleared. To be honest, I'd hoped for somewhere better than that hateful bland room. She was there, looking as she always did, nothing but our two plain chairs to offer bodily comfort. I felt no fear or anger, until I noticed a frightening difference. One complete wall had become a swiftly moving black cascade the consistency of blood. No longer was it hidden through a doorway. I shrank from it, remembering how its likeness had consumed me as if I'd been an apathetic lemming.

'Be still,' she said, 'and tell me why you've not found him.'

For a second, I wondered if she meant Charity's *glorious Prince*, but that couldn't be it. He meant nothing to me. The only one that mattered was the one who had blown my life into this abyss of mind-boggling torment; my nemesis.

'I'll get him,' I said arrogantly, not the least bit willing to own up to my own weak persistence and easy distraction.

'He's with you now.'

Immediately I checked, already roused for a showdown. Seeing no one, I squinted at her, my nose crunched in annoyance. 'Another of your riddles?'

'Not this time: an answer. You're the one who's been seeing only what you want to see and hearing only what you want to hear. You're the one who allowed them into your soul ... allowed them to exploit your weaknesses. Think how they nurtured your many failings; how they set their snares then watched you run headlong into their traps. You've been searching for yourself, Ronald.'

No way was I prepared to accept that! 'I didn't cause my own panic,' I retaliated. 'Neither did I wipe away my memories or make time and reality bounce around like befuddled blimps in a storm.'

'Accepted,' she said, catching me out.

I was about to pile in again when she held up her hand.

'You must listen carefully, Ronald.'

She waited for me to settle, which took a while. Once I had, I soon sensed something terrible coming. My heart practically seized.

'What you remember as panic was not panic at all,' she said. 'It was the birth pangs of transition; your transition. You were leaving your old self behind – your physical self – not your soul. It all happened at the juncture of your last breath. It is still happening.'

That absolutely freaked my chicken. I stared like a glass-eyed dummy. In my head were a million screams and a million more questions, yet I couldn't so much as twitch.

'The body is more than purely physical,' she went on patiently. 'It has a mind. It has a soul. If the body is nourished and exercised, it will grow healthy and strong. If the mind – the intellect – is stretched, amazing things can be achieved. If the soul is not fed – if it is neglected – it shrivels and sickens. It becomes vulnerable.' She paused. 'Do you understand?'

What could I say? The whole concept of *understanding* had just been stood on its head and jumped on. Yet the key point had penetrated. Dimple hadn't been lying, and neither had the message carved on Frank's chest. I was dead. At least I wasn't alive in any way I could tag as living.

I tell you, even with nonentity woman's explanation clanging in my ears, I still had to wrestle hard to believe. But there was no point in fighting it. Something deep within me had finally caught on.

She hadn't finished. 'All the things you remember and all you have experienced during your transition are unique to you, except for one thing. Understand, Ronald, many have crossed over before you and many more will follow, yet you all share this one thing in common. In life, you were all marked in Christian baptism, your foreheads anointed.' She became sorrowful. 'Those who are not anointed tread a different path as dictated by their beliefs ... or the lack of them.'

My ears pricked up at the mention of foreheads. I ached to pin down why Charity and her pals had reacted so badly when I'd rubbed mine, but I held off. To compensate, I focused more keenly on my surroundings.

My thoughts soon scampered back to the question I'd first asked. 'Where am I? If it's heaven, it sure doesn't look like it.'

'Not heaven,' she said. 'You're at the boundaries of life

and death; heaven and hell.'

Thanks a bunch, I thought. That tells me diddly-squat. 'So what about me?'

She nodded. 'The path you've been allowed to travel in transition was a gift in love because of your baptism; an opportunity for you to recognize your weaknesses and—'

I cut her off. 'You mean I'm on my way to heaven, proper heaven?'

She looked sad. 'Despite your baptism, in earthly life you had no belief in the One Who Saves. If you had, you would not be facing judgment.'

That stunned me. Actually it ripped out my heart.

She saw. 'It's not I who will judge you, Ronald, and certainly not those creatures you've been with.'

'Creatures,' I echoed. I'd never thought of Charity or the others as anything like that.

'Yes, creatures,' she repeated. 'They speak with reverence of their Prince as if he can reward with everything anyone could desire. Yet I tell you they worship the Devil – the father of all lies – the one whose fleeting touch burned you the first time you came to this room.'

My eyes spread wide. Chloe's transit from Dimplesford General had been pain free, mine as if all my senses had been fired up and consumed in unrestrained torment.

She saw my realization. 'You've already experienced a taste of being cast into the pit. Charity's goal was to send you there permanently, in Simon's footsteps. Her promises were utterly false and vile, as is everything tainted by her Prince.'

'I didn't understand,' I whispered, remembering Frank's dying words. Made me shudder to think how blind I'd been to everything between the lines. 'I never—'

Her glance silenced me. 'What efforts did you make to understand while you were alive?'

I gaped. 'I don't know. My memories only start with the charity, the conference room.'

She came back at me. 'What efforts did you make once you'd ceased to live?'

'How can I answer that!' I protested.

'Oh, Ronald,' she said, 'you're still so deaf and unseeing. You must understand. Only the mark of faith bestowed on you at baptism gave you this last chance to open your eyes and ears and seek the gift of salvation. How do you feel you've used it?'

'Well enough,' I said sulkily, 'considering the way I've been treated.'

'Then I'll answer my own question for you,' she said firmly. 'Your soul has never been free of thoughts of revenge. You—'

'Hang on,' I interrupted. 'I was being manipulated by *creatures*: Charity, Susie and Dimple for starters. Reckon there were more too, like Bridget and that quack husband of hers.'

She looked deep into my eyes. 'There's a difference between being manipulated and allowing yourself to be manipulated. The creatures to whom you refer were required to fulfill a role. You were under no such constraint. Their function was to tailor scenarios that brought you face to face with your weaknesses in life – your major sins – and so give you chances to confront them, show contrition, and open your heart. Yet you never seriously challenged these scenarios ... or what you were being asked to do. You just moaned and wallowed in self-righteous self-pity, neither standing up for yourself nor against things you knew to be aberrant.

'Think. While you were naked in the conference room after that vainglorious celebration of your supposed bravery, Charity told you plainly. She spoke of her obligation to demonstrate that lust, pride, avarice, vengeful intentions, deceit, anger and all your other transgressions could only lead to your downfall. Yet you saw nothing but *her* potential weakness.'

'Okay,' I admitted sullenly. 'I was mislead.'

She came back at once. 'That's not good enough, Ronald. You rejoiced in lusting after the flesh, including demon flesh. You allowed your temper to rule. You were eaten up with pride and vanity in equal measures, even to worshiping your own image. You let yourself be a medium to the living and involved yourself in their lives. You cheated, lied and manipulated purely for your own gratification. You used others, abusing them, never attempting to help them unless they helped you. You cold heartedly murdered. You—'

'That's not fair,' I butted in. 'I didn't murder anyone.

According to you they were only *creatures*. Besides, I saw Susie afterwards, alive.'

'Can you not see, Ronald,' she said somberly. 'Your intention was to murder. You believed you had. You ignored the struggles of one victim and the pleas of another. Even your final refusal to join Charity was bedded in spite, nothing honorable.

'On the few occasions you asked for help, it was always totally self-centered. You had no sense of offering anything in return: no remorse, no sense of service, no questioning of how you landed in the situation.' She looked gently upon me. 'You were like a drowning man too busy thrashing about to realize you were deepening your own troubles ... and I so wanted it to be otherwise. I wanted your redemption. I hated to watch while you cast away every opportunity to rise above petty temptation and seek a better way.'

The sheer breadth of her indictments hit me hard. 'Who are you?' I asked.

She seemed to notice a difference in me. Maybe it had showed in my tone.

'I am a servant sent by the One Who Saves,' she said, 'by the Anointed One who wants to save you.'

I stared. There was nothing I could possibly say.

I'm not sure how long we sat quietly together, but I know that when she spoke again her voice sounded different, like a subdued breeze. I didn't expect her words to be so challenging.

'There was a multi-gifted man born to earth in the seventeenth century,' she began, startling me with her baffling choice of topic. 'His name was Blaise Pascal. Among other things, he was a philosopher, mathematician and physicist. What matters to you is that he posited a wager that captures the essence of your situation.'

I nodded, unsure what was coming.

'You need to think carefully about his wager, Ronald, and know that, in life, everyone must participate, intentionally or by default. It concerns the existence of God. People either believe in Him or they don't. Sitting on the fence is not an option. There is no half way. This means the wager has just two alternative positions: belief or non-belief. The stake, of course, is life itself; eternal life.' I gulped as she held my gaze.

'If you believe that God exists – if you *wager* your life on his existence – but then human death proves you wrong, you lose the reward you had hoped for, but that is all you lose. Yet if death proves you right, you gain everything; an everlasting life of happiness and peace.

'But what of the other position: wagering that God *does not* exist? The reward for being proved right is a life lived in your own way, nothing more. But the cost of being wrong is extreme. You forfeit your immortal soul and forever lose your place in paradise.' She smiled. 'Therefore, in every way, the wise choice is to wager your life on God's existence.'

I could only say, 'Yes.'

'But there's a problem,' she said earnestly. 'Making a wise choice is not the same as having belief. It may be professed as belief, but it could easily be insincere, possibly entirely false. So I ask you: is it likely that God could be fooled by such a ploy? I tell you, no, not for a single moment.'

'Suppose not,' I said.

'And there's one more important thing,' she went on. 'Even though you may desire to believe, there's no switch that turns that desire into genuine belief.' I frowned at that. 'You can't *make* yourself believe, Ronald, even if you want to, and neither can anyone else.'

My nerves tightened as her eyes filled with compassion.

'So you see the conundrum: the safest play is to believe in God in the hope of being rewarded with eternal life in heaven, yet no one can force themselves to believe, and God cannot be fooled by counterfeit belief. And so we turn to you, Ronald: the things you did in life; how you chose not to believe; how you wagered against the existence of God.'

'No,' I said, frightened, 'not deliberately. I never thought—'

Her sigh made my words dry up. 'As I told you, everyone in life must participate, intentionally or by default. You made the unwise choice – the unwise wager – and now it's no longer a matter of what you believed. You have seen beyond. Your post-life experiences have overtaken your failure in life to seek evidence of God. So the wager gets superseded by a question: have you learned enough to let your eyes and ears be fully opened to the One Who Saves, or are you fit only for the Devil's charity?'

That completely blew my mind, more so when she stayed silent. It was obvious what I was expected to say, but equally obvious that merely saying it would count for nothing. Unable to bear the strain, I blurted, 'What happened to Chloe?'

'I think you know,' she answered.

'Okay, what about some of the others? Frank, for instance, and that security guy at the hospital? Were they creatures or people like me?'

'I'm touched by your concern, Ronald,' she said softly, 'if it is concern and not idle curiosity. What matters now is you. In due course you will be judged. You must think about my question, about what you are going to say.' Her sudden smile warmed me. 'Maybe you should also think on His grace and mercy.'

I closed my eyes, striving to imagine how I could even begin. Yet there was something buried inside me, a compulsion to tell my story. I really wanted to break through and stop others making my mistakes. I wanted people to know, anyone who would listen. Then I understood. I'd left it too late. My desire to speak out could never be more than an insatiable hunger. But that didn't stop me.

Glancing at nonentity woman, I began cautiously, my words not really meant for her. Perversely, they were for people I could never meet. 'Don't get me wrong,' I said. 'I'm not after sympathy and I'm not making excuses. I made my choices same as everyone else. We all have free will. I guess that's the point.

'I could put a gloss on the way I used to be. I'd like to, but you'd soon see through it. You're not daft. But I have changed, finally, though getting you to believe me is a tough call.'

About the Author

Robert D Turvil likes to take intriguing and unusual ideas and spin them into stories with an edge. That's what he's done with *The After Death Afterlife of Ronald Foster*.

He has offered up a world beyond our own and opened a window. We see a place in which normality has been stood on its head and jumped on. But there are also some compelling human questions. Not least: is there an unavoidable wager, a bet we have to make about the existence of God and eternal life?

Happy reading!

13563094R00137

Printed in Great Britain
by Amazon.co.uk, Ltd.,
Marston Gate.